THEY WEEP YE
©
C.P. HILTON

A HAUNTING LOVE STORY
ADULT THEMES
CONTAINS SCENES OF MODERATE SEX AND VIOLENCE
2023

Linked with
'GHOSTS GENTLY WEEP'
©
C.P. HILTON
2023

PROLOGUE

(i)

In twilight the young lady was wet; fiery red hair extinguished, her shawl, everything was wet, and laden. Drizzle had been persistent leaving the dark cobbles shiny in the curved line of streetlamps.

A bottle clattered.

She cursed the broken gin bottle, turned a corner and was gone.

In the silence a white fox crept from the edge of night. The damp air with the light from a church vestibule created an aura about it while a bell began its heavy lament, rocked by a wind that drove the rain into the trees.

The fox raised its head and sniffed. Wrapped in a blanket in a cardboard box on marble steps within the vestibule's shelter, a baby's eyes shimmered.

(ii)

The air was heavy with desert dust, it came in beneath the door and formed a carpet over the clay floor grazing the back of his shaven head. He was pinned by knees on his chest, hands of body weight on arms and legs.

Spittle landed on his cheek; hoarse words hovered.

"On this day you will leave our land. And though you may dwell in your darkness, you will not hide this brand from anyone's eyes."

The dull blade scarcely glinted; he scarcely made a sound.

He was cut; two lines up the side of each nostril.

(iii)

Circling a mansion then between two cypress trees a wind rushed, escaping through the bushes and out between the gates of the white walled garden, down to the deep waters of the loch. Someone inside the building was closing shutters, working from left to right throughout each room until there were no eyes.

"Now," he spoke, "we are on equal terms."

"I think not, Yefimovich," she said.   "There is no mistaking the scent of a match with freshly lit candles."

Six flames flickered, they cast a moving pattern of shadows over his shaven scalp and the scars running up each nostril; easily confused as a trick of that light.

"But still," he said, "you enjoy a blindfold."

"You are too heavy."   An incubus, Yefimovich squatted on her chest.   She, too, was naked; her frame taut, spread as a star, tied to ropes fixed to rings bolted to the floor; all perfectly symmetrical with the inscriptions carved into the bare boards beneath her.

Yefimovich reached behind, his fingers playing between her legs, "You always like that."

"Not now," words were gasped.

"Are you watching, Major?"   Yefimovich considered one of the impassive faces of the black robed audience of five, each with a candle at their bare feet, with his at her head in the wood-panelled room of heavy furniture, two swastika flags flowing from poles each side of the sealed door.

His hands tightened around her neck.

C hapter 1

Touch was as sensual as night.   Caress became arousing, quickly tainted by guilt.

Revulsion slipped its way in and created a need for escape. The intruder must have sensed it; the change that awakening brings. A dream slipped away.

In a dawn's yellow fog, he rolled out of bed and thumped into the bathroom to stand over the toilet bowl; the odour of urine rising as it dribbled on the floor.   Hands crossed to opposite shoulders, he squeezed overworked muscles and looked into the mirror.

***

"Mister Ashington, thank you for coming. I am Frank."

"Call me Church. If that's allowed."

"Church it is, then."   A featherweight with a long reach, Frank stood even taller than Church had imagined.

Church stepped into the deep carpet, challenged by a high ceiling, a glass lamp shade suspended on a long chain offering a mute greeting.

"Please, Church, choose a seat," Frank pointed to two chairs offset in the centre of the room.

Church tried a laugh, "I'm more used to stools at opposite corners and I thought I'd be on a couch and you behind a desk with notepad."

"Boxing ring? An interesting analogy. But a couch? I do not work that way. Desks and notes are barriers and so are clothes," Frank gestured to the similarity of shirt and jeans.

"I nearly wore my suit."

"You chose not to."

Church sat, Frank sat; mirror images, poised.

"As I say, Church, thank you for coming. Before we begin, I would like to inform you that the session is limited to an hour."

A clock ticked. It was somewhere in the room.

"Plus," Frank carried on, "anything we share will be treated as confidential."

"You mean I mustn't tell anyone."

"My mistake. You can tell anyone anything you choose, but I will not, although I do seek the support of my supervisor."

"I get it."

"I'm wondering if there is anything you would like to share."

Silence stretched for Church. It became uncomfortable. "Are we waiting for your supervisor?"

"Again, my mistake. I meet with my supervisor outside of these sessions."

Silence did not hesitate to return, gloating, conspiring with the clock's tick. The clock; this had happened before; it took him Jasmin's family home.

The tick became a nag.

"Jasmin, that's my wife, she said I had to come for counselling."

"Jasmin said you had to come."

"Well, no. Hearing it that way," Church folded his arms and leaned back, Frank did not move, "Jasmin was right, I needed to come."

"You needed to."

"Hard to talk about but...yeh well...I get these dreams you see." Church rubbed his nose. "They take over during the day. Like having someone following me all the time. Turning and no one there." He realised he was wringing his hands, "It's all the time."

"Turning and no one there. Yet someone from the dream follows you, persistently."

"Yeh that's it," Church leaned forward, so did Frank.

"But no, not someone, it's something. Something dark."

***

Church drifted back to bed and clutched his pillow, inhaling perfume as stale as fading flowers. He drifted into a domain, a forlorn place which held vague distinction between dream and a reality.

Was that him laughing?

It was horrible.

She was there again, the young lady in a shawl, droplets of water on her fresh cheeks, her red hair drenched and heavy, she held a baby in her arms which she placed to the ground and pleading with her eyes, she placed a rope around her neck and faded into darkness.

And from that darkness, from beneath the bed, hands snatched up to his ankles. He was locked, everything was locked; shocked and frozen by a grip as cold as a grave. Air began to rasp. No, not the air, it was the sound of his body tugged over the bed, sheets yanked with him. With each tug over the coarse mattress, with each rasp, he was being dragged to a crypt. He felt no pain but impossibly his feet and ankles contorted to curve under the foot of the bed, then calves, then knees, his thighs; all bending like rubber. He grasped the spars of the bedhead. The covers slipped aside; naked for an invisible drooling audience in the cooling air. Eyes wide, accustomed to the dark, the so familiar ceiling passed along. The room was disappearing. He tried to scream, to howl; he could only whimper. Arms elongated, fingers tied in clever knots to the bedhead, his shoulders then his neck; all was entering a deep darkness.

C hapter 2

A ghost drifted by the banister above the stairway which descended to the entrance hall as vast as a ballroom. Suitcases were lined down there, on the black and white tiles. She floated into an empty bedroom. Through gaps in the white-painted bow window, the thin air whispered; a distant voice encircling; a growing vine, entrapping. She swayed gently, staring out of the window.

The quick December twilight matched the mood of the sea. In constant rhythm, waves closed onto the stones of the beach. The saloon rolled along the road and she watched it coming to the entrance below; the railings covered by droplets of moisture merging as chameleons with bubbles of paint concealing the rust beneath.

She watched him step out of the car; bulbous, his black shadow coalescing with his form to become one entity.

The ghost stopped moving.

Beside the suitcases a grandfather clock clunked, its pendulum slicing off another segment of time, oiled cogs moved, forcing the coiled spring to relax yet another increment.

"You invited him?" A voice betrayed by sorrow ran from the room.

"Willow," he spluttered through his moustache, "you worry so, growing old before your time."

"Thank you for that."

"Brothers need no invitations." He patted his pockets then retrieved his sherry from the mantlepiece, retreating from the heat of the fire. "And we need someone to keep an eye on the place. Blitz looters."

"Philip," Willow placed her hands over her belly, "the war is over, barbed wire is away from the beach."

"Don't trust anyone."

"Yet you trust him."

"Willow," he spluttered again, "you mustn't exert yourself in your condition," then he turned, "ah Taversham."

"I let myself in," heavy words rolled across the floor, he held the key, taunting. "You had best make haste for your trip to bonny Scotland. Here are the train tickets I procured."

"Procured?" Willow challenged.

"Yes," Philip intervened, "well done."

"Good evening, my dear Willow," he bowed. "Still radiant with India's sun."

"Ceylon."

"And if I may say, being with child so becomes you." With a blubbery smirk he offered the tickets to her. "When you arrive, please pass on my condolences to your dear sister. If I can be of assistance."

"Poppy can manage."

"I am sure she can but without her husband it may prove difficult. And having recently attended a funeral of a very dear friend I am acutely aware of the pain."

"Sorry to hear that," Philip tried.

"His move to here was considerable, remarkable. It is said he had a brother; both fled the threat of the Russian revolution. He dwelled with Bedouins, then between the wars, coincidentally, he lived in Scotland. That's where his ashes are destined, to fulfil his wish, beneath two trees at his old home." He simpered. "Death caught up with him."

"I say," Philip suggested.

"Tickets," Taversham offered them to her.

She put her hands down a toilet bowl.

Upstairs, the ghost lingered, with no place else.

C hapter 3

Sleep became a conflict; dreams returning or thought's arguing. Church swung his legs from the bed, indifferent now to whatever lay beneath and turned on the table light. A smashed red telephone was scattered on the floor. He stared at the framed photograph on the oriental cabinet; a handsome young woman with straight black hair, a white flower behind her ear giving a defining hint of overseas; the photograph picked that out. Church grabbed the perfumed pillow, lay it on his lap, placed his head into the crib of his hands and wept.

***

"Hi."

Church spun. "Sorry; thought you were talking to me." It was a battle to look just at her face, those eyes drew him.

"I was. Saw you on the train this morning," head to one side, long black hair hanging, she was smiling.

"Yeh? Er...yeh, good old London to Brighton." He flexed his neck; a ploy to look down to take in the jeans and leather jacket, and her tight white vest. He realised he was moving closer, pushing the edge of his tray into her flat stomach, "Sorry." He backed into someone, "Sorry, mate," he was granted a grunt.

"A long queue just to get a sandwich," she was not disguising her scrutiny, magnifying it by raising an eyebrow.

"Especially if you want only a coffee."

"What are you studying?"

That smile was powerful.

"Me? Er...technical drawing."

"You look like you belong in the gymnasium."

"Really? Er...thanks. Used to box. Er...you?"

"Often thought of wrestling."

"Pardon? No...er...I mean what are you studying?"

"Art and design."

"Oh, er right," he was drowning, "sounds nice."

"It is. Giving me so many ideas. What about you?"

"Me?"

"Technical drawing?" Do you enjoy it?"

"Beginning to. Only started it to keep out of trouble."

"Hey, I'm giving up on a sandwich. Nice talking. Stay out of trouble."

"Hang on," Church blurted. She waited. "Sorry...er. Will you be on the train tonight?"

"I'm Jasmin without an e. Jasmin Jamison, folk call me Jay Jay."

"Er...Jasmin's a nice name, even without an e. I'm Church Ashington but prefer Sandy. Not an e in sight," his laugh felt lonely.

"Not an e in sight but plenty of ers."

"Pardon?"

"See you on the train."

The impact of the oncoming express thundering past first shocked then rocked the carriage, all subsiding to the original slow rhythm, houses disappearing backwards along square windows.

"Do you remember steam trains, Church?"

The motor cycle Madonna was looking at him, the train's steady motion giving a knowing nod to her head.

"Never been on one, Jasmin. Wish I had."

"Really?"

"Never bothered at the time. You know how it is; you live to regret it." The curve of the track pushed the evening sun into her eyes. Iridescent; they were iridescent.

"I want to travel more one day," she leaned back and sighed, "If I don't, I know I'll live to regret that. Funny, isn't it?"

"What?"

"I'm already looking back on my future and seeing the possibilities of regret."

"I think I know what you mean," Church wrung his hands.

"You don't."

He looked down, he was being studied, her head tilted as it was that morning.

Church forced himself to look at her, "Do you have a motorbike?"

"The jacket? My boyfriend was a rocker, I was his biker chick. Did it to freak out mum and dad."

"You boyfriend is a was?"

"Is a was?"

"I think I've got it now though."

"What are you talking about?"

"No, I mean, what you were saying earlier; looking back on your future; it must be like seeing your own ghost."

"Too much for the end of a day," she went completely silent.

"At least I haven't been saying er this time." He reverted to staring out of the window, his lonely reflection slipping by.

"Hey," she dipped forward and touched his knee, "I'm just tired, don't look so glum."

***

"Something dark is following. Frightening."

"It is Frank. And I don't mind admitting it. But if a bloke off the street tries it on, I can deal with it. But this...."

Silence threatened.

Church submitted, "Don't get the wrong idea though, I mean I don't want to have to use violence, that's why I stopped boxing." He pointed to his damaged nose. "But if someone tried it on at the orphanage...well that's when I realised, I had to teach them. Yeh," Church readied to search Frank's face, "I was raised in an orphanage."

"At the orphanage you learnt how to stand up for yourself, but these dreams are something harder for you to handle."

***

"No good crying over spilt milk, Sandy."

"Who said I was crying?"

"You spilt the milk."

Church looked across the plastic-pine café, trying to remember who 'down and out' was and how come he knew his nickname. Giving up on that he searched his own table, to the base of the milk jug, "Just a dribble."

"Never mind," the bloke stubbed his roll-up into the full ashtray, "haven't seen you in here for a while. Church, isn't it? Unusual name but cool."

"That's right," Church winged it, "busy. You know how it is."

"It's a shame about the parting of ways though."

Church defied the intense stare.

"Now that is something to cry about," the intruder persisted.

"Don't know what you mean."

"The Beatles splitting up."

"Oh that, just a rumour that is. That group will go on for ever."

"The name's Jake, if you forgot. Most people do."

Jake then seemed to have lost interest, paying more attention to rolling another cigarette, or maybe he realised that he did not know who he was talking to. Or whatever. Church sank back to where he was; peering out of the steamy window. So close to the glass; he was the street entertainment.

Only a tramp with begging bowl hands passed by to leave a deserted theatre so Church turned to the stark interior, intrigued by the old man thumbing through a map book, his fingernails seeming incredibly old, even though they had only recent history.

"I said, no good crying over spilt milk."

"What? Jake what are...? Oh Jasmin," he adored her

face. "Didn't hear you come in." The door's sprung bell was still clanging while he tried to peer into her sunglasses.

"Are you ready for this?"

He stood, the chair legs grated across the floor, the waitress turned to watch him leave. His money was on the table.

Just that tilt of her head. Jasmin was in front in bright sunlight as they went out through the door to cross the street. Just that tilt of her head was enough. Church looked to where she glanced and saw him, him at the jeweller's doorway, him with his blond curls. A pebble dropped into a deep pool, the ripples expanding, that was all it took for the event to dwell; down into that deep pool; deeper and deeper reflections in deeper and deeper worlds, Church sank.

"Hey, keep up," Jasmin's shout reached him.

He crossed the road while she waited at the office frontage with windows of etched glass; patterns of lace with one engraved word; *'Taversham.'*

C hapter 4

'*...stones set in rhyme...*' Paintbrush in hand, the other hand loitering by his boiler suit pocket, the tousled urchin sang to the taped music, bobbing along with the ascending bass notes, dabbing white gloss along the scaffold pole lying the full length of the bench.

'*...the Caledonian water line...*' He squinted at his work, trusting in the cobweb-filtered daylight coming down through the roof's small skylight.

'*...a path flowing down from the moon...*' "Oops," the brush was tawny.

'*...we dance one more time...*'   "Could be worse," he considered the mug, the white film floating over his tea.

"Jimmy, we need to go."

He barely heard her above the music and the screech of the barn door sliding open.

Turning off the cassette player, dunking the brush in a jar of turps, he stuffed both hands in his pockets and blinked at the dazzle from outside. "Sarah." He hid the mug.

The warm day flowed in, stirring up the sadness of last summer's sweet hay, leaving her silhouetted; a sphinx in a calico dress. "I don't know why you are doing whatever it is you are doing but you should do it outside, get some fresh air in your bones."

"I know," he jigged. "But where have you been?"

"Over giving Gran some goat's milk."

"And how is she? Gran, I mean."

"Frailer than ever."

"Nah, a tough old biddy, love her to bits," Jimmy eyes

dipped to the floor.

"She asked if you could see to her front door."

"Do it now," he gathered up tools, throwing them into a wooden box.

"Can't, I just said we need to go."

"That time already? Zimmy?"

"Scoop him up as we go. Hey," she gestured, "paint lid. And bring the mug."

Chapter 5

Church stepped out of the bathroom, water soaking into his dressing gown. He passed beneath roof timbers through the murkiness of the upper gallery and turned on the lights for his cathedral.

He pounded down the bare stairs pausing by the splashed coffee stain on the wall. It resembled an abstract painting. He sat on a stool at the breakfast bar. Unwashed dishes were stacked in the sink and splintered wood piled at the French doors.

His faithful hound; a bleak mood came padding down the twisted stairs.

***

In a silence unusually pure, Church sipped his pint of *old ale.* That it was *in season* reminded him of the passing of the years; a medieval way of being in touch with ancestors; the pub's beams and stone walls bringing on that thought.

"Yeh," he spoke into the glass, "another time another place sounds good." The beer lapped over the rim.

***

"Boys, don't worry, she won't capsize."

"But Grandad, the sea's coming in over the side."

"Gunwales," the whiskered face scowled, "it's coming in over the gunwales. But you three lads spread yourself out about more, put us on an even keel. And I'm not your Grandad."

"But you are as good as a Grandad. Better."

"Right Nick, right Eddie, we'll leave Church out of this."

"Yeh he's away on one, again."

"We will take the yacht out next time, "Grandad continued, "teach you how to sail. But my next lesson in seamanship is how to tell which way is North. Well Nick?"

"With a compass."

"Nit wit; compasses are for drawing circles."

"How then?"

"Put your finger in your gob then stick it in the air. The coldest side is North. But don't tell your teacher because you're meant to be off school with a belly ache."

"Too many apples," said Eddie.

"That's right, Grandad."

"And don't call me Grandad."

"Nick, how come he's catching more fish?"

"Dunno. Hey, Church."

Church had to shut off listening; his school, his life, all was different to theirs. He looked about the endless space wondering if the salt from the sea was giving the air that crystalline colour. And he wondered if, somewhere way beyond the glorious sun-setting horizon, the sun had to be rising in the West. But he knew that the dark shadows moving under the boat really were the monsters Grandad described from his voyages around the world.

"Church," Eddie's shout gave no echo, "rod's dipping; you gotta bite."

"Another one," Nick added.

"Church? Hello?"

***

"Hello." A round face was smiling.

"Hello," Church chucked it back but the polo-necked flash git was not going.

"Listen," Church tried, "this seems to happen more and more, people talk and I haven't a clue who they are. Not trying to be rude but who..."

He was halted by hands in surrender. "I apologise, meant no harm; just that I'm new to the area and a trip to the local seemed the best way to meet folk." He gestured to turn

17

away.

"No, no please." Church pointed to the bar stool and offered his hand, "Sorry about that. I'm Church, though I'm always called Sandy."

"I wonder why," he smiled at the hair. "Richard," they shook hands, "but please don't call me Dick."

"Asking for trouble. New to the area, hey. Live nearby?"

Richard nodded through the opened door to across the green.

"It was you who bought it." Church did not turn to see the property, "Original leaded windows and a thatched roof; a lot of upkeep but a good sound place, well sited above the flood line. Well done."

"A voice of knowledge?"

"Architect. And what do you do?"

"Hey Sandy," the slap on his back hurt.

"Hey Sandy," the second was no kinder.

Church turned to the two grins, "Yeh, hi Nick, Eddie." They were both giving Richard the eye. "This is Richard."

"Hi Dick."

"Hi Dick."

"How come you know Sandy?"

"We go back years." Church put his hand to the side of his face and spoke gruffly from the opposite corner of his mouth, "Richard, tell 'em nothing."

"See this," Nick was holding pieces of hacked lead; rough coin shapes. "Gonna try these in the juke box." He nodded to Richard, "Made em myself."

"Really," Richard calmly turned to Church as the pair peeled off. "Seem harmless."

"Believe me, they are not."

"Oh?"

"Never mind," Church avoided scrutiny. "So, Richard, what line of work are you in?"

"See, you don't know him, do you," the other two had returned. "I reckon he's James Bond."

"I'm a dentist."

"Aaagh," the pair screamed, backing away with hands over their mouths.

"Known them since we were lads," Church tried.

The explosion from the jukebox speakers shook the walls, dense music making conversation impossible, augmented by the pub becoming full with a boisterous crowd. He watched Richard stand and finish his drink.

"Look, I'm sorry about all of this," Church shouted in Richard's ear. "We're having a party next Saturday, be nice to get to know you properly."

"No need to apologise," Richard shouted back, "Been in far worse situations. Believe me, this pub is a doddle."

"I was apologising for my mates."

"Like you say; harmless...or not. But I must say a party sounds good. How do I find you?"

Church already had a business card in hand, "Next Saturday. Bring you wife or whatever."

"Single."

He watched him leave. Familiar melancholy returned. He spent the rest of the evening swirling the dregs at the bottom of his glass.

***

"Extremely hard to handle," Frank reiterated.

"Yeh hard to handle, dead right," Church thought about it. "And these dreams, these feelings, I keep it all private. I must or everyone will think I'm a loony. Always been easier just to hide it away." Again, Church studied Frank's impassive persona.

"Sounds like this goes back some time."

"Childhood." *'And further,'* he thought.

"And you don't tell anyone about it."

"What...? Sorry I was miles away. Well, my mates; they just say I'm going off on one."

Church laughed and noticed Frank did not even smile.

"You say you were miles away," Frank paused. "And

your mates have a form of understanding but you keep it all private, for fear of ridicule."

C hapter 6

"At least it's not raining," Willow offered a shallow laugh. She adjusted her headscarf and considered the tight buds of the daffodils growing beside the path then turned to her companion, "Alice, you still look as young and as pretty as ever."

"Don't feel it."

"But I suppose this is the best place to meet and catch up after so long, then say goodbye."

Both reflected on the grey headstone; it was set in clipped grass opposite their bench beneath trees.

'Mimosa'
'1922-1940'
'A flower never fading'

"How I had to fight," Willow sagged.

"As always."

"My choice of resting place; a fight against his family and that brother."

"Be grateful.   All those investments," Alice gazed into the distance, "with a palace by the sea."

"Sooner have a bungalow." Willow sighed.

"Try and be happy."

"I was jealous, you know, you with your pretty face and my baby sister, best friends."

"Best friends, maybe."   Alice retained that distant look. "But it was you who looked after her when your parents died."

"Left with no choice."

"You've never forgiven."

"But you helped."   Willow faced her, "Yes, I may have been jealous but I did appreciate you befriending someone like Mimosa."

"A gifted girl."

"Not everyone saw her that way."

"Some people have to be nasty."

"But I still refuse to believe it."

"You need to move on."   Alice shifted awkwardly, squeezing Willow's hand with each word.   "Look at your big sister."

"Poppy."   Willow shrugged, "A free spirit."

"You have a wonderful thing.   Another flower, your very own Jasmin."

Both turned to the two tots playing on the grass.

Willow's laugh drifted high, "Look at Justin with his blonde curls.   No need to guess where they come from."

"Ali still hasn't a clue," Alice closed her eyes.

Willow hesitated.   "But it is good you married Guy in the end.   Did he ever suspect?"

"Who knows?"   Alice produced a hip flask from her bag and took a swig.   "And he'll never know once we are there, nor Ali. I'll be safe then. Safe," she swirled the flask.

"Willow sighed, "Can't believe you are actually going."

"Not far."

"Not far? Too far; blooming brain drain. Always top of the class; another thing I hated you for."

"What best friends are for."

"Second best."

"Willow," Alice paused, "have you never considered going away?"

"I once said goodbye to going away."

"Sad."

"Huh, Philip's brains really have gone down the drain"

"Don't be so hard on him.   What he went through; you should be proud."

"I am proud and I think...I think I love him. But..."

"How far back does that go?"

"Pardon?"

"You and Philip, when did you start to think...?"

"Look at those two now," Willow tittered.

Hand in hand, the tots were toddling down the path, protecting each other from tumbling. "Justin and Jasmin; prince and princess. They could live in your palace by the sea." Alice passed over her flask and reached into her bag, "Hang on, I'll take their photo, still got my trusty Brownie; sort of keepsake, from Ali."

"A photo of a beautiful reunion. Wish you weren't going." Willow sighed.

"Always sighing."

"Sighing and wishing my life away." Willow drunk from the flask.

C hapter 7

The young girl's cropped hair flickered as silver. In her sweet pinafore dress, she came out from behind the heavy curtains and pressed her ear against the door. The wood created a mellow tone to the voices within the room.

"Don't worry," father was talking. "It's good to be different."

"She will need to be," that was mother. "Being cute guarantees nothing except being someone's wife, then a mother, then a housewife." With long fingers, she would be embroidering.

"She's strong, she'll find her way." She pictured his stance; glasses on his long nose, hands moving as if conducting an orchestra.

"At least being cute guarantees being able to pick and choose the right husband."

"You certainly did," he would be smiling at the ceiling now. "But for certain the twins will grow into having a solid career."

The girl heard sniggering from behind.

"Listening in."

"Naughty little girl."

She felt a set of fingers poking her back.

"Very naughty," another set poked.

"Pack it in," she turned and swiped them away.

"Wallace and Wallace, two little titties," they were poking again.

"That's not nice," Wallace snapped at them, "don't touch me there. Stop it. Snitch and Snatch; twin terrors."

"Don't call us that," the poking became harder.

The identical boys were side by side in front of her. She altered her stance, turned her palms up, pulled her elbows back and with tight fingers, thrust hard into their solar plexus and beyond. Both tumbled. She ran into her bedroom and threw herself on the bed burying her head in the pillow. Her white tunic with black belt swung on its hanger on the slammed door.

***

"Wallace, like, you are so weird."

Wallace pulled the sheet up to her neck and propped herself on her arm to watch him dressing. "But that didn't stop you." She struggled now to admit how much she had enjoyed his tight physique, his downy beard and that strange feeling of him inside her; an invasion. It was still sore, stinging, and wet. Something special abandoned.

He sat on the edge of the bed and pulled his black jumper over his torso, "Hey listen, I mean don't take this the wrong way," he was not even looking at her. "I mean, I like you..."

"But," Wallace squinted her blue eyes and screwed her fists. She challenged the side of his face.

"My friends, they think you are weird as well, I mean your short hair, you look like a boy, at eighteen you haven't even got real tits. Even your name."

Wallace buried her head in the pillow. Before he could stand, she slipped her bare leg from the sheet to yell and violently kick out at him. He rolled toward the door.

Her yell fading, she lay on the bed in an empty room.

C hapter 8

Air was thick with the oil-laden history of the station.

"Old carriages," Jasmin was squeezing his hand, jumping as a child in her sandals and summer dress. "No corridors, do the mean look, stop anyone joining us."

The train moved even before they sat, their feet skidding on the gloss of discarded magazines, momentum throwing them in a heap on the bench seat. She was making the entanglement worse, wriggling on top of him, her breath increasing. Hands at his belt, she was gnawing his ear, "Get them down," she was panting, tugging at his underpants, doing it for him without ceremony, leaving him feeling a nasty coarseness of the stained seat on his buttocks. She raised her dress, she had no nickers, she sat on his lap. He felt sweat from a hot morning dash to catch the train, the softness of her flesh, warm moisture from between her legs. Her hands reaching down, her fingers tangled in his pubic hairs, he could not stop himself jumping with the electric pulse. She raised herself then in stages lowered, "Bloody hell, you're even bigger than I dreamed." He felt her damp heat surrounding his erection, discovered that untried intimacy, so tight, so personal, squeezing to be fully inside her. She raised herself again, then lowered to pause. She balanced, her quivering legs taking the weight, grabbing his arms to bring his hands up inside her dress to discover her stomach. Exploring, sliding his hands up and over each pointed breast; he ejaculated quietly. It was private; a pumping rush, swollen, exquisitely painful. She would never know how quickly it had happened, the train took over, a beat, faster, increasingly frantic, breasts slapping into his palms, her head bobbing, bent double, she gave a coarse grunt, continuing her frenzy until exhausted.

She rolled onto the seat and collapsed over him.

Heads bumped.

The train was slowing to enter a platform causing them to transform to a tidier existence. They jumped to sit on the opposite bench.

Church searched the stern face of the lady who entered their carriage. She sat where he had sat. He felt remnants of his semen oozing inside his underpants. Hair clinging to her sweating face, Jasmin laid her head on his shoulder. He put his arm around her and drew her close, then looked out of the window. He now had his back to forward motion and the familiar landscape slipped away.

***

Even though it was setting, the sun was hotter than yesterday, only so to make it unbearable for him and him alone, Church Ashington, to wear a suit, a black one. Wanting to tear it off, Church tugged at the tie around his neck, wishing he had bought a larger shirt but had to escape from the shop. Church did not mind the bloke being queer but he did not have to make it so obvious he fancied him.

He held on to the black railing feeling the paint flaking in his palms. Looking up the seven steps he saw the black door beginning to open.

"Mummy, promise, please," it was Jasmin. She opened the door fully and from above was looking him up and down.

"Wow," he said it first, trying not to make use of his low vantage point and look up her white mini dress. Hands on hips with legs apart, she could only be enticing him, dipping her pelvis forward to give a glimpse of white panties.

"You look great," she nodded. "And thank you." She offered her hand to lead him up the steps.

The hallway was vast and as an act of kindness, it was cool. And it was silent; which the grandfather clock's ponderous clunk accentuated. It seemed a premonition, or recollection.

Jasmin was squeezing his hand. "We can do this," she rose high and led him across the black and white tiles to the only room with an opened door. Jasmin went in first and before following, he turned to look along the high curve of the staircase, drawn to the bannisters above. But Jasmin was pulling him in.

He was lurched to land under the scrutiny of a lean, moustached, man. Hand on tweed jacketed hip, the other at the mantelpiece, he stood at the empty fireplace.

"Good afternoon, Sir," Church did not hesitate, this was going to be easy and he was not going to faulter, marching toward him with the purpose of a handshake.

"Ah."

"Allow me to introduce myself, Church Ashington."

"A handsome name," came a woman's voice, "for a handsome young man."

"Mother," Jasmin hissed, "you promised." Hand crooked through his arm, Church was led, "Church, this is Mum."

"Pleased to meet you." Church tried the proposal of another handshake and with it offered, "Mum."

In a dress too formal, Mum tittered and put her fingers to her mouth.

"Sherry." Father gruffly rescued him, both confused as to whether a handshake was still a good idea. Jasmin clearing her throat was sufficient to warn Church not to down the tiny sherry in one, yet from the edge of his field of vision he caught the mother doing just that. "Jasmin tells me," Father grunted each word, "you are training to be an architect. White collar, admirable."

"That's my plan."

"Lot better than that arty farty stuff."

"Language," it gave Mum the opening to pat a seat for Church. Jasmin dipped her head instructing him to sit next to Mum. "Would you care for tea and some of my cake."

Perched on the edge of the sofa, balancing tea cup with teaspoon on a saucer and the slice of cake on a plate, Church knew if he sat back then the soft cushion would complete an engulfment by the suffocated parents that somehow belonged to his honeyed girlfriend.

The clock chimed and before Church could finish counting, Father charged.

"Need to be off," he patted his pockets at Church's eye level. "Golf club AGM for me and WRI for you my dear. Convenient."

"But it's tomorrow..." Mother was led away to leave a room full of space.

"Bloody convenient," Jasmin flung herself beside Church. "We've got three hours."

"How did I do?" He was being dragged somewhere.

She stopped, turned and hugged him, planting a sloppy kiss on his cheek. "Brilliant. And thank you. Get them off my back for a few weeks. Thank you," another sloppy kiss.

"Seemed easy."

"Only one thing though," Jasmin was facing him.

"What did I do?"

"You just had to say it."

"What?"

"You just had to say; *Mum...this is fucking good cake.*"

A naughty child was being led up the staircase. Something followed. Along the upper hallway, waiting by the bannisters; an invisible audience. Jasmin had gone. He crept into a dark and empty room which was haunted.

"This was Aunt Mimosa's," Jasmin turned on the light, transforming the room from a dark void to a brilliant, sharp edged white. The ghost was grey, standing in the corner.

"Never heard you mention her."

"She died."

It was her ghost.

And they were still there, the audience; slobbering and distended, causing Mimosa's ghost to fade then disappear.

Church resisted the unbelievable urge to swat them away as bloated bluebottles.

The evening air whistled through the opened window. The net curtains drifted. Jasmin caught them, entwining them to form a rope, supporting her upper weight as she bent to look out. She wriggled her hips; an invitation. Denying the existence of any perverted spectators, Church took off his jacket. Taking his time, he loosened his tie and undid the top button of the despised shirt. He undid his suit trousers and stepped up behind her, leaning over, pressing into her tight bottom. "That's nice," she said. "Bloody hell, feels like you're everywhere, oh yes, do that, wet a finger, slide it up my bum. Use two. Hurt me." He was not touching her. Trousers and underpants at his ankles, already erect he slid up her skirt and began to pull down her panties, still struggling to reject that other hands were there, too. He felt vulnerable.

"No," Jasmin commanded, "leave my panties on, pull them to one side." She was reaching behind to grab his dangling tie, keeping him under her control.

"Ram it straight in hard. Do it now."

He plunged into her, feeling that closeness, that all-consuming tight warmth, her dampness and sweat. Her smell.

"Yes," she squeezed out the word, pushing back to gain his full length. "Oh shit, it's Dad's car. They're coming back. Finish me, Church. Do it."

Church did not have to move, in rapid gulps she was doing it for them, he ejaculated, that pulsating devouring fire, he did it prematurely, without announcing it, timing his false groans to coincide with her series of coarse gasps.

Car doors slammed below.

Church dressed himself watching Jasmin smile at him while squirming to adjust her wet nickers. "That's what I wanted to feel."

He pulled her away from being a display at the window and held her close, her breath slowing, he protected her from any dark entity either in the room or outside.

Taunting, the shadowy audience silently congratulated themselves.

She let go of the curtains.

***

Net curtains delicately moved in the window of the cream cottage. Philip failed to notice as he stood beside his car in the forecourt amongst the stack of rusting wrecks. The workshop door was open and that was his focus. "Ah," someone was coming. He stretched his tweed jacket about himself. He felt so cold.

"Nice car is that."

"Wah..." The accent was a shock. Philip quizzed the greasy face, peering into oily spectacles.

"Aye a right fine car."

"Oh yes er...," Philip snorted through his grey moustache at the greasy rag used to open the fuel cap and the greasy bib and brace leaning against the wing.

"I remember went they were on at beginning of that police programme."

"Oh." Philip looked down and in to Willow, her greying hair sneaking out from her white headscarf. And she was fidgeting with the map book. Again.

"No 'iding place, that were it."

"I say; we are making our way back from Scotland. Got a bit lost. Am I on the road for the A1?"

"Best fill her up then."

Willow had stopped fidgeting; the map book lay on her lap. She seemed to be gazing into nowhere. He rapped on the window. She did not react.

***

The large ball of orange was rapidly setting, creating flaming streaks across the deepening sky, the heated air poured down the rounded hills of the tea plantation.

It was cooler on the veranda of the bungalow.

The fading light gave an olive-green hue to the skin of

the young servant in white shirt and black trousers. Willow searched his enchanted face. He was admiring her.

"My dear Ramesh," Willow spoke quietly; a face was near the window. And as Willow spoke, she forever adjusted the headscarf of the sari, it flowed with shades of white, like the flowers beside the garden path, all meandering into twilight, "I do not think she approves of me wearing the sari and I do not think she approves of me talking to you."

"Surely common curtesy would allow me to converse in saying goodbye. And besides the sari was my mother's and I thank you for wearing it. If you will permit me to say so, you look as beautiful as I ever dared anticipate." He looked to the window, "And it is worth a scolding for such an opportunity."

"I think she's gone," Willow raised her voice, "we can skip formalities."

"Thank goodness. My beautiful Willow tree, I just want to hold you and kiss you one last time."

"Too many eyes."

"But you are so beautiful."

"I'm not sure If I'm wearing this properly. You say it was your mother's but I am not that much older than you. Am I?"

"You are misunderstanding me; my mother wore it when she was young; like us. It was her wedding dress and now it is a family heirloom, sacred. There is no one left in my family worthy, so I want you to treasure it."

"Now I feel even more uncomfortable."

"I wish I could have helped you dress but please believe me when I say you look beautiful. Yet you seem as uncomfortable as you did in your military uniform."

"Do I? I'm sorry."

"Please do not apologise. A willow tree gains its strength by bending to any adversity, bending gracefully."

"I shall apologise gracefully in future."

"You are using clever words," his voice sang, almost in sweet rhyme, "but I think you were more at ease without words, without clothes, lying in long grass, together, without care."

Willow blushed as he stepped closer. He held a white flower by its stalk between finger and thumb, she smelt exquisite perfume. He was close now. Perhaps it was the cooling air but she trembled. She felt his hand, delicate by her temple, the scarf rustling loud in her ear as he adjusted it to place the flower behind that ear.

"Will my life ever be complete without you, Ramesh?"

"Will I forever be waiting for you, my Willow tree?"

Looking into his brown eyes, she tenderly kissed his lips.

He stepped back and brought his palms together at his chest. He bowed to her.

She closed her eyes forever seeing his young face, forever smelling the perfume of the garden of Jasmine.

***

Philip rapped on the window again, "You have the map upside down."

She opened her eyes and wound down the window, using a finger to pull her scarf away from her ear, "No need to shout."

"It's a Wolseley int it?" The attendant persisted.

"A1?"

"Is it a 6/80 or 6/90?"

"Wha...?" Philip could smell petrol convinced it was from the man's breath. He rapped on the window again which Willow wound down again. "Money."

More fidgeting. Willow handed out a handful of coins. Philip passed them to the outheld greasy palm. "A1?"

The chap blew his nose on the greasy rag, counted the coins, dropped them into his pocket then shuffled back to the workshop.

"Well thank you very much." Philip blasted until he was behind the wheel and pulling out of the forecourt. "As cold as this wretched air."

They passed two trees; each dying in solitude.

"Pardon?" Asked Willow.

"I think this is the right direction. Check the map, do."

"Why didn't you ask the man? His back looked so painful, the way he walked and held onto the car."

"Map."

"I didn't mention it before," Willow's face did not turn away from the map book, "we never had time to ourselves. But she's aged so."

"What?"

"Poppy."

"Yes well," Philip huffed, "it's been many years since we last saw her. Took the train. Think Jasmin was soon to be shipped off to boarding school. Remember?"

"Yes," she sighed. "Seems like yesterday we visited was when I was pregnant. A sad time with her husband's funeral."

"Yes well."

"Time seems to have passed so quickly. So many sighs so many wishes."

"Ashington seems the good type."

"Always looking over his shoulder. Even at their wedding."

"Needs to; someone has to keep an eye on that girl."

"She looked beautiful in the sari."

"What? Yes...well...Never saw the point in that."

"Someone once said I looked beautiful in it."

"Yes...well..."

They slowed, creeping forward now. The road narrowed. Reptilian, with scales of stone walls; it snaked out before them across the dale.

"Are we lost?"

"Not sure but it's so dammed cold," he reached and slid the heater full over to red.

"Going to be dark soon; cold and lost."

The sun was setting ahead, beyond the horizon, casting no hues; the sky a sheet of iron.

"Wait," Philip brightened. "Look." In the distance, dots of colour rolled from left to right, right to left. "Lorries, looks a busy road. Must be the A1. Sure, it is. Will it be right turn or left? Check the map, old girl." He patted her leg.

"A glass of wine would be nice."

Philip dipped the accelerator.

"Please be careful Philip, those walls." Willow was retrieving the map book from the foot well.

"Well? Is it right or left?" The junction was dark with bushes swaying in the slipstream of the lorries sweeping by, left and right.

"Are we here already?"

"Left, or right?"

"I wish I knew."

"Wait a minute," he guffawed, "worked it out old girl; sunset straight ahead, left south. Military precision."

In a jubilant burst, Philip checked to his right and swung out to the left.

Time altered its pace.

A heavy shadow moved over them.

A gigantic tyre. A red cube exploded; a concussion with ear bursting force.

Silence.

Philip looked out through where the windscreen should be. Willow was a ragdoll, her white scarf floating to the ground. Without preamble, thrown into a world of broken glass, upside down, tarmac so close to a chewed face, petrol intoxicating, pain unbearable, tossed to dungeons of torture, walls dissolved, light muttered; Philip finally felt warm. He closed his eyes and was running, then he was flying.

C hapter 9

She closed her eyes, leaned her back into the park bench and held her breath to retain it all.   The warmth of the sun was delicious. She could hear birds chattering in the trees above.

"Dappled light with dappled sounds; that would make a lovely painting."

"Hmm," lazily she turned to see who spoke; a fledgling middle-aged lady; jeans, boots and purple hair. What a grin.

"Do you mind if I join you?" She slid in close. "Saphire tinted eyes. Love your hair. Is it naturally silver?"

"Yes," she smelt Patchouli, turned and thinly smiled, squinting into the sun. "And thank you. But I'm envious of yours."

"I was thinking of cutting mine that short so don't be envious, yours is gorgeous. I'm Lee."

"Wallace," she offered her hand, pleasantly shocked by the way it was accepted, soft and delicately brushing, palm to palm.

"What are you reading?" Lee was gently against her, twisting to see the cover. "Tao."

"And you know it's pronounced '*dow*'; impressed. And you?"

"Winnie the Pooh," she held it up.   "I wonder what character you would be.   You in your smock, you are," Lee touched her chin, "Christopher Robin."

"Oh. But he was a boy."

"Have I offended?"

"No, no."

"Too forward?"

"It's ok I'm catching up."

"Too fast then."

"I was just half asleep, dreaming."

"What do you do?"

"Studying law."

"And reading Tao?"

"That's why I was dreaming. And you?"

"An artist."

"That's why you said I would make a lovely painting."

"And you would."

A young man walked by and Wallace responded to the eye contact, "Sweet." She whistled through her teeth and watched him walk away, waiting for the head to turn; it did not.

Lee had her hand on her shoulder, "They will make you hurt."

"Tell me about it," Wallace looked to the ground.

She was only just inside her field of vision, Wallace knew Lee was staring at her, she turned to equal the gaze, then the smile. Lee's hand was still on her shoulder and she reached up to place hers on top.

"Wallace, can I take you home?"

Sheets were hung by a cane over the window, soft light flowed down through the large square roof light; a framed painting of a perfect sky above the bed; a mattress on the floor.

Frankincense must have been burnt and still there was the Patchouli. It smelt and felt of Heaven on Earth.

Wallace sensed Lee's arm around her waist, so delicate was the touch. She did not know who was trembling, perhaps both were.

Paintings lay stacked against an easel. "Wow," Wallace moved away to step around them, "they are just like photographs."

"Photorealist, or if you want to sound really good, hyperrealism."

"I used to paint by numbers."

"Probably sell better than these."

"These don't sell?"

"I do try at exhibitions but what I really need is a shop window, a permanent display but in the right place, offering commissions. But who can afford that? And…" she swung her hand across the room, "…this is my display, permanent chaos. Think Travis has the best approach."

"Travis?"

"My husband or should I say ex."

"Ex. Oh, I see. But what does he do that is the best approach?"

"What? Oh, I see what you mean." Lee folded her arms, "He's tidy for a start, which is why I like the mess but he's a writer, a poet. Just needs a table at a book fair or whatever he does, or says he does."

Wallace saw the way she was being looked at.

Lee softly spoke, "Don't look so confused." She smiled. "Relax."

"Am I that easy to read?"

"Far from it."

"It's just that you don't come across as being a married woman."

"Thanks," Lee pouted, leant forward, her shirt dipping to expose her cleavage and blew a kiss. "But then he is a permanent far-away ex."

Wallace felt a flush rising. "Is Travis a good poet?"

"You said my paintings are like photography. Travis says that photography is painting by light and his poems were paintings by words."

"Nice words?"

"Nice words, all in a line, all of them good ones, all of them lies."

"Oh."

"There, see what men can do. But enough of Travis."

Wallace was melting beneath a teasing scrutiny.

"Wallace, will you be my muse?" The voice was husky.

"Will you paint me?"

"Being a muse entails lots of things." Lee moved to stand in front of her, edging toward the bed.

"Things?" Confusion became gentle; an arousal, an invitation, a dare to back away.

"You haven't answered," Lee was closer, Wallace could feel her breath at her neck.

C hapter 10

The grey reception office was patterned by sunlight passing through etched glass.

"Good morning, Misses Ashington, "with her neat hair tied back, the sultry receptionist looked up from her desk. Perhaps a prerequisite for the job; perched on the end of her thin nose were half-rimmed glasses.   Leaning forward in her blouse to adjust the paper in the typewriter, she pressed against the desk's edge, exposing more of a teasing red bra. Church realised he was under scrutiny from the figure in the corner and did a double take. She belonged to Carnaby Street. Pin stripe suit, collar, tie, cropped silver hair; she looked like a boy.   He struggled to comprehend the elf but had to look away from the demolishing eyes. She suggested a smile while sliding the filing cabinet drawer shut with just one swing of her hips.

"Taversham is expecting you," the receptionist said. "You know the way."

Church pulled himself from the enigma.

The corridor was long and brown.

"Guess I don't exist," Church said it loud enough to be heard back at the reception area.

"Too old for you," Jasmin matched the volume.

"What about the other one."

"Behave."

The ancient varnished panels looked sticky.   Church checked by dabbing then focused on walking.   In the advancing darkness was a deep hole; he was convinced. "Hey Jasmin, you should let me go first."

"We're here."

The door was the largest of all the doors they had passed. It swung open.

"Ah, my beautiful niece," with his blubbery smirk, the greying giant beckoned.

Heavy, the room and every piece of furniture, even the air, the light; all was heavy and the same dark sticky brown. The couple followed and sat opposite him at the desk.

Church took a deep breath, "You may remember me at our wedding." Church remembered a leering blob. "I'm Sandy...um I mean...Church Ashington."

"I am so sorry for your loss Miss Jamison. Or, without seeming presumptuous, I should say it is our loss."

"Nice to see you again, Mister Taversham," Church wanted to kick his teeth.

"Taversham." There came a pause and a hint of a glance. "Friends, family, associates; everyone refers to me simply as Taversham."

"Sounds distinguished," Church lamely offered.

"Now, Miss Jamison, if I may proceed to the delicate matter of the will."

"Misses Ashington." Church amplified it by scuffing his boots across the rug.

It awoke something.

Church was diminishing. Words faded, merging into mumbled sounds and mocking laughter; a pulsating obscenity, his nightmare was bubbling from a deep black pool at his feet.

C hapter 11

Kicked dumbbells scattered out of his way across the garage floor. Breathless, Church paced, wrapping thick bandages around both fists. In one movement he turned, extended his arm and hissed, rotating his wrist to slam into the punch bag, twisting to follow on with the other fist; a fluid motion of punches rolling, wave after wave.

Outside, the sound of each punch, the sound of each hiss turned beneath a heavy sky to surge against the house.

***

Jasmin put the mug of tea down on the desk beside the French doors, "What happened to you in Taversham's office?"

***

"I don't understand what is happening, Frank. But it's nice to have someone who listens, someone who knows what they are talking about."

"At last, a relief to find you can be open."

"Yeh," Church reflected. "Funny though, talking about trying to be tough at the orphanage shows me how I've moved on, don't need to prove myself anymore, even got my own business, settled down and married."

"You have moved on."

"Yeh, but it's like I'm always apologising for my past."

"Regrets?"

"No, not so much that. Guess I don't feel worthy."

Church ducked. Frank ducked and threw in, "Not worthy?"

"Bound to be. If you were abandoned as a baby, who wouldn't be?"

"You were abandoned."

"Dumped outside a church.   That's my name, just to remind me.   That's why I chose a nickname; Sandy," he pointed to his hair.

"You chose to be called Sandy because it is a diversion from your name's reminder, a reminder of that sense of being abandoned."

"And not worthy.   Raised at an orphanage, don't deserve a wife as good as Jasmin, she could do so much better.   And I can't forget that it's her money that got me started so quick."

Church sat upright; Frank copied and listened, "How did I end up talking about all of that?"   He quietly shook his head, "Only came to see you to fix a bad dream.   But what do you think?"

"You are wondering what I think."

"These things from my dreams; are they in my head? Am I going mad, or are they real?"

***

Not before he finished scribing the hard pencil line and turn off the swivel lamp, did he look up from his drawing board.

Her eyes were a whirlpool.

"Well?" Jasmin persisted.   "I mean you just shut down in that office."

"He is a walking obscenity.   Doesn't he make your flesh crawl, the way he looks at you?"

"He is my uncle."

"Yeh, keep it in the family.   Taversham?"   He scoffed. "How come its' not Jamison if he's family?"

"His first name.   But why should that matter?"

"Concocted."   He folded his arms and swung away from her.

"Sulking? Left out of the conversation, were we?"

"Please don't taunt," he rubbed his bent nose, "I did try, you saw I did.   But it's hard to be a dog on a lead.   Except for this," he nodded to the drawing board, "I'm nothing."

"That is beautiful," she studied the details.   "Those

arched windows, your trademark. But you know you are more than any of this, don't fall back on playing that old game. Something seems to be going on with you."

He felt the soft touch of her hand on his shoulder.

"Yeh, I know," he looked up beyond the gallery to the high ceiling and tossed his pencil to the desk. "I dunno, it just seems to take over. It's always been around me yet I still can't explain properly. Can't find the words. Guess I really should see Frank again."

"You keep saying that," she said it and he closed his eyes on hearing the kindness in her words, "I wish you would," she whispered. "Or I'll go for you."

"Or maybe you'll find me on the end of a rope one morning."

"Never say that again. Or I will see Frank and tell him you said that."

"Yeh," he snuffled, "suicidal. Tell him I hear murmuring voices and seeing things, having a nervous breakdown and have me put away in the looney bin. Sorted."

Jasmin was now so far away.

"Hey," he touched her thigh and quietly spoke. "You do love me, don't you?"

She was unreachable.

"I'm messing this up completely," he nodded to himself, "I know I am. I'm so sorry about what you are going through; really sorry. You believe that don't you?"

She showed no response.

"Been meaning to ask; the party?"

"It will do us good," she finally spoke, "we need it. But for now," she sighed and looked down, "I must think of the funeral and we need to get ready. Please wear your suit."

He searched for any hint of a forgiving smile.

***

Church moved from the graveside, moved from making pointless conversation with pointless people. And as the convoy paraded off, he remained, studying Jasmin at the cemetery's far end. The heavy bulk of Taversham was moving away from her, away to his car. Jasmin walked to sit on a bench alongside a lady, a detached part of Taverham's shadow loitering behind them.

"Mum often spoke about you, Alice. And she was right, you are so pretty."

Alice quietly smiled, "I may have been pretty then but I'm a lot older now." She took Jasmin's hand, "This is where you mother would have wanted to be, alongside Mimosa."

"Something told me that, Alice, like something told me to seek your opinion." Jasmin nodded to the three stones. "Don't know if dad would approve."

"Don't you worry," Jasmin felt Alice squeeze her hand with each word. "You are coping so well."

Jasmin dabbed her eyes with a tissue. "It's my way; not showing it." She took a deep breath, "I don't know, but somehow we were not," she searched, "somehow, we were not close. And that makes it harder because now we will never have the chance to be near each other." She looked up to the high sky then turned to Alice, "Thank you again for coming all the way from Australia. And Justin."

"How well do you remember Justin?"

Jasmin put on her sunglasses and Church followed her gaze, drawn to a figure on a mound. He stood beneath a yew tree, his blonde curls down to his shoulders.

C hapter 12

The gravel on the overgrown playground wailed of grazed knees. Alongside the upright derelict school, the caravan window almost parted from its rusted hinges as the chequered-shirted scarecrow forced it to close from the outside.

He adjusted his baseball cap and stroked his ragged beard, watching the red van slip away, the air whistling in the slipstream. He savoured the envelope, "Hey man, *'par avion',*" he swayed, "now that is a good sign." He opened it and pulled out a cheque, straining to read it. "Sweet sister, you are so good to me," he held it closer, "oh you are so good to me." He kissed the cheque. "Ibiza."

The first splat of rain caused the cheque's corner to flap and bounce back. The second hit the top line of ink, "Oh sheeit," he took off his cap and felt the third drop on his bald pate confirming that it was raining. The fourth hit square in the middle of the cheque, "Goddamit." The ink was running off the page. "Oh man." He genuinely cried.

"Hey there Floyd," with an exaggerated Oklahoma accent, Jimmy was shouting from the playground's edge. "What's going down man."

"Goddam rain," Floyd hoarsely screamed, "that's what's going down." He wrung the cheque, "Sheeit," and forced it into his back pocket.

"Stopped now," the air was turning humid in the returning sun. "Come and join us and get really warmed up."

"Hello Floyd," Sarah gently called, "Zimmy says hello as well," she rocked her babe in arms.

Together they walked behind the school.

Clouds completely parted.

The hollow was in a clearing of hawthorn. A large fire was established; it roared, creating its own wind of searing heat. Cooling wet grass lapped at them as they neared the dip.

"Greetings my brothers, greetings my sister." The bespectacled lank-haired man stood tall, height exaggerated by the vertical stripes of his kaftan tied at the waist by a white sash, "You are most welcome." He gestured to a low dome draped in tarpaulin, branches giving its form protruding through the top.

"Hello Isaac," they responded in disjointed harmony.

A duo with dreadlocks appeared with a wooden wheelbarrow which they placed beside the fire.

"Welcome stones," announced Isaac, "such noble stones. I thank you stone gatherers and keepers of the fire." Using long handled pitchforks, the duo placed the stones into the heart of the fire, their faces quickly turning red.

Sarah headed across to an open-fronted hut where ragamuffins spilled out. She moved toward a flaming-haired rounded woman. "Sweet Rosemary," Sarah kissed a freckled cheek. The embrace was prolonged until Sarah swung away to place the bundled Zimmy amongst the children on a sheepskin rug in the hut. "You please look after him beautiful angels and call me if you need."

More people appeared; a rag-tag crew who lovingly greeted each other. Then apart from the stone gatherers and keepers of the fire, they all removed their clothes, piling them beside the hut where the children watched and giggled. Then, either oblivious or not acknowledging the smell of body odour, they stood in a circle naked beside the fire and before the low dome.

Isaac thumped his staff's end to the ground.

C hapter 13

"Lee, please don't close the curtains."

"I need to, the light."

"Won't the window in the roof do?" Wallace shivered. The air flowing from the window above was a cool shower over her skin, "And don't look at me like that. You know what it does." A marble statue, she opened her arms and stood, allowing her nakedness to be seen without restriction.

"Do you want me to paint you or...?"

"Or?"

Lee's long white shirt was unbuttoned, as it had been since they rose from their bed. Her hard purple nipples teasing in glimpses and with paintbrush between her teeth, striding in white boxer shorts, she was advancing.

"But I still want the curtains open."

"It excites you doesn't it, the thought that someone just might see us."

***

Outside, pedestrians floated by, shapes and colours murky, sound a drone through the grey patterned glass.

"You were annihilating poor Mister Ashington." The receptionist swivelled her chair, turning her back to Wallace.

"Who?" She played with her voice, "Innocent little me?" Pulling up the sleeves of her pin striped jacket, Wallace moved like a cat. She walked her fingers along the back of the chair. "And what were you doing to poor Mister Ashington, Janice?"

"Me?"

Wallace reached over and continued walking her

fingers slowly down to the buttons of Janice's blouse. "See what I mean; naughty lady; so many already undone." Wallace slid her small hands inside the fabric. Janice squirmed in her skirt, exposing hints of stocking tops and red silk. Inside her bra now, Wallace could feel Janice's breasts becoming clammy. She tenderly squeezed. The sun was sweeping low, piercing in, causing a beam of dusty light, spotlighting the pair. Wallace breathed into Janice's ear, "Will they see us from outside?"

"Is that what you want? Push the chair to the window then."

"Shall I?" Wallace teased, "You're just going to have to wait for the next time." She blew in Janice's ear and moved away, pausing at the mirror, tidying her suit while Janice stood, adjusting her clothing. Anyone entering would know nothing but dare suspect everything; their charged energy filled the room.

"Same time tomorrow," Janice was efficiently tidying papers and locking drawers. "Checked the diary, he's in court again so we can carry on where we left off, see how far it takes us."

Wallace saw the smile, "Well, Janice, that's something for you to think about when in bed with your husband," she checked that the stationary cupboard was locked. "In court, is he? While I'm stuck here." She took her coat and fedora from the stand.

"Stuck here? You've got me. And you never know, one day I can watch you stand in court. Now that would be a turn on."

"Never going to happen. If only you knew what a struggle it is for a woman working through law."

"If only you knew what a struggle it is for a woman working through marriage."

Wallace gently helped Janice finish pulling her blouse together and buttoned her coat. "Remember what I've said; I'm on my own and I can get up to anything if you are not there to keep an eye on me."

"And you remember what I've said," Janice was eye to eye, "you can get up to anything you like but," she pecked her, "you've awoke so much in me, I want details."

They tightly cuddled and over Janice's shoulder Wallace saw their reflection in the mirror. She swivelled so that Janice could see.

The door crashing shut and the clunk of the lock echoed throughout the office.

Seconds stretched. Another clunk took place and the store cupboard door opened, barging against Janice's chair.

Taversham's gloom filled the reception area.

Humming a *'rom pom'* tune, he fumbled with the Minolta as he waddled down the dark corridor to his office.

Chapter 14

"Should know better," Jimmy clanged around the workshop until finally becoming trapped in tangled junk. He had tugged at a roll of wire wool to give himself a small square. It tore into skin, cutting between finger and thumb, drawing blood which congealed with grime. Ignoring it, he continued polishing lengths of copper tubing, removing dull corrosion to create a shining set laid out as organ pipes.

Selecting three, he dabbed the ends into a jar of flux, the acidic paste biting into his cut. Instinct told him to flick his hands but he held on to his treasure, stamping his feet until the pain eased with the echoes.

He slid the coated three ends into a 'T' joint of the same polished metal and lit a blowlamp, kicking away anything that may ignite. Playing the flame over the joint, the copper turning blue, he watched closely, coughing against the fumes to remove the flame at the first sign of solder running like quicksilver to drip onto his boots.

He picked up the work with a cloth, offered it to the confused arrangements of pipework on the bench, gave it a quick wipe and placed it at an appropriate place of the jigsaw.

With folded arms he considered the task, "Floyd's gonna love this."

"Do you think he will?" Jimmy jumped. Sarah was there. "Is that going to be what I think it's going to be?"

"Sarah, I'm not going to lie to you." He shoved his hands in his pocket, whistled and walked out of the workshop.

"What about Gran's door?" She shouted after him.

"Fortnight Tuesday."

***

The clink of a teaspoon against bone china filled the peat-smoked kitchen. Sitting at the stove by the contorted fluepipe, her cheeks rouged, straggles of grey hair sprouting from her beret, she stirred and stirred her cup; the last unbroken one from the dresser.

"It's when the corncockles flower that I remember him most," her cracked voice floated through the door, across the flag stoned lobby to the adjacent room, the candle flame steady by the window. "He found the strength, he always did. He worked that mare hard, far harder than she could work him." Closing her eyes, she saw him come in at dusk through the front door; grimy sweat causing his collarless shirt to cling to his torso, with skin tight about his face.

Washing her cup in cold water at the butler sink, she silently dried it and placed it on the dresser beside the last unbroken plate.

A click.

The front door gently opened, inviting a ghost to enter; his. But only the night air came quietly in; an old friend. Face to face with grained red paint, she used her spindly shoulder to persuade the door to shut.

She turned and grasping the rail, made her way, one step at a time, up the steep stairs.

The door clicked open.

She went to the top hallway to turn back. The turning motion continued, giddying. With one last cry she bounced down each step, her head cracking loudly on the flag stones.

She lay for a moment, her tangled body partly on the stairs, partly in the lobby.

She found the strength, she always did, and managed to claw herself down the stairs until she lay fully on the flagstones.

The night air a shroud, her rouged cheek on the cold floor, the candle faded.

C hapter 15

"What the?" Church stood at the door, gawping.

"Good evening." At the threshold, Richard offered the bottle of wine. "May I come in? I am not lucifer."

"Bloody hell," he stood aside and rooted, watched Richard enter. Church considered his own jeans and shirt then looked Richard up and down.

"Church? You seem troubled."

"White suit."

"Oh that. Well," Richard offered a shrug, "why not?"

"Well...er come right in then, nice to see you, I thought you may not come."

"I'm a bit late but we didn't agree on a time. And. Well to be honest I hate being the first guest to arrive. I hope I'm not the last though."

"Funny you should say that; Jasmin is here but hasn't appeared. Still upstairs getting herself ready."

"Again. Why not?"

Church studied Richard as he viewed the room.

"Couldn't see much from the outside," he was gazing up.

"Yeh, I know, need to fit outside lighting, lots to do out there," Church rubbed his nose.

"But inside," Richard nodded, "I am reminded of a cathedral."

"That was my intention."

"Intention?"

"Built from scratch at my specs."

"Specs?

"Specification."

"Your design. Your own business?"

"Yep, I think it's going to work. The signs are looking good, have a few customers with work in the pipeline. I'd show you my drawings but I've tidied the desk and...."

Richard was eying the civilised groups of guests, drinks in hand, their conversation a low hum.

The phone rang at the breakfast bar, all heads turned to Church, "Don't they know what a phone is?" It stopped. "Been doing that all day."

"Nick and Eddie not here."

"Not yet. Hey sorry I'm boring you please come in properly and I'll introduce you to folk."

"No please, I hate that approach. If you don't mind, I'll just mingle. But please, you were not boring me and I've one question. The stairs, they are new but...?"

"Green oak. Not a new concept, just an idea I'm trying. They will continue twisting as they dry more, should be effective."

"I see. I..." Richard stopped abruptly, staring at the stairs.

"Are they collapsing already I..."

At the head of the stairs, the long red dress with a deeply plunged neck was attracting everyone's attention.

"Wow."

"Church," Richard offered, "your jaw is touching the floor. "I assume this is Jasmin."

"I think so."

Walking the catwalk, Jasmin slowly came down each step, her legs subtly exploiting the long slit of the dress.

"Good evening," she hooked her arm around her husband but was addressing Richard, offering her hand.

"Good evening," he accepted her hand.

"I'm Jasmin."

Church had never heard it said that way, so seductive, like the perfume.

"Richard." He endlessly held her hand.

"Church has mentioned you. A dentist?"

"Just taken over the town practice."

"A new kid in town. Are you alone?"

"I am."

"Come with me, there is someone I would like you to meet."

"Er, no, er. Richard doesn't like to be..."

They walked off and Church watched her bare back. How she moved. "What the...?" Lights outside took Church's full attention.

He went to the French doors.

On the lawn it was chilly and very dark. Coarse rubble on the driveway pushed through the soles of his moccasins. Goosebumps on his bare arms, bent low, he approached. Torchlights were cutting the night; searchlights in an air raid. Tossing aside shovels and spades, he tore an axe from a tree stump giving it a practice swing. Ducking behind shrubs, he could make out where they were; beside his red Volvo at the garage's widespread entrance.

A banshee wail, a charge; a mad axe man.

Two stood, rooted.

"Right then," Church commanded, "Nick, jack the car back up. Eddie remove the bricks and put the wheels on."

"It's a fair cop," they touched their forelocks.

"I'm going back in, I'm cold."

"Are you seriously annoyed?" One called.

"Nah."

"Lucky for you then."

Church realised he was still swinging the axe when he came in through the French doors, he shrugged at the gawping faces, "Gate crashers." It was tossed into the corner and he searched to see what was going on.

"We just love the whistle," Eddie was already there and had cornered Richard.

"Whistle?"

"Whistle and flute."

"Of course; suit. And thank you."

"You're welcome," Nick encroached.

"We hear you don't like being called Dick."

"If you don't mind."

"Richard it is, coz you are a mate of Sandy and that's all it needs."

"We did try calling Church by the name of Dinger, but he didn't like it."

"We only did it once."

"Dinger?"

"Church, Church Bell, Bell; Dinger."

"Oh yes," Richard sipped his wine, "of course."

"Plus, we don't like it if anyone calls us Dicks."

"But they only do it once."

"Grandad taught us how to deal with that sort of thing."

"Grandad taught us a lot."

"Grandad? You two are brothers?"

"Almost but I'm Razor Eddie and it's Nick the Greek. Sandy called Grandad our...What was it, Nick?"

"Our mentor, that's what Grandad was. That's how we met Church."

"Mentor?"

"Welfare come probation officer."

"An ex-con."

"Reformed he was."

"And he taught us how to stay on the right side of the law."

"Just."

"A fine line."

"Razor fine."

"Ah," said Richard; "And Nick, you are from Greece?"

"Nah we are both locals, a long line of wreckers and smugglers; Hawkhurst."

"Hawkhurst?"

"Notorious."

"Legendary."

"I see," Richard searched their blank faces. "So, what do you two do for a living?"

"Wrecking"

"And smuggling."

"Interesting. And you all met at school?"

"Nah. Our mums have been mates forever."

"Inseparable."

"We all live in a big house by the sea."

"One big happy family."

"Inseparable."

"And Church?"

"Church; well, he had a different background."

"And he is different. Grandad started to show him how to live with being different."

"Yeh, he missed Grandad the most."

"What happened to Grandad?"

"Hang on," Eddie raised his hands.

"A bit of a nosy sod aint yer," Nick advanced, "reckon you might be the law."

"Yeh."

"Or a copper's nark."

Both crowded.

"Good job you a mate of Church."

"There you are." The skimpy and sinewy blonde locked onto Richard. "Thought I'd lost you."

"No chance of that."

"Ah," Nick backed off, "so you've met Avantha."

"You know Avantha?" Richard held on to her.

"Everyone knows...oomph," Nick was halted by Eddie's elbow in his stomach.

Church stood in the gallery looking down, sounds a babble, the horde of colours a kaleidoscope spiralling up. He was determined to appear in control but could not move. He had already dropped the empty bottle of whisky; it had bumped down the twisting stairs, a slow and crooked step at a time.

He closed his eyes, his body spinning.

He woke somewhere in the night.   He was in bed. Jasmin was there; breathing delicately, her slender bare back glistening in the low light.   He wanted to tenderly stroke her downy shoulder, wake her to tell her how beautiful she was, how much he loved her.   His arm flopped on top of her and he sunk.

C hapter 16

Sarah tucked her hair behind her ears and flexed her fingers. On her haunches, skirt billowing over strong thighs, she could feel her toes curl with each squeeze of the leathery udder; milk splashing into the pail.

The goat stamped a hoof.

"Nearly finished. Be patient."

There was a sadness in her lilt, matching her eyes.

She straightened her neck and looked up to the roof, drawn by the corrugated iron creaking and flexing with the warmth of the sun outside. "And don't eat that." Moving the pail aside, Sarah stood and pulled the hay net from the goat's mouth. "Off you go," free from its tether, the goat skipped over the cobbled floor while she ambled to the house.

In the stone walled lean-to, the door was open to let in daylight. She filtered the milk through muslin draped over a small churn in a sink of cold water.

Walking down the sapling lined lane, through white clouds the sun was a gentle warmth on the top of her head, air exotic with the coconut hinted aroma of yellow gorse. Wellingtons chaffed her bare legs and her shoulder was already sore from Zimmy's weight in the sling. Before she entered the shady dip, she stopped to adjust herself, changing the milk churn over to the other hand.

As she progressed further through the rising bank the air cooled, the sound of bubbling water overpowering. Her footfall became hollow as she stepped on the wooden bridge. Down below, endless, the brown water hurled past, creating a froth.

"Hi Jimmy."

With a grin, he straightened his back and walked to hug her.

"Tell me later what you are doing."   She nodded to the neat pile of white scaffolding.

Jimmy pulled an apple from his pocket and sat on the tool box, making room for Sarah, offering a nibble to the drowsy Zimmy.

"Goat's eating the hay net," she tucked her skirt under her lap and reached to bite at the apple.

"Nice idea though, baler twine hay net.   I'll make a wooden rack."

"And," Sarah cringed, "I'm sure the woodworm holes in the byre roof are getting bigger."   She stroked Jimmy's arm.

"Diesel and engine oil," Jimmy spoke with authority, "that'll sort the buggers out."

"Well, I can help by cleaning it down first."

"Aye, long handled broom will do that."

"So much to do, hey Jimmy."

"Could always give it up and buy a wee place in the country," he snuggled inside her.

"We've done it, living our dream," Sarah lay her head on Jimmy's shoulder and sighed; a sad distant breeze.

Zimmy started wriggling and burbling. "Best go."

"Give Gran my love," said Jimmy, "haven't forgotten her door either."

C hapter 17

Taversham was breathless after closing the heavy shutters in his office, he fumbled his way to his desk, slumped over it and turned on the lamp.   Light was sombre.   He began investigating the workings of the camera. The flash went off, startling him. Podgy fingers surprisingly agile, he wound the film and opened the back to retrieve the reel.   Rising slowly, he went to a framed certificate on the rear wall and prodded a small button on the frame.   It swung away with a click to reveal a recessed metal cabinet.   Tip toed, the key chain attached to his belt loop just long enough, he opened the safe to place the camera and film in. He paused, patting, savouring the mixed contents before closing it then collapsing in his chair.

He poured a brandy.

**

"Think we deserve a brandy," the bald Yefimovich used the dual scars on his nose as a signal of might, defying anyone in Taversham's murky office to challenge his suggestion.

"We all need one," Taversham sided.

Perfectly centred over an ornately carved system of triangles and circles on the floorboards, was a corpse; a young woman, her hair in ringlets. Except for the triangle of black pubic hair, her bare body was as pale as the wax of the six candles, grey eyes forever retaining the look of disbelief, staring up at them; six ogres.

"Shame it had to end."

"Couldn't go on forever, too risky."

"Probably pregnant, been five weeks."

"Five weeks you say? Best dress her."

"A final photograph," the flash was harsh.

Grunting, fondling, probing still, they slipped a flimsy dress on her, taking delight in sliding up soiled panties.

Limp limbs flailing, they rolled her onto an oilcloth and wrapped her into it.

An odour of linseed oil filled the room.

"You know what to do."

"When I've finished, she will look as if she took a direct hit."

"Fortuitous that Jerry dropped his load on the town."

"Why don't they get a move on and invade?"

"Inconvenient." Taversham was folding a flag with swastika emblem.

"Still a shame it had to end. The girl I mean."

"I do believe she was beginning to enjoy it."

"Retarded or not, she could have talked and someone may have listened."

"Pregnant, you say? That would have scuppered things. Too many questions."

A heavy rug was rolled over the markings on the floorboards.

"Another brandy," Yefimovich insisted.

C hapter 18

A monotonous jousting match; overtaking lorries hungry to overtake, tarmac a treadmill, an endless roll split down the middle by white lines, eyes open; it was all he could see. Eyes closed; he saw the same. And an endless noise to shout above. "I think we should stop; coffee would be good." The road was wet, he squelched past a tractor belching black smoke.

"You're finally admitting it," Jasmin said, "I was ready to grab the wheel."

"Just not used to it anymore, that's all."

"But what a time to start. No wonder you're tired."

"Yes," he snapped, "here we go again. I wanted to get through London before the rush hour. I'm sorry. Ok?"

Church briefly took both hands off the wheel and looked at her, seeking some form of solace.

"Hey," Church jumped, "did you see?" The image flashed past over her shoulder. Parked in a layby was a car, it was their car, a red Volvo, the driver was himself, he was desperately alone, their eyes locked. It was gone. "Wha...?"

"Watch the road."

He blinked, "Yeh need coffee."

Church followed a vintage vehicle into a car park at a siding lined by oak trees.

He stopped and turned off the engine. Silence was a roar. He had to lock his shoulder and lean sideways to apply his weight in clicking up the handbrake. He turned to Jasmin, "Sorry."

"Forget it," she opened the car door.

"Bloody Oaks," Church read the sign and stretched,

fresh air was delicious. "This is where King Charles is meant to have hid before they chopped his head off."

"A nice thought," Jasmin marched off.

"I'll hide in the trees then."

"I need a wee that's all."

"Me too," the blue rinsed lady warbled.

"Mentioned it two hours ago," Jasmin strode with her ally.

"They never listen."

With coffee and cake still bubbling in his stomach, the backcloth of scenery had progressively changed; the road was passing through a wide rolling plain of green with dotted bare trees.

"Don't remember seeing the border, now the signs clearly say Forth Road Bridge, ten miles. So where are the first, second and third?" Church turned. Jasmin was asleep. A vendetta; he dabbed the brakes and sneered at the flashing headlights in the mirror.

"Where are we, Church?"

"Had a nice nap, have we?"

"Is that the Forth Road bridge on the horizon?"

Yes," he said "you've missed the first, second and the third. And the border."

"Really?" Jasmin looked out of her window.

"Have you got the money ready?"

"Money?"

"The toll?" Church offered.

"Toll?"

Hanging from a sweeping arc, taught steel cables wove past. Looking way down to the wide river, he beat the steering wheel in time with the tyres drumming over the bridge's sections. "Twang, gonna fall down one day."

"Not funny."

"Bad design, can't maintain it properly. Should have copied that one." He nodded to the symmetrical tangle of iron. Brilliant that one. Paint it red then start all over again."

"That's for trains."

"Yep.   Let the train take the strain.   Have you got the money?"

"Money?"

"How did we get here?"

"Do you want the binoculars?"

"The signs clearly said *'route avoiding city centre,'* I have followed them religiously since the bridge and now no more signs."

"I know where we are."

"Yes," said Church, "Edinburgh City Centre."   He regarded their regal buildings.   "And it's rush hour."

"Should have left home earlier."

"Have you noticed, cars snort and snarl in a traffic jam."

With every inch further north, the sun set a little more.

"Walking pace."

"Huh?" Jasmin did not turn to him.

"The seasons advance at walking pace.   If you leave Brighton when crocuses are just in bloom, and walk north. They will be just in bloom all the way up."

"Assuming someone had planted them along the road you intend to walk."

"A long walk."

"Long and lonely."

"Dark now. Gonna be dawn when we get there."

Church was thankful that there were no oncoming headlights to blind him, he could drive down the middle of the single track. The muddy ditches each side looked hungry. He peered to his right, "Wonder what it all looks like?" Flickering paraffin lamps, that distinct colour, distant lights through windows of the sparse spread of houses conveyed to him that this was their domain, their history, not his; keep out. "No shops."

"We have lots of food and drink, I put it all in the boot."

"The headlights are becoming dim, best stop and clean them."

"Church," she touched the back of his hand, "thank you for driving me all this way."

"Anything for you. I do love you; you know.

Her hand slipped away.

"And I guess you love me," he shrugged, "though I can't think why you would want to."

"Yeh, go on; undervalue yourself."

"I've had enough."

Eyes closed and under a blanket, Church knew it was dawn. He remembered; *'The darkest hour is right before the dawn;'* that darkness always made him feel empty and nauseous. And he was cold. He started the engine and turned on the blower.

"You hardly slept. I've been studying those mountains. Is that snow or clouds?"

"I think it's snow, look."

"A cresta run for you."

Ahead, in a shaded hollow beneath a low sky, snow was piled each side of the road; weeks of grime, frozen.

"Unbelievable," Church said, "from Spring to Winter."

"A long walk."

"Lonelier and colder."

A bare Rowan challenged in acres of slumbering wilderness.

"Guess this is the way."

"Straight on and turn right by the ruin."

"You remember?"

"I remember the ruin, used to think it was haunted."

"It still is," the gaping windows looked starving.

Their way became a potholed track. Church steered the car around each hole, full with black water of unknown depth. Ahead was a stone building; two windows aside a red door, two windows in the slate roof. The perimeter of the tangled garden had a low wall with a gate for the path which led to the house. And dominating, still retaining golden autumn leaves, was a beech tree.

"I used to climb that, didn't think it was that tall."

"In films," Church said, "there would be a swing hanging from a branch and it would still be swinging."

"There was a swing."

They stopped.

"Best pull in a bit more, people may want past."

"There's houses down that track?"

Church opened the boot to pull out his anorak, passing Jasmin hers. She was shivering.

"You ok Jasmin? It sure is cold."

"Just a bit strange being here again."

"I bet," he put his arm around her. She was rigid. "I can only guess how hard this is for you." The gate struggled to open; equally as welcoming.

A king and a queen; the dormer windows looked down.

Hushed and waiting; all was hushed and waiting.

"I was praying it would be there," Jasmin retrieved a rusting key from beneath a flower pot of lavender, grey shoots sprouting. The lock opened easily, poised. And the red door swung in after only a touch.

C hapter 19

Throughout the gorge, the roar was a loud and continuous companion for Jimmy perched on the bridge edge over the boiling stream. Mudslides were common, the same mud that soaked into the knees of his dungarees. He scarcely put his weight on the brace and turned it; the sharp bit cut easily into the wood. Bright orange; the clean waste spilled out. The odour of tar rose; a retention of when the wood was once a railway sleeper. He aligned metal brackets over the holes and inserted coach bolts, spanner poised over the square heads.

"Ok it's time to come clean, Jimmy," soft words originated close to his ear, no need to overcome the noise of the water, her breath was sweet.

"Sarah." He turned and kissed her, "Sorry I slipped away, did look for you."

"Knew this is where I'd find you."

"Is Zimmy with Rosemary?"

"She loves it."

"Nature's Mother."

"Ok Jimmy," hands on hips, she jaunted, "come clean."

"Simple. Won't be long before Zimmy is walking."

"A while yet. And?"

"Look at the drop. Gonna erect barriers."

She nodded to the neatly arranged pile, "Out of those white painted scaffold poles?"

"You got it."

"Why don't you ask the council?"

"How many times have you asked them to upkeep our track?"

"And when will this be finished?"

"Fortnight Tuesday. Why?"

"See the bath in the kitchen; I'd love it if water came out the taps."

"Twenty-two-millimetre pipe on order. Dole next week."

Sarah encroached coming close to his cheeky face. "This is a wonderful life."

They held each other.

"Have you got over the shock?" He gently asked.

"Sort of. Miss taking the milk over. Emptiness."

"As long as it didn't bring up other stuff. Wish I'd done the door while she was there to see it. One last cup of tea."

"Not to be. See you later."

Her kiss and warmth remained while he watched her. Plodding now, she went up the hill and vanished amongst the pines.

The throb of a diesel engine rolled down. The tractor was held back by the reins of gears and power of the engine, heavy black tyres slowly crunching over gravel. The engine died.

"Well well Jimmy. Fit like?" The holler came from inside the cab.

"Aye aye Willy, nae bad. Yersel?"

"Jist glorying on." The ruddy farmer dropped out and swaggered on his pelvis. He stroked his stubbled chin, "Fit you up to?"

"I'm building a barrier, to stop the wee yin toppling in."

"Oh," he stood back, "but that's right fine. A guid job as usual. But the council, they should."

"Waste o' time, ye ken that."

"Oh well, I suppose, I'd best check the gimmers."

The tractor grumbled to life and Jimmy stood aside, watching the giant wheels circle past.

"And I have left something behind and it haunts me now," Jimmy sang then jumped with the blare of a horn.

"Aye aye Jimmy. Fit like." The postal van could get no closer.

"Didna see you, Alec." Jimmy looked in at the postman's big nose.

"Fit you up to?

Jimmy sighed, "Barriers."

"Aye but the council should…."

Jimmy's raised hand stopped him.

"Well, I'd best finish the rounds. Nothing for you but one here for the 'Old School'. And it's *'par avion'*.

"What's in it?"

The van took off, the wind whistling in the slipstream.

Hands on hips, Jimmy looked both ways. "Anyone else?"

He tried to orientate himself, struggling to pick up thoughts which he left in the toolbox. An unmistakable and unique clatter advanced. A rusted campervan shunted, juddered, then stalled to a halt. Isaac stepped out. "Good morning, James."

Jimmy looked up at Isaac's eyes, magnified by the lens of wire framed, glasses.

"James," Isaac solemnly spoke, "are you going to attempt another joke about tall Dutch men?"

"I'm working on one involving windmill sails."

"I have to duck."

"That's my line of thought."

"What are you doing here?"

Jimmy sighed, "Can I tell you later, please?"

"Of course, James but you are always working."

"No other way, habit of my short lifetime."

"Many lifetimes," Isaac nodded.

"Goddamit Isaac," the hollering did not have a source until Floyd rounded the corner, "Did you not see me waving?" His straggly hair, his beard and his shirt flapped as he waved his arms; all demonstrating.

"Of course, I did not."

"Hiyah Floyd, good to see you man."

Floyd scrutinised the sky, "Nope, aint raining. See this thing here my dear sweet Jimmy," from his back pocket he pulled an envelope.

"'*Par avion,*'" said Jimmy.

"Sure is. My sweet sister, I thank you. I can get to Ibiza now."

"Don't leave me," dropping to his knee Jimmy feigned a sob, "you can't," he kissed the back of Floyd's hand.

"Goddamit, Jimmy."

"Floyd needs his dreams" Isaac stated. "We all do. And I thought you would be going to the Isle of Wight, James. '*The Boy*' is alive and will be there, though they all want him to be someone he used to be."

"I liked him the way he was."

"Some people are not allowed to change, while others promise they will."

"I know," Jimmy sagged, "Sarah said it was okay for me to see Dylan but so much to do."

"You are truly grounded. And Sarah's darkness has moved away, she is surrounded by Angels of bright children, the old lady is with them."

"Yeh," Jimmy scuffed, "thanks Isaac."

"It is not my doing, James. Floyd; you want a lift to the bank?"

The noise of the campervan gone, Jimmy nodded, "Yeh, thanks Isaac." He started to throw tools back in the box, "Try again tomorrow?" He looked around, "Nah, enough of the day to do a bit. No point tho, gonna be a coach load of folk lined up at the top. What do you think Jimmy, I don't know James what do you think? The BBC, maybe an outside broadcast crew is on the way, be on telly. Should set up a stall, sell our wares."

A shadow at his feet made him shut up and turn.

The anoraked Sandy haired fellow was regarding him with his head to one side. Jimmy then realised there were two. The lady was also in an anorak. Matching anoraks.

"I'm sorry to trouble you," she was stunning, thought Jimmy, but scared.

"Hi," Jimmy tried to reassure with a smile, "we were just talking to myself."

"Hi," the Sandy haired fellow stepped in, someone not to argue with. "Don't know if you can help us, we are looking for someone." He checked with his lady, "Sarah?"

C hapter 20

In near darkness, Taversham watched intently, bringing the image into focus in the shaking camera lens. Wallace stood facing him; her boyish face, mischief in her eyes, her tiny breasts fully revealed, palms of both hands brushing the top of her cropped hair. The camera clicked. She finished opening her shirt down to her delicate navel to line up the buttons which resembled her nipples. The camera clicked. She neatly closed the shirt. The camera clicked.

"What do you think?" Janice was out of sight, her capering muffled. "Next time; in his office?" Lights were turned off.

Taversham waited in that darkness until convinced they had left. Turning on the light in the claustrophobic stationary cupboard, he adjusted his trouser belt, leaned on a cabinet and wheezed. Scarcely recovered, he placed the camera aside and fiddled to slide a plywood section along a shelf to conceal the mirror's back, placing reams of paper in their original spot.

***

Two bulks filled the empty cupboard.

"So that's what a two-way mirror looks like." Yefimovich chuckled. "Heard about 'em. Could have done with one up in Scotland. Shame, I cannot go back."

"I fully intend to keep an eye on things," Taversham said. "Creates knowledge and of course, power." Taversham regarded the shaven headed monster, "It only seems to work if dark this side, light in the reception."

"Ah, I see." They spilled out of the crammed space, "So

this is going to be the reception?"

"Yes, change it. Now that it is," Taversham searched the ogre's face, "procured."

"Well done, Taversham, an admirable acquisition. Shame about Blenkins." Yefimovich laughed, his body wobbled. "Fell off the pier, did he? Pity no one can fall off the pier now, lifted the bloody boards, barb wire, mined the beach. Damn them all I say."

"No one noticed that his lungs were filled with bath, not sea water. And no one noticed the bruises on his ankles. How comical he was when I pulled him under. Thought he would never stop wriggling. All his bits," Taversham chortled, "wriggling, bubbling. Wriggling over. Bubbling over. No more senior partner."

"No one noticed, you say; nods in the right places is what I say. Shame about these bloody windows though, all boarded up."

"I'll have them replaced when the war is over. Shutters in the office; privacy."

"Yes privacy; that's what we need."

"I do believe there is a cellar."

"A cellar? Good show," the ogre rubbed his hands.

"But for the rest, I rather fancy etched glass, it can be made to look like lacework."

"Mind you," Yefomovich jabbed, "all boarded up; get up to all sorts of things."

"We may have a recruit. New beginnings for our new circle. A photographer."

"A photographer? Better all the time. Be even better once the invasion is done with."

"Doorways open, the path laid out." Taversham stroked his double chin, "In the meantime, as you say, a good place to get up to things, private things and a good place from which to pass information across the water."

"Told 'em the about the pier and the beach. They said they want more delicate information. Bit of a romp this spy business, hey."

"Trust my brother to spy on the wrong side," Taversham tutted.

"Told em about that too."

"Oh? Oh, I see."

Chapter 21

"I can never thank you enough," said Jasmin.

'*I, not we,*' silently challenging, Church sat opposite.

He shifted his attention to the crammed room steaming with an odour of boiled nappies, the bowed ceiling, scarcely an inch of concrete to stand on, piles of unopened boxes, plates, buckets on the table. And the bath. It sat at his feet.

"This place is so quaint," Jasmin continued, "I love that window, so tiny."

Church looked at it. It was sealed with dried and cracked putty, out of alignment above the kitchen sink.

"It's the least we could have done, we were both so fond of Gran," Sarah poured tea. Church hated that sound.

"Gran? Is that what you called her?" Jasmin quietly asked. "Sounds a fond name. Always been Aunt Poppy to me."

"We loved her like she was our Gran," Sarah closed her eyes.

And," Jimmy rocked in his chair, Church switched his attention to him, "we made sure she had a good send off. We can show where she is rested, next to her husband."

"Thank you for doing all of that," Jasmin folded her arms, "we couldn't get away in time. And I'm sure you knew Aunt Poppy better than I did and what was right for her."

"It's the least we could do," Sarah distributed the mugs.

"Are you sure the money was enough?" Jasmin was using her overkindly voice.

"More than enough, we owe you some," Jimmy stood and opened the sideboard drawer, Church shifted in his chair to give some space. "Thanks," Jimmy tentatively nodded to

Church.

"No please," Jasmin held her hands up, refusing the envelope.

"Please," Jimmy stood fast.

"Are you staying long?"

Church realised Sarah was speaking to him.

"Back tomorrow."

"Where is it you are from, Church?" Jimmy teamed with his wife.

"Same place as Jasmin, near Brighton."

"What about you?" Jasmin asked Sarah, "Not local. Where are you from originally?"

"I'm Irish origin but we came up from Oxford," she reached over to touch Jimmy's hand, "It will be a year next week."

"Yeh," Jimmy added and looked to Sarah, "moved up to get out of the rat race."

"Self-sufficient," Sarah joined in, "living off the land."

"Wow," Jasmin beamed, "good for you."

"How do you manage?" Church saw everyone looking at him, expecting the long-awaited oracle. "Money?"

"Church," Jasmin cautioned.

"No, it's a good point," Jimmy rubbed his forehead. "Child benefit and yeh I'm on the dole."

"Uh huh," Church nodded.

"But I'm working at doing odd jobs, helping out here and there to make enough."

"And we hope to sell our surplus," Sarah contributed.

"Wow," Jasmin continued, "I think that's a great plan. Isn't it Church?"

"Yeh."

"Yes," Sarah continued, "Jimmy is a plumber but he can turn his hand to anything."

"The bath?" Church was giving no hint of emotion; none to give.

"Well," Jimmy laughed, "I'm trying to convince Sarah,

we should plumb it in right here in the kitchen, save on pipe runs. The Aga has a back boiler. But really, I gonna drag it into the bedroom and fit it in there."

"So that's what an Aga is," Sarah considered the stained enamelled contraption. "And is that peat?" She reached to touch the earthy brown bricks piled in a basket.

"So how many rooms do you actually have?" Church challenged.

"This room and the bedroom through there, he pointed to the new tongue and grooved door. "But and ben."

"Sorry?" asked Jasmin.

"But and ben, this type of house, that's what they call it up here," Sarah smiled.

"So, you will run it to the septic tank."

"We are still investigating that, Church. There is an outside toilet."

"And a milk parlour," Sarah added.

"Should have a demolition order on it."

"Church." He refused Jasmin's frown.

"It's ok," Jimmy intervened. "It has," he turned to Jasmin, "It means that the council want us to do work and bring it up to standard before we can live in it. But we are living in it, so…. tough for the council."

The door to outside opened, squeezing into the last bit of available space.

"Rosemary," Jimmy trumpeted.

"Inevitable," Rosemary beamed.

"Zimmy's home."

***

Cold and bare, the very bones of the house were cold and bare.

And waiting.

A frail light came through the glass pane above him. Church stood at the top of the stairs, head down, empty, staring at the flagstone floor below, dark in the shadows. He walked over creaking boards through one of the two doors facing each other. The room was bare. He turned and went through to the other.   The bed was stripped to the mattress. Two wardrobes stood each side of the window, their doors open; waiting.

"So rude." He heard Jasmin's snap from behind.

"So nice and chatty." He did not bother to turn.

"Of course."

"Of course? How come you can't be that way with me?"

"What do you mean?"

"You know what I mean, the whole journey up here and before that."

"Before?"

"There's something," Church added.

"Something?"

"Something else going on with you."

"Like what?"

"I don't know but there is something, he paced, "something about you."

"A fine one to talk. But I don't know what you mean," Sarah folded her arms. "And before we go, I want to see Gran's grave."

"It's Gran now, is it? Go on your own."

C hapter 22

"What actually happened to Aunt Mimosa?"

A hesitant breeze dipped across the grassy mounds of the cemetery, Alice closed her coat and swivelled on the bench to look directly at Jasmin. "She was killed in the war. One of the first bombs to fall on Brighton."

"I knew that bit. But why all the mystery?"

"Well," Alice shifted uncomfortably, "you see," hesitation created an empty space. "I don't think you know this bit but Mimosa was little bit simple; backward."

"Backward?" Jasmin jerked to look directly at Alice, "I never knew that."

"It wasn't a secret, more that the family never admitted to it."

"Mum never said."

"Away with the fairies, your father always said."

"Hey," Jasmin smiled, "sounds a nice place to be."

"It was. Mimosa was always happy. I loved her to bits," Alice bit her lip.

"But I felt there was something else going on surrounding her death."

"That's the thing," she quickly nodded, "Mimosa disappeared."

"Disappeared?"

"Four, no it was five weeks before, before her body was found, she had disappeared. And," Alice hesitated once more before blurting, "there was a rumour that she was pregnant. It probably would have been overlooked had she not been missing."

"Pregnant?

"Just."

"And no one knew what happened?"

"The nearest to an answer was that she had become confused and disorientated and..."

"For five weeks?"

"With the war going on there was so much turmoil, especially in Brighton. We expected the Germans to invade."

"The war, yes. Mum was in the WAAF and Poppy went to Scotland with the land army but Dad; well Dad never spoke about the war."

"He was dropped in France, helped the French resistance. He was a spy."

"Dad? A spy? Really? My Dad? No."

"Got captured. Really brave."

"My goodness."

"Don't think your father liked me."

"That's my father." Jasmin turned to the three graves. "Never that close, we didn't talk like we are now." She smiled at Alice, "It's like you're my Mum."

She felt Alice take her hand, "I sat here once," Alice said, "with your Mum. You and Justin played just over there. Devoted." From her bag she passed Jasmin a small black and white photograph.

"Devoted." Jasmin looked up at the sky.

"But your mum; maybe I shouldn't say this but I sensed that she was always on the point of admitting she was wasting her life."

"Really?"

"She was in Ceylon toward the end of the war," Alice was squeezing her hand once more, "A hint of romance, although she never said. But I knew her well enough."

"That fits now, somehow." Jasmin thought about it, "Mum always had that faraway look, always on the point of telling me something."

"That's what your mum often said of me. Giving clues,

apparently."

"Mum asked," Jasmin continued, "no she begged me to wear her white sari at my wedding."

"A white sari, that sounds beautiful."

"It was. I'll find some photos and send them; they are all together now, in a box, the sari and old letters; my memories alongside my mother's. Sounds sad, doesn't it?" Jasmin was asking herself.

"Exquisite sadness."

"I felt like a far eastern princess."

Alice quietly laughed, "I once said you and Justin were a prince a princess."

"I think Church liked it; he had enough trouble coping with the day. And Dad never really noticed. It made me feel like it was a wasted day. And two best men?" She hid her head, "Why did I agree to that?"

"Shame to waste a day. Shame to waste a life."

Jasmin slipped the photo in her pocket, put on her sunglasses and swinging her legs, looked up.

"Thank you," said Alice, "thank you for sharing this time together before we go back. Going to have to go back, keep putting it off and I think Justin likes being here."

"I'm gonna miss you. And Justin. Wish you weren't going."

"Your mum wished something like that. Always wishing, always sighing."

C hapter 23

In her floral dress, the young woman with grey eyes and hair of ringlets stood by her bed at the white bow window, lace curtains drifting with the draught.

"Hello my dear Mimosa," someone had taken her hand, stroking and squeezing with every word. "Nothing to be scared of."

Heavy shadows descended.

She looked up at them.

***

The phone on the breakfast bar rang, Church was already at the door. It stopped.

"Jasmin," he was bellowing up the stairs. "Off to meet with a new client; John Airedale."

No reply came.

Rain began to hit the windows; droplets rolling down.

He left.

She came down the stairs in her dressing gown, bare footed and bare legs. Tears rolled, clinging to the hair at her cheeks. She sat at the bar stool and stared at the floor.

The phone rang again. She picked it up.

"Hello."

"Jay Jay, it's Justin."

"Thanks for calling back."

"Look, I know what we agreed but I need to see you again. Jay Jay; please."

"Tomorrow morning. Same place." She put the phone down and spent the day looking at a creased black and white photograph of two tots smiling and holding hands, him with his long curls.

***

In the bare room at the white bow window, Jasmin shivered in her floral dress, she rummaged in her handbag and drew out a miniature of white rum. She swigged it down in one and let the bottle fall to the makeshift bed; a blanket, their encampment, the remains of his stash, the shared joint. She wrapped her arms about herself and stared along the beach road.

"Justin," she sung his name. He was forever walking away, down that road, taking his tenderness.

The remaining smoke from cannabis still lingered, she inhaled and closed her eyes, falling asleep, still standing, still feeling Justin's embrace; his touch, his smell, carrying her away.

A wave engulfed; arms about her, too many arms for one person, their strength overpowering everything, especially fear. She felt herself lifted, hands exploring, squeezing her breasts, sliding up her skirt, her thigh. A seeking finger explored her anus, she allowed her weight to drop, the finger slid inside, supporting her whole weight, all emotions controlled, suppressed, except for one; obscene pleasure.

A darkness deepened.

"Good afternoon, Miss Jamison."

"What," snatched from nightmares Jasmin turned and staggered, she felt an arm stopping her fall. "Justin, you've..." She stared up.

"Forgive me if I startled, young lady," Taversham jangled keys, taunting. "Force of habit from the war. I always have checked over the property anytime it is not occupied. Security, you know."

C hapter 24

"Sandy, you've come back."

"Yeh," Church remembered Jake sitting across the tables exactly in the place when last he was in the steamy café.

"Didn't know you smoked."

"Started again," he lit his cigarette determined not to cough in front of the unwelcome onlooker.

"Bad for you, or so they are starting to say."

"Yeh, yeh." The door's sprung bell clanged, "Bloody hell," Church locked onto the silver-haired suited girl marching in.

She was challenging his stare.

A duel; this time in his own territory, Church was not going to back down. She ordered a coffee and waited, fingers drumming the counter, her eyes still matching Church's gaze. Carrying her cup, she strutted directly to him and sat at his table.

"He's ripping you off, big time."

"Pardon?" He stubbed out his cigarette and searched her blue eyes.

"Taversham, you shouldn't be using him for a start."

"What? But he's Jasmin's uncle. What's the problem with that?"

"Unethical. But he's ripping you off."

"What? How?"

"He's very clever about it. Not just the obvious stuff like cash in the bank, although I'm sure he's taken a slice off that. But it's hidden stuff, family investments. Not sure what he's doing with the properties."

"Woah, slow down. Are you saying Taversham's, what's the word, embezzling Jasmin's inheritance?"

"She really needs to read what she's signing."

Church grunted, "She's on another planet."

"Taversham is good at that."

"Hold on a minute, this is too much, too fast. He's a slimy turd, that's true. What do I need to do here?"

"What you called him is an understatement. But he's clever. Never lets me in on any dodgy dealings. I'm just doing his boring stuff."

"Dodgy dealings? Can we fight him?"

"You can but it's a long and complicated process, could be expensive. He also has people in high places who he has a hold on."

"What sort of hold."

"A corrupt hold. Things for blackmail."

"Things for blackmail?" Church had to repeat it to comprehend what she was saying.

"You can beat him though, don't think his reach extends that far."

"Sounds like a battle."

"A long and dirty fight," Wallace nodded.

"Why are you telling me this?"

"Survival."

"What?"

"I'm Wallace," she offered her hand.

It felt so tiny.

"I have to go. This never happened."

Church sat alone, "Did that really happen?"

The door's bell clanged through his brain.

C hapter 25

"It'll be like the old days." Eddie slipped off the stool and steadied himself on the bar. "But shush, landlord may hear." He staggered, obviously disorientated by trying to hold his head high, aloof. "Blackmail implies accumulated evidence."

"Eddie, you've got it," Church shook him by his shoulders, "finally."

"Yers," Nick slurred, "accumulated evidence; that's what we need to accumulate, then we've got him by the balls."

Church slapped Nick's face, "Finally, you've got it, too. How long has it taken me to get your brains to work out what I've been telling you?"

"About six pints," Nick waved his empty glass under Church's chin.

"Leave it to us Sandy."

"Absolutely not, I'm coming with you."

"Why don't we just torch the place?"

"Eddie, piss brain," Church slapped him again.

"That would destroy the accumulated evidence," Nick shouted.

"Well done, Nick."

"When?"

"Now?"

"No not now," with outstretched arms, Church held them both by the throat, "we need to be sober. Tomorrow."

"Then we've got him."

"And not a word to Jasmin."

"Not a word to no one."

C hapter 26

Yefimovich could not move, pinned by a person at each arm and at each ankle over the ornate legends painted into the concrete floor. Beneath a low wood ceiling, Taversham stood over it all, his weighty legs protruding from his black gown; they all wore black gowns, except for Yefimovich. He was naked and bruised.

"Why?" Yefimovich spat blood.

"Shall we say; a coup." Taversham knelt across his chest, his mood darkened, "Hold him tight, he may kick."

Yefimovich did not kick, nor did he make a sound while Taversham throttled him, his own screwed face red with expended force.

The last breath from Yefimovich filled the dingy air. They coughed, retching with the stench.

"Hurry up and be rid of his stinking remains." Taversham stood and placed a handkerchief to his mouth. "Burn it." At the base of wooden stairs, he twiddled his fingers at his comrades, "I shall do away with any suggestion of an autopsy, have him cremated and see to it that I have his ashes." At the shadowed trapdoor at the top of the stairs he wheezed to himself, "If we fulfil his wishes then we can only hope that he will fully depart."

***

She stepped out of her office into the gloomy corridor.

"Ah, Wallace."

Taversham blocked her path.

"I have a task for you, my dear."

"A task," she placed her hands by her side and dipped

her head, eyes holding him.

"My office light...it keeps...," he twiddled his fingers, "flickering."

"And?"

"And I require you to arrange an electrician to remedy the issue."

"You want me to arrange it?"

"This old building has so much history; even before my time of occupancy."

"I'm busy, if you don't mind," Wallace indicated that she wanted by.

"Beneath your very feet is a cellar, all sealed up. So much history, all sealed up."

"Really," she judged the space available; too narrow to pass him.

"I have been wanting to speak to you."

"In a corridor?"

"So much history, becoming lost."

"Taversham, that is the nature of history."

"My circle of associates is diminishing, time passes, people...well they grow old, they die."

"And that is the nature of people."

"And I am seeking to build up a new circle."

"Circle?"

"Of associates."

"Taversham look I..."

He halted her with a raised hand. "I wonder if we, you and I, would begin a new circle."

"What?"

"I've taken up a hobby, joined a camera club. Night school."

"Well good for you. Now I..."

"Useful it is, to have films developed of a, shall we say, delicate nature. Would you like to see them?"

She saw him leering at her and altered her stance. "Certainly not. Let me by or...."

"I think you should," the mood changed; deepening, threatening.

"I beg your pardon?"

"If you saw my interesting attempts at photography, I feel sure it would change your mind in assisting me in the new beginnings of my circle. It would become our circle."

"Let's be clear," the whites of her eyes were sharp in the gloom, "we are work colleagues, which itself is unfortunate. But that is far as it goes."

"Here. Tonight. Midnight." He stepped aside.

C hapter 27

Traffic and pedestrians diminished with the day's passing. Three huddled in the street outside the recessed front door.

"No torches, Church," Eddie snatched it from him.

"Night vision," Nick added.

"But it's not dark yet," Church pleaded.

"It will be inside."

"Too early.   We should have come later," Church persisted.

"That's when the rozzers are out."

"Blend in will you, Sandy.   Take that balaclava off. Gloves on."

"Bloody hell," stooping at the door, Nick beckoned Eddie, "antique."

"It's a Jeremiah."

"Nah it's a Charles."

"What you two on about?"

"The lock; 1818, Jeramiah and Charles Chubb."

"Look," said Church, "I didn't invite Arthur Negus. Open it, will you."

"Did that five minutes ago."

The grey reception was hollow; the glass door rattled shut and the lock was clicked behind them.

"Bloody hell," said Nick.

"This place is creepy," Eddie wisely concluded.

"Wait till you see the rest. This way."

They inched in the dark, down the corridor, "I'm still convinced there's a deep hole here," Church used the wall to guide him until his hand struck the doorframe. "We're here.

Not locked." They entered and clustered in the office doorway, closing it behind.

"Pitch black."

Someone turned on the light. It was brilliant.

"For Pete's sake," Church halted mid scream then grated, "you said no torches."

"Look," Eddie calmly pointed.

"Shutters," Nick continued, "light not coming in."

"Light not going out."

"Just look at this place, what's going on?"

Floorboards had been lifted. In the brown office of bookcases, heavy desk with chairs, snips of wire and tools lay strewn around a step-ladder.

"Worth a bit."

"Put the wire down."

"Look at that."

Church stepped back and continued walking back, passing through the walls to stand alone in an empty street. It was dusk; an immediate confliction of lights. Reality rushed him back inside. The rug had been lifted and fully exposed on bare boards, in the spotlight of a new bulb, was an ornate pattern of triangles and circles.

"Beautiful bit of carving that, craftmanship."

"Seen that sort of thing in a blue movie, devil worship, sacrificing virgins."

"Never find a virgin round here."

"Please," Church quietly spoke.

"You alright Sandy? What's up?"

"He's away on one."

"Please," he struggled to move his eyes away from the carving, "let's do what we came to do and go."

"Right," Nick and Eddie rubbed their hands. They scanned the room.

"Nothing obvious."

"Desk drawers?"

"Nah."

"Bookcase too heavy to move."

"Floor?"

"Could be."

"Nah."

"Wall hangings," the two said in unison.

"Only one."   Nick walked to the framed certificate, "Another giveaway, see, floor just a little bit worn here, same as under the desk."

"Prolonged use."

"Hope you're paying attention, Sandy. Grandad's tricks of the trade."   Nick pulled at the frame then ran his hands around it. *'Clonk.'* It swung away from the wall.

"That's a Henry Brown."

"1886"

"Doddle."

The safe was open.

"What is all this?" Nick was pulling at a neat display of papers and items from slots in the opened safe.

"Slow down," Church picked everything off the floor to arrange it on the desk.

"That's a swastika," Eddie waved the sheet of paper.

"Just loads of documents and bits of junk. No dosh."

"Waste of time."

"Church called a halt.   "Just slow down, let's not spoil this. It may seem worthless but I'm positive it means a lot to certain people."

"Accumulated evidence," the two lads proclaimed.

"Hey, I've found the holy grail," Nick brandished a chalice.

"Slow down, I said."   Church raised both hands, "We need to organise ourselves. You are not looting tonight."

"Ok boss, respect. What do you want us to do? We need to get out."

Church sifted.   "This means nothing to me, can't find Jasmin's name but…well…Take some of the stuff but leave stuff behind. Make it obvious…"

"He'll know that we know what he's up to," offered Nick.

"And we've got some of his stuff as evidence should we need it. Right Boss?"

"Hey look at these," Nick neatly laid out photographs on the desk.

"Bit blurred and fuzzy, but what are they doing. That looks like a boy."

"That's a pair of tits, that's definite."

"They could be the virgins."

"Let me see. Looks like the reception but different." Church flipped through the pile and became withdrawn. "I'll take all of these," he quietly insisted and investigated the safe. "And these," he picked up rolls of film. "And as for this," he threw the camera down and stamped on it.

Marching to the bookcase, he slid books and envelopes off a shelf and selected a red box file, emptying the contents on the floor. At the desk, he placed into the box all the photographs, film rolls and a selection of the safe contents. "Let's go." As a last thought, he picked up a large key and tossed it in.

Church surveyed the reception while the lock was being picked again. "One more thing," he wrapped his balaclava around his fist, walked to the mirror and smashed it.

"Out and lock the door."

"Can't trust anyone these days."

C hapter 28

Orange light from the streetlamp came in with Wallace, her feet crunching on glass.

"Someone's been here," Taversham stood whining.

"As I see," she saw the smashed mirror. "And no doubt you require me to phone the police. I'll let you explain as to why we are here at midnight."

"Wait," he stared, "close the door and lock it."

Wallace complied but maintained her distance, continuously side on as he circled.

He shot a finger to her, "This is your doing."

"Who do you think you are?"

"Come with me."

Wallace held back but followed and stood in the corridor, watching from outside his office.

He progressively dissolved.

"It may have been the electrician," Wallace entered and quietly pondered, "but unlikely."

"Pathetic diversions." He rose. "This was you."

"You call me pathetic," she strode and inspected the office. "Only you know what's behind all of this. I think I will call the police. A full investigation. Would you like that?"

He picked up the broken camera, turned and hurled it at her. It struck her temple, she staggered. He launched himself with surprising speed. She felt the disgusting touch of his hands about her throat, his open mouth close to hers, his breath foul. Rocking on her heels she shifted her stance to be angled to him. In circular movements, she forced her arms high inside his grip, the hold was broken, she rolled back, bent her elbows, swung her hands palm to palm and pushing forward with a piercing shriek, lunged up at his chest, the explosive force emanating from her whole being. He staggered. Her palms parted, arms completing a circle, she rolled back on her heels then forward to explode her hands on his chest again. A tree was felled. The floor shuddered as he smashed down on his back. Her arms completed the arc to rest by her sides, dissipating the remnants of energy. It took two blurred seconds.

"Zhongguo wushu," she bowed, "a far more worthwhile night school than your camera club." She checked that he was still breathing; his chest like bellows. "That's why I can go anywhere at midnight."

Wallace calmly checked through the mess. Taversham raised an arm. "Stay down," she commanded, "or you will never get up."

"Nope," she picked up papers and tossed them around, "can't find anything concerning me. Some fascinating stuff though. Love the carvings on the floor. I think I'll just leave you to sort it. We will be here in the morning, business as usual, create no suspicion. And should you call the police, I will speak the truth the whole truth and nothing but. And from now on, hear this, I will be the one in control."

Eyes closed, Taversham lay.

He was racked by a pain, especially the back of his throbbing head, it had struck the floor. By sound he could visualise Wallace leaving; her efficient footfall clicking down the corridor, passing over the cellar and into the reception. "What?" She was at the smashed mirror, "Sick bastard." The door was unlocked then left open.

Night crept in; pattering through the building to his feet.

He opened his eyes, shocked by brightness. Rolling to his side, it took many efforts to rise to his knees, then his feet. Groaning deeply and panting, he squeezed his chest then flopped over the desktop to recover. Referring to the ceiling, he clattered the step ladders to beneath an ornate hook; a remnant from a gas lit era. Taversham bent with difficulty and rummaged through the discarded wires selecting a length of braided flex. He managed to tie a knot, creating a loop. He placed the loop around his neck. Holding onto the wobbling ladders, it took many efforts before he was able to ascend. Puffing loud, precarious, he was at the ceiling with arms aching, fingers clumsy, his shadow obliterating everything. A pig's squeal. Ladders crashed sideways. He had managed to secure the flex to the hook and hung for an instant, his form filling the entire room, limbs lashing, until he thudded with a kettle-drum-beat to land on his feet, lurching, just keeping his balance. The snapped flex had tightened around his neck. He slid his fingers inside the hold. He could not escape it. He fell to his knees, wheezing, his face turning blue. Gouging, he struggled to free himself from the grip. Self-inflicted, Taversham was being garrotted. In a frenzy he fell to his back, bent legs trapped painfully beneath. His eyes bulged. He rolled to his side, kicking the air. All stopped. Only for and instant. Began a rhythmic dance of flaying limbs, hands and feet drumming; a terrible crescendo.

On the inscribed floor he lay; a mouldering corpse.

Rotting air rose about him, entwining with the memory of every obscenity committed in the building; all snatched by the night to dash back out through the opened door.

Chapter 29

The train bounced over the points.

"What do you see?" Jasmin's voice pulled Church from his trance.

"Sorry?" He looked at her sleepy morning face.

"When you look out of the window?"

"Oh that. Well, I guess it's too much college but all I can see is different patterns of brickwork; English bond, stretcher bond, Flemish bond," his words were laid in time with the clattering over rails, "English bond, stretcher bond, Flemish bond."

"Oh."

"And you?"

"Train lines running parallel, together for ever, then sometimes one goes off to travel in a different direction. All so fast."

***

"That was exquisite," Richard lowered his head to kiss Avantha's ever moist lips.

"A perfect gentleman, not squashing me." She pushed her head back into the pillow to look up and focus on him. His eyes were roaming down to her breasts, still rapidly rising and falling with each breath.

"By any other name," he was looking at the tattoo.

"That's been said before."

"I'm sure it has." He shifted and rolled over to reach for the glasses.

They lay side by side, bolstered by the pillows, sipping champagne.

"I must thank Jasmin for introducing us. I wonder why she did it."

"Always been intuitive." Avantha turned to Richard, "She's leaving him."

The champagne dribbled down her neck, to her breast, her tattoo; a rose. It was blood red.

***

Jasmin reached for the red dress, again. Coat hangers swished along the rail, as they had been for over an hour.

The phone rang and swiftly Jasmin reached to pick it up from the bedside table.

"Hello?" She sat on the bed comparing the colour of her dress to the red telephone.

"Jay Jay, it's Justin."

The red dress slipped through her fingers; floating as a feather, never ending, spiralling into the depths of an abyss.

***

Jasmin sat at the dressing table in her dressing gown. She could hear Church fussing downstairs. The phone rang.

"Hello?"

"Jay Jay?"

"Yes."

"It's Justin."

"Justin," she put her hand over the mouthpiece waiting to hear what Church was shouting; *"I'm off to meet with a new client; John Airedale."*

"Justin, call me back." Like rain against glass, tears began to roll down her cheek.

***

"Now you are making me feel bad."

"Why?" Jasmin looked over her wine glass to Alice.

"Because it was me who got you two together."

"What made you?" Jasmin emptied her glass.

"Just a feeling," Alice hesitated and searched the wine bar's triangular-tiled floor as if seeking sweepings for an answer. "It's the way you were talking at the cemetery,

99

it reminded me so much of your mother; hinting at being unsettled. And I know Justin is a good listener."

"Yes, he certainly is. For the first time in my life, I found someone who listens."

"But I didn't intend or plan it to go this far." Alice also emptied her glass and waved to the waiter.

"We never thought you did. Nor did we. After many phone calls we met and then…Well things just happened."

Alice took over from the waiter and arranged the fresh glasses. "And now I could be going back to Australia alone."

***

He slammed his bare fist into the punch bag until blood caused his torn skin to skid over the bag's leather.

***

Church screamed, "You're my wife," he flung the mug, it missed Jasmin, missed the stairs and hit the wall; the coffee spattering to form a wet brown stain trickling down like rain on a window pane.

He stood as a child.

***

Endlessly high; he could not answer why but the two evergreen trees at the entrance had always made him scared from the very day he had arrived; the very day they had put him in the orphanage. But Church loved the building; a symmetrical confusion of windows and arched recesses, all held in check by an overseeing clock tower.

He loved the building; the two dark trees mystified him but he hated everything else.

Lined up in shirts and short trousers along the grassy ridge, the boys obeyed Matron and raised their arms, then down. He needed a pee.

"And up," she sang, "last time, and down. Well done. All dismissed for porridge making."

"Churcheywurchy," he heard it but did not turn.

"Churcheywurchy," the jab at the small of his back was too much.

Church turned, raised his fist, moved to the right to strike to the face.

***

"Do you think we are doing the right thing, Alice?"

"Jasmin, believe me; I am not one to judge," Alice stubbed out her cigarette and lit another.

"But I, we, we need to hear it from someone else."

"I can tell you this," Alice emptied her glass and poured more. "I wanted to move to Australia to escape."

"Escape?"

"And I used Guy to get there. We soon parted. He was not Justin's father; he never knew that but Justin did from an early age."

"Oh," Jasmin hid behind her empty glass. Alice filled it and waved the empty bottle to the barman.

"The point is I don't feel guilty. Indeed, I was bad," Alice stalled, "yes, did bad things, indescribable things." She halted and paused. "But I did the right thing for us. Guy said I used him, trampled on him. But he got over it."

"What about Justin's real father?"

"Ali? Don't dare go there." Alice darkened. "He died from cancer, painfully."

Jasmin ducked. "Sorry to bring up stuff for you. And to burden you."

"So many secrets, too many secrets. That's the burden I carry."

"You look tired."

"You have no idea."

"That's confused me more."

"Sorry, just telling my truth, or part of it. But never mind that," Alice reached to squeeze Jasmin's hand, "It's not easy but you have to do what is right for you. Listen to your heart. There is a voice inside you that speaks your truth; listen to it. And drink up."

***

He tentatively touched his nose. After two weeks it still

throbbed, he remembered the red mist descending and taking aim with both fists, relentless.

"Ashington."

Church stood to attention in the dock.

The sombre figure regarded him. "I have considered your unfortunate beginnings in this world. But that is no excuse. The very best has been done for you. You are mixing with the wrong people. You should already be prepared for your future. Learn a trade, go to college. Find yourself a direction in life. At least get a job. Have you considered the army? Irrespective of this, if I see you in here again, you are going down."

***

The interior of the police car was saturated with vinegar on chips. Uniforms matched the night. A single headlight's beam swung across the windscreen; a motorcycle roared past. They watched the red tail light curve away.

"Have him?"

"Did that one last night."

"We can have him again."

A car slurred past.

"Have him," the driver started the car and accelerated through the gears.

***

"What's his name?" The nurse glanced at the box on the counter and smiled at the young constable, helmet under his arm.

"How should I know?"

The nurse gently searched, cooing at the baby, "You seem a troubled soul my little one. We will have you checked over in a moment." She nodded to the constable, "Sometimes there is a note. The last one had a name on a label tied round her ankle."

"This is my first one."

"Congratulations; it's a boy. Ok, where did you find him?"

"At the church."

"Where do you live?"

"Me? Near Ashington. Why?"

"Sorted. Any idea who the mother might be?"

"The Sarge thinks he knows but she scarpered; reckon she doesn't want to end up in the loony bin."

"You policemen seem to get younger and younger."

"Er...I think he needs changing."

"Clever of you to work that out. You could make detective."

"I fancy the flying squad."

"I fancy a drink." Elbows on the counter, fingers cradling her face, she smiled sweetly. "When you off?"

"I'm in a hurry."

"Why rush?"

***

"In a hurry, are we?"

Church wound down the window, the stuffy air escaped while he blinked at the flashing blue light. "So what?" He couldn't make out anything except a pale face.

"M.O.T., insurance, licence," the face snaked in. "Been drinking, have we?"

"That's another rhetorical question."

"Don't get smart with me. Where are you going?"

"Who knows? Who cares?"

"Listen," the face hissed.

"Look," Church snapped, "do what you have to do, lock me up, throw away the key." He cupped his face in his hands. "I don't give a shit anymore."

"Problems?"

A softer face was at the window.

"Yeh, I guess so. Look I'm sorry. My wife, she's left and...Oh, what's the point," he reached in the glove box and shovelled out scrambled papers.

Church could hear them talking outside.

"Drink?"

"Smells clean. Domestic, I reckon."

"Hey," Church heard a gentle voice. "It's nearly daylight, stop for a cuppa. Things will get better. Believe me, I know."

Church took the returned papers and watched the car disappear.

***

Church sat at the dressing table. Loneliness was a pain in his stomach. The phone rang and stopped. All he could see was red. In a snarl he picked up the phone and flung it to the ground, it bounced, he leapt, picked it up and threw again, this time it shattered, fragments of plastic everywhere. No recollection; he was beside the French window standing before his splintered desk, his knuckles torn and red, dripping blood. The axe slipped from his grasp. He moved and sat on the stool, arms wrapped around his head, face squashed against the breakfast bar, tears gathered in puddles.

***

Church was dismayed by the stack of unwashed crockery and part-eaten meals at the breakfast bar, "What day is this?"

He picked up the phone and dialled.

"Taversham solicitors," a sweet voice said, Church felt sick. He restrained from slamming the phone down.

"Er, this is Church Ashington, can I speak to Mister Taversham, please."

There was silence.

"Hello, can I speak to Taversham."

"I'm sorry Taversham is...unavailable."

"Oh, er well what about what's her name; Wallace? Actually, it's her I really need to speak to."

"She is unavailable as well. We have your number. Someone will call you soon."

He slammed the phone down. "Just what am I thinking?" Church hurled a pile of plates into the sink, water splashed at his feet.

***

"Getting wet."

"Never noticed it was raining," Church found it strange hearing his own voice in open air.

"Right fine car."

"What? Oh yeh. Thanks." Church stood in the forecourt, gathering thoughts. The dismantled wrecks stacked high like dishes seemed ready to collapse. He smelt petrol and watched the guy fill the car.

"Going far?"

"North."

"Not rightly sure how far North is."

"Pardon?"

"Sorry, a bad habit," the guy turned and laughed, "used to joke with Dad, to try and cheer him up. He was a grumpy old git with a bad back."

"Yeh, I need cheering up alright. I'll just drive on and see how far it gets me."

"Sounds nice. Freedom."

"Sounds nice?"

"A pound per hundred miles."

"What?"

"That's what I reckon, if you drive canny like. Three gallons for about a pound and that does you roughly a hundred miles."

"No idea how many hundreds of miles I need."

"Best fill her up then."

"Er, is the A1 that way?" Church gestured with his head.

"Aye, left out of here, straight on then you're there. Right for the North. Being upgraded to M1. Gonna be chaotic with road works. Building a slip road. Black spot."

"Thanks. Thought I had it. Does seem familiar."

He drove off the forecourt passing two standing dead trees; forlorn figures, waiting for decay.

**

As soon as he pulled into the layby and switched off the engine, Church fell into sleep, the car rocking with the shock of lorries charging by.

He partially woke at some point; he did not know the cause; perhaps he was dreaming. Passing was a Volvo, it was red, it was his car and he was driving. Jasmin was with him, it looked as if they were arguing. And they saw each other, him, and the driver; eyes locked for an instant.

***

"I have calmed down. I'm sorry I threw the mug. I'm trying to be sensible." He tore at his hair and let his fingers drag down his face. "Jasmin, please." Church paced and watched her; hands at her side, fingers playing with her floral skirt. "This just doesn't make any sense. How can you just leave? With him? You hardly know him." He felt his rage rise. "How long has this being going on? Has he been here?" He held himself back. "But I love you. Don't you love me anymore?" He wanted her to hold him; to feel that touch once more. He wanted to scream, lash out. Fists clenched; he began to stamp and scream. "Try and make sense. What about this house? All the plans? What are you going to do? Where will you go?"

"Travel."

"Is that all you can say?"

Head down, she stood as a child.

***

The beech tree stood, benevolent. The girl shrieked with joy, flew off the swing, fell to her knees, rubbed them and picked herself up to run to the ball.

Standing at the red door, she threw the ball up, it thumped and bounced off the upright window at the roof, she caught it and threw it up at the other, she caught it again and threw it again; faster and faster came the bouncing thuds; endless.

***

Church lay on the bare mattress, giddy through exhaustion. The first thud merged with whatever he was dreaming; perhaps the first thud was the dream. The second had the same effect, then the third. Again, and again, he heard it faster and faster and faster; an endless beat.

His pulse quickened, his heart thumping.

He sat and filled his lungs.

"No."

His scream split the night.   Like an arrow, it flew forever.

***

Jasmin tipped the rucksack upside down and shook it; the contents spilled over the floor, some rolling to beneath the stairs.   With an impatient sigh, she repeated the process, placing some items in the rucksack, slinging others across the room.   There came a hard thump at the door.

"Richard."

"Hello Jasmin, just called by to thank you for a great time I had at your party.   But actually, I would like to chat with Church, thinking of having some alterations.   Is he in?"

"Come in."

***

Two wardrobes stared; impassive observers.

He lay back and drifted toward oblivion, his pulse still pounding.   He was parched.   Taunting, downstairs, came the dripping of water; a tap leaking into an enamelled bowl; a crack bell's thud.

The thud became louder, a threatening rap.   The devil himself was beating at the door.

"Church."   His name.   "Church."

He was walking down the stairs.   Or was it a dream? Perhaps it was someone else's dream.

"Church."   He stood at the red door.

"Church."   He opened it.

"Thank goodness."

"Richard," Church fell into his arms.

C hapter 30

'Closed.'

"Always wanted to hang that on the door."

Wallace slackened the silk scarf from around her neck and sat back, her tiny white-socked feet on the reception desk. "That's a relief though, Janice," she adjusted her fedora, sliding the brim over her eyes, "just spoken to the electrician's wife. The doctor's been, he's sedated and stopped screaming."

"It looks like we got away with it." Janice turned to Wallace.

"Got away with it?" She took off her hat. "Janice, we did nothing that we had to get away with." She shifted, put her feet to the floor and leaned forward to touch Janice's knee.

"Janice, I can see you are worried."

"I'm scared."

"It's ok to be scared but nothing to be scared of," Wallace spoke softly, "I've spent a lot of time with the police. They have made their minds up. It's suicide. Can't work out why he did it though. No one can."

"Suicide? Why?"

"Why, exactly. They did try to pin it on me but the broken flex still hanging and the hook just about off its screws; plus, the knot and the all-round pressure bruising of the flex added to it. And besides that," Wallace considered her thoughts, "I reckon someone from higher up just wants the case shut."

"Really?"

"Probably open too many secrets. Implicating others."

"Corruption?"

"In high places," Wallace nodded to herself.

"And he attacked you."

Wallace removed the scarf, revealing her neck, "Showed them what he tried with me," she dabbed at the bruise on her temple, "plenty of theatrics."

"What did you tell the police?"

"I told them the truth. If I lied, it could have backfired at any time; someone could have seen me enter or leave. At midnight." She sucked her breath and shook her head. "Wouldn't look good."

"But why did Taversham want to meet you at midnight?"

Wallace put her feet back up, "He was up to something bad, that's for sure. I could find nothing connecting me," she looked at Janice, "or you. But then again what was there to find?"

"What was stolen?"

"That's the point. We just don't know. Found some strange stuff chucked about the place. Hey," Wallace put her face to Janice's and lowered her voice, "I think he was a spy in the war; pro-Nazi that's for sure."

"Really?"

"If he was a Russian spy, I reckon the police may have been a bit more interested. A lot of weird stuff though. A touch of the occult, I reckon. Strange connections with different personalities. But that doesn't surprise me."

"Lucky the burglars didn't go into your office."

"Yep, the main safe. And I've got the key to that now."

"What's next?"

"Well, I'll have his office, move my files out of my small safe to the big safe and...."

"No, I didn't mean that."

"Negotiate, merge with another company, let them be the ones to sift and find out what nonsense he was up to. Let our clients contact us and we can refer them on, one at a time.

They can deal with it. We stay in the clear."

"There have been a few calls," Janice searched her desk, "here is the list."

"Let's have a look.   They mean nothing to me except Ashington.   Could you call them, please; I'll talk to them. Especially him."

"Still reckon you fancy him." Janice offered a smile.

"He was interesting."   Wallace rubbed her neck, watching Janice dial. She watched her for a long time.

"No answer."

"Ok."   Wallace leaned over and stroked Janice's arm, "Something else is troubling you." Janice removed her glasses and Wallace saw the tears.   "What is it?"   Wallace took her hand, come on you can tell me anything. You know that."

"Did you say anything to the police about…"

"About us you mean?"

Janice blew her nose and nodded.

"I did."

Janice winced.

"I had to. If they found out any other way, they would only wonder what else I had to hide."

"How did they take it?"

"Confused; I think that's the word?   Were they interested? He kind of seemed that way.   But she certainly was." Wallace flickered her eyelids.

"But isn't it illegal? But I suppose it's not anymore."

"Consenting adults, you mean. That never did apply to women."

"Really? I wish I'd known."

"Maybe that would have spoiled the fun," Wallace poked her.   Then she turned to the broken mirror, "That sure has spoiled it though. Just what was he playing at?"

"Apart from that, it was fun wasn't it, Wallace?"

"Was?"

Janice's head went down.

"Janice," Wallace stroked her knee, "I knew it was

leading up to this. If you want to stop its ok. It was fun but we knew it wouldn't go anywhere. Didn't we? That's how you saw it, didn't you? Janice?"

"I think so but."

"But?"

"Well, I'm sorry but…"

"But what?"

"I told my husband."

"Oh."

"Sorry," Janice cringed.

"I'm even more sorry; your marriage. It's the last thing I wanted."

"Not your fault, we are consenting adults."

"How did he take it?" Wallace saw Janice dip her head further.

C hapter 31

Ghosts did not come beyond the garden gate.   Watchers always stay outside; intimidating, knowing the most intimate of secrets. And Church did not want to face them. He nudged the flower pot with his foot, it moved just enough to expose the tip of tarnished metal. The edge of the door step lurched at him when he bent to pick up the key. The door's red paint was a flaking chalky skin; aged by the sun. It was not locked. He heard Jasmin's voice asking him check it when they left. He clung to her voice but could not move his thoughts to calculate how long ago that was.

He stepped in, onto the dark flagstones.   The sweet smell of soot conveyed images of an alien yet familiar warmth; safety and security; he allowed himself to welcome that.

He did not challenge the need for so many contortions of the pipe as it left the stove to eventually disappear through the ceiling, leaking joints stained with tar and that same smell of soot.

Church granted himself permission to acknowledge the need to drink and borrowed the dressers' cracked cup.   The brass tap squeaked, brown water flowed and spilled into the cup. It tasted metallic. He could not manage to turn the tap off completely and sat at the scrubbed table, hearing the drip into the enamelled basin.

Church sat throughout eternity; it passed so easily.

Now Richard was there.

"I struggle to remember being here with her but I remember coming in alone. I remember being upstairs. The rest is numb."

"I was grateful to find you."

Church chewed the torn off length of loaf, crust cutting into his gums. He sighed at Richard; it caused him to choke on the crumbs.

"Slow down. Here." Richard passed the beer bottle. "Couldn't find glasses. Help yourself to cheese, please." He rubbed his arms and nodded to the stove. "Chilly. Dare we?"

Church looked around the room, "I didn't take it in at all when Jasmin and I were here. It was brief and I wasn't in the mood, apparently." 'Jasmin,' he heard her name and hid his face behind his hands. He forced his head up, "Sorry. No melodrama. Promise."

"It's ok." Richard was at the stove. "Need paper, wood. And what's this stuff?"

"Peat," Church did not move. "Shall I look outside? Bound to be a shed or something."

"There is a whole line of outbuildings. I've already had an explore, wasn't sure where I'd find you."

"On the end of a rope?"

"Never."

"I did threaten that once."

"I'm going outside, Church. I may be some time."

Alone. Church stood and wobbled, his legs ached, he rubbed and loosened them, wandering into the adjoining room. It was empty, save for a burnt-out candle in its holder on the window sill and a mirror on the wall. Church gazed into its sepia tones, shocked by the aged reflection.

"Success," Richard sounded a long way off and Church had to check that he was there.

Smoke soon filled the house, no escape.

***

Jimmy sat and waved away midges. The coppice was secluded, lime green, no obvious pathway in or out, not so for the midges. Not even the sky was permitted through the bud-tipped branches. It was a stupa. At its shrine, green stained copper, composed, was a domestic hot water cylinder with a complicated arrangement of gauges, taps and steam. From its top a coiled pipe led to a bucket.

"Can't get plumbing like that anymore," Jimmy sucked at a healing cut between thumb and finger. "Shame it's got stained green, had it gleaming."

"Verdigris." Isaac towered even when sitting cross legged on the damp earth.

"Third degree?"

"Verdigris, Floyd; the word for copper's green staining. It oxidises in the air to from copper carbonate."

"Take a swaller," Floyd forced the jar under Jimmy's nose.

"I think he would prefer to drink it through his mouth, Floyd."

"No Isaac," said Jimmy, "it's more of a sniffing vintage is this one."

"Not for drinking, you mean," Isaac soberly nodded.

"Oh," Floyd smoothly sang, "don't you be disgraceful about my liquor."

"You mean disrespectful."

"Disrespectaful is what I mean."

"This is why I love these meetings," said Isaac, "meaningful and worthwhile."

"Go on, Isaac," Jimmy swung the jar toward him, "just for once."

"You know my answer, James. Besides, it should be distilled three times with proper temperature control."

"That's pure alcohol," Jimmy insisted.

"But it has many other chemicals, distilled as an azeotrope," Isaac lectured. "It is not pure ethanol."

"Ethel who?" Floyd slumped.

"Ethyl alcohol. C two H five O H."

"That's my blood type," Floyd gave a whoop.

"Nah. It's good moonshine this, dripping well," Jimmy nodded at his handywork then coughed at the smoke. "Dagnammit Floyd, don't use no green or rotten wood, they get you by the smoke. And don't put the cylinder directly on the fire, burn a hole no time."

"I am gifted," said Isaac, "I know when no one listens to me."

"Oh now," sang Floyd, "cool it. Both gonna give yourself a hartatach." He eased back, pulled out his harmonica and began blowing and sucking.

***

"How did you know I would be here, Richard?"

"I didn't. We worked it out," Church saw Richard's penetrating look, "Jasmin and I, we worked it out."

"Oh."

"I called by, innocently. And she told me what was going on."

"That's great. I'm glad someone knows what's going on. I couldn't tell you how long I've been here, just about know where I am, haven't a clue how I got here, haven't a clue what she's up to. I don't know...." Richard's presence, rock-hard, told him to stop.

Richard was smiling now. "A raging storm, dead and flat, blind fury. You want to scream, cry, hide, tell the world, talk to no one, plead and destroy."

"You should be a psychiatrist."

"It was a long journey for me to become single, Church, long and hard."

"What did she say?"

"She's gone."

"Gone."

"Was there, when I came to see you for a chat. She was packing a rucksack."

"A rucksack?"

"Look," Richard drew a breath. "We talked. Or rather she spoke. She said a lot."

"Never said a lot to me."

"That's the point. Look, Church, I'll give it to you square. I don't know what you two had at the beginning and

I'm sure it was good. But for her, well that spark has gone."

"Was he there?" Church felt rage rising.

"No.

Look, whatever Jasmin is going through, I'm sure he represents escape; a path, a way of fulfilling unfulfilled dreams. Whether it is permanent, who knows."

"Yeh, and I'm expected to wait while she…"

"Of course not."

"I bet she never even mentioned me."

"Yes, she did. Oh yes, she did. It's hurting her. Sent me here to find you."

"Very touching."

"A question, Church, from me. You have built up your own business, I'm sure it is with Jasmin's support. But Jasmin; what does she do?"

"Do? What do you mean?"

"Exactly. She said she had so many dreams when she first met you. Her art her designs. What happened?"

"What? That wasn't my fault. You didn't know her parents and when they died, she became tangled with finances, investment and property. Not my fault."

"And she's not blaming you. But she has been leading an unfulfilled life."

"Why didn't she say."

"Why didn't you ask? Why didn't you listen?" Richard poured wine with a smile, "I remembered, I brought glasses and bottles with me."

"Cheers." He closed his eyes and rocked. "I always told her how grateful I was to start my own business so young and so easily. "Yeh," Church nodded to himself, "it was because of her cash input to support me."

"She mentioned that but said it didn't help you build your own esteem alongside it."

"So many clever words not said." Church shook his head while still rocking; to and fro. "I halfway got to know her on our train journeys to college. They were simple hours.

Should have listened then to what she was trying to tell me. Guess I never had the chance to get to know her after that; even though we were together full time. It's like she's back on that train now. Without me. But I was just a kid then...."

"Church," Richard shifted to attract Church's full attention. "I laid it on hard with you. I had to."

"Yeh...face reality. But I wish, I wish I could simply be back on that train."

"I tried it with Jasmin. And, well, sorry, but she was in touch with reality. She mentioned investments, the house, other property, including this place. She asked me to pass this envelope to you." Richard raised his hands. "I know what's in it. She told me it contains cash so that I would take care of it. She said that she would contact solicitors when her was head was clear. And yours."

"Solicitors, yeh Taversham."

"Taversham? That rings a bell. But listen to me; you may think your emotions are settled, not nice, not what you want, but settled. But believe me it's all going to come round again for you."

"Guess I need to think of my business too. Oh god." Church raised his arms high, "Is that what I really want to do anymore?"

"Can I help?"

"I should have my diary in the car. Make a few calls to tick things over. Do they have phones up here?"

"I'm not sure. Do you think they have pubs? Shall we?"

A sombre evening created an alien sky above the track they walked.

"Look at those mountains, Church. Are they clouds or is it snow?"

"I remember Jasmin saying something like that. Hey I said her name without boiling." Church realised Richard had stopped listening. "But this was a bad idea. Those clouds and snow are tinted red. Sundown."

"It's becoming dark, Church and we passed that tree

117

twice."

"Can't see the way back."

"Are we going forward? I need a drink."

"What's that noise?"

"A haggis?"

"Follow me."

"Richard, you actually have a waxed jacket and green wellies with a buckle."

"Stopped on the way and bought them. What exactly are you wearing?"

"Army surplus. Jasmin hated me wearing it. No more matching anoraks."

"Hush," said Richard, "I hear singing."

"I smell burning."

"And what is that noise?"

***

"Now I am just an outlaw," Jimmy sang, "left my fambly all behind."

Floyd smacked his harmonica on his palm, "Clean her out a bit."

"Are you genuinely from Oklahoma, Floyd?" Asked Isaac.

"All my life," Floyd wiped a tear.

"Shush," Jimmy slurred, "I hear footprints."

"It'll be the Feds," Floyd picked up a shotgun.

"Put that down," Using one finger, Isaac calmly forced the barrel to the ground.

"My goodness," Richard burst upon them.

***

"Inevitable," Sarah was stirring a pan.

Rosemary was bouncing Zimmy on her lap. "Like, what did you say?" She reached up to move a nappy along the line and poked her head through the gap.

"I was going to say," Sarah looked at the beaming face, "I'm wondering where the boys are. And now I can hear them."

"Sound way off, this is far out," Rosemary agreed with

herself.

"Sound very loud. Arguing?"

"Inevitable."

"I know what I'm talking about," Jimmy stumbled in backward waving his finger to whoever was outside.

"Oh me," Sarah forced a smile. "Church."

"Inevitable," Rosemary nodded wisely.

***

Dawn passed without being noticed until Church realised that the day was coming in through the window, highlighting sweaty chaos in the kitchen. He was nauseous.

"Would you like another coffee?" Sarah was whispering to him.

"Yes please. That moonshine...it's deadly." Church saw a sadness behind Sarah's brown eyes; the sadness of distant cries caught on a breeze.

"Where's Jimmy?"

"Bed," Church nodded to the door. "He did say goodnight to you but didn't want to wake you. Isaac and Rosemary, they left. That Isaac, he..."

"He can be very intense. Likes to read people and you are a new book for him."

"Hey, I wonder what happened to Richard."

"Rosemary?" Sarah asked, "Did she take Zimmy?"

"No Jimmy did. Zimmy? Is he Rosemary's or...?"

"Zimmy belongs to me and Jimmy," that sadness was still there. "But Rosemary?" Church saw her look at him, "There is a lot more to her that meets the eye, a lot more," it was an assessing look, "but she's just so broody."

"Oh. Hey thank you so much for the hospitality, the food."

"You were starving." Sarah was still looking at him, "I know I've said it already, but with so much noise I want to make sure you know. I'm so sorry to hear about you and Jasmin. She seemed such a nice girl."

"She is, at least I thought she was." Church searched the

ceiling then turned to Sarah. "But now that it is quiet. I want to apologise. When we were here last, I was a right twat. I bet you are thinking *'good for her'*."

"You were a bit blunt but now it makes sense; stuff must have been going on between you. But we try and make a point not to judge. We came up here to get away from that sort of thing."

"I said my apologies to Jimmy, too"

"And I'm sure he came round; in the end."

"Right on."

"You were arguing though, when you came in."

"Was I? I'm sorry. Not right I should argue with someone in their own home."

"He was going on about swatting the midges flying around biting people and you thought he meant midgets."

"Really?"

"I think so. But I really am sorry, Church. For you and Jasmin."

"Well as they say," Church bravely inhaled, "always someone worse off."

"Think of the last guy."

Both jumped.

The pile of clothing on the table erupted.

"Think of the last guy," Floyd's bald pate rose, "you said always someone worse off."

Church saw a bleary-eyed beard with finger pointed straight at him.

Floyd lurched, "But there has to be a guy on the very end of that line; the last guy."

"Oh, it's a guy, is it," said Sarah.

"Well, no, sweet lady, I do believe you can have last ladies too. Always was one at the last waltz at college. Hey," Floyd looked down, scuffing his boots at something under the table.

"Please be gentle," the mumble came from deep below.

"What the...?" Church and Sarah caught themselves

gazing into each other's eyes.

Bumping his head on the table, Richard emerged. "Good morning, everyone. Why I must have crashed down there. Crashed. See, I'm learning the lingo."

"Hey Ricardo," Floyd assisted him to a seat, "said I'd drink you under the table. I was talking about the college last waltz. Did you go to the college?"

"Of course."

"Didn't see you there but what did you study?"

"Well, actually, I'm a dentist."

"You gotta be shitting me. I too..."

"Would you like some coffee, Richard?"

"I too..."

"Oh yes please, Sarah. And thank you for an extraordinary night"

"I too..."

"How are you feeling, Richard?"

"I too...."

"A doddle thanks, Church. Now Floyd; your eye tooth? Show me."

"Goddammit," Floyd slammed his fists on the table. Zimmy and Jimmy gave one cry from the bedroom. "I kindly thank you," said Floyd, "now that I have your attention. I would like to share something with my new found friend, Ricardo."

"Go ahead," Richard put his arm around him.

"What I was going to say was..."

"Yes?"

"I too," Floyd drawled, "I too am a dentist."

"NOoooo..." Jimmy's denial floated through.

"Fully trained and qualified. Yep," Floyd sat back. "Still got my own clinic back in Oklahoma City, me and my sweet sister. That's why she sends me them ol cheques." He nodded to the audience. . "Sheit man," he jumped, "just realised; I should be in Ibiza. Flying today." He looked at Richard, "Is it today yet, or is this still yesterday?"

"Could be tomorrow," Jimmy's suggestion came through and became lost in the room.

"Ibiza," said Richard, "I fancy that."

"Hey man," again Church saw Floyd's finger pointing straight at him. "Before I go. Let me tell you something, mister last guy."

"I'm ready."

"You wanna bring yourself down from this bum trip you're on?"

"I'm ready."

"Think of your death dance, man."

"Think of what?"

"Think of the day you are gonna die and the place you've chosen to dance your death dance. And make that place a good ol high majestic mountain, with the wind flying and an eagle crying through a cloud tipped sky. Think of your own death, man.; the day you're gonna die. Then you gonna know that all this shit going down don't mean a shit."

"Was that you speaking that, Floyd?" Jimmy's question trailed in.

"Listen to him, Church," and Richard had to contribute.

"Hey what time is it?" Floyd searched his wrist.

"Five."

"In the morning?"

"Yep."

"Sheeit, there aint no such time." His head thumped to the table and Richard gently put his cap on him.

***

"Goodbye Richard."

"Only for now," he started the land rover.

"Can't thank you enough."

"There's still supplies in the box I bought. Remember what I said; emotionally it's not over. Be something wrong if there was. Remember that bit as well."

"I do feel much better."

"A two-day hangover. But I feel happier now I've met

the people around you. They are a distraction from reality."
    "A separate reality, Isaac calls it."

C hapter 32

Church freed himself but held on to the dream to make sense of it before it withdrew from an existence that day brings.

Solitary in a vast wilderness, the dream was familiar, as was the feeling of being watched, assessed, turning but no one there, yet someone was there and had been for a long time. Was all withheld in one dream? He had seen a white fox at marble steps and at some point, that white fox had sat at his feet; deep eyes holding images he was yet to see.

Precarious, he sat on the bed in the upstairs room, pining for the feeling of familiar routine. He jerked to stand and swung shut the wardrobe doors to stop them watching. Perhaps it was them in his dream. And standing between the wardrobes he scratched his stubbled face, looking out of the window at the lonely shadow cast by the beech tree.

***

Not another house stood within sight, except for the abandoned ruin that Jasmin said was haunted.

Now Jasmin haunted it.

So much open space, bare wire fences and sparse saplings; Church felt conspicuous with no place to hide, except to duck behind the buildings or the low garden wall; which was tempting to avoid the constant wind.

A clamour rolled around the empty barrow when he threw bare branches in.

The secateurs he had found in the byre were rusted and blunt, so was the saw. His wrist ached and muscles of his arm burned. He stood on the path, the only clear space on which to stand and looked again at the walled square which was the tangled garden.

Church emptied the wheelbarrow at the pile he had begun in the centre of the interwoven grass, combating the argument that a bonfire would burn and scar what was once a cherished lawn. It made him think of Poppy and it was the basis of a friendship with a lady he never knew, yet, somehow, was beginning to know.

He turned, not expecting anything but disappointed when no one was there. His dream visited. He turned again, almost seeing something, so real, a figure, a grey figure. It was a young lady, that much he knew and it annoyed.

Clouds gathered bringing a foul mood.

With a rising wind, transition was swift and complete.

Irritated now, angry, it fuelled his task, quickly becoming a blind rant, frustrated by poor tools. Clean cuts were no longer a priority, he hacked and tore at branches, especially those that stabbed his eye; a witch's curse. He circled his pile, emptied the barrow and always, always behind him, opposite in the circumference, there was a wraith, a pleading frail form. Invisible, she was always there. The shadow of the beech tree grew. Something had been lurking, a being, darker than any shadow. It spread over Church and the wraith shrank.

He ran.

Church collapsed at the kitchen table, exhausted by the hurricane force, a whirlwind that he had no recollection of escaping.

He found himself at the sink filling a pan.

Discipline created a structure caned into him at his orphanage. It built a wall of protection. He searched Richard's box, rattled around the cupboards relieved to find a pan; a two ringed hob in the corner of the worktop. Vague was his involvement; he did not know if it had been used by either Richard or Jasmin. He tried various switches on the wall and bit his lip with frustration until a feint red glow grew on one of the rings. Stirring his porridge, content that it was simmering, he felt an emptiness inside, not from hunger although it resembled that, more of a pain and he knew that it was because Jasmin had entered his thoughts; or he had allowed her in.

Outside the sky's canopy lowered, thickening, sweeping across. The darkening day caused the window to act as a mirror. He saw himself alone in the kitchen.

The hairs at his nape stood.

Behind his reflection a black shape was growing. It spread up the wall to the ceiling, spreading above him, about to drip like molten tar. Church picked up the pan of porridge and turned.

***

"Jimmy," he heard the urgent thud of her feet meeting the wooden bridge.

"Hi Sarah," like Sarah he shouted above the sound of the stream below. "Come to see the finished masterpiece?" A fog was forming from the rising droplets. "A fortnight Tuesday as promised."

"That's really good," she tugged at the lattice of white pipes.

"What's wrong," Jimmy saw her face.

"Church called in, looking for you."

"And?"

"He said the water was off."

"That's not a problem. Why are you looking so worried? You know he and me have kissed and made up."

"I know you did, no problem with that."

"So?"

"You didn't see his face."

***

Church did not know if the bang at the door was real. He stood rigid in the kitchen's furthest corner with no will to challenge nor defend. He expected and accepted the worse.

"Church?" Jimmy peeked in.

Time and light curved away into infinity but came an

ending.

"Thanks Jimmy." Church emptied the glass of whisky.

"More?" Jimmy offered the bottle.

"No more thanks. Er, are you sure Sarah's alright? I think I scared her."

"You did but she's ok, more worried for you."

"Urggh," Church buried his head in his hands and spoke from that shelter, "Dunno what's happening to me; ghosts and nightmares." He slid his hands down and looked at Jimmy, "I've always been this way and kept it to myself but now it's just boiling over."

"Like the porridge you mean?" Jimmy was avoiding eye contact and inspected the splattered walls.

"Yeh, I know what you think. I'm a loony."

"I dunno." Jimmy was staring at the floor.

"I'm really sorry Jimmy. I know we got off to a bad start and..."

"It's not that," Jimmy smiled at the ceiling, "I'm just not very good at this sort of thing. Should have brung Sarah."

"I am sorry though."

"Right," Jimmy abruptly stood, "no more, 'sorry.' Deal?"

"Deal."

"I didn't bring Sarah, but with the whisky, she gave me this," he pushed a rolled up sleeping bag across the kitchen table. "She realised she had stripped the place and guessed you wouldn't be thinking of bringing sheets and stuff like that."

"Yeh me and Richard realised that sort of thing but didn't get round to it."

Jimmy stood tall, "Listen to me," he adopted a strange foreign accent, "you must make efforts to ground yourself."

"Isaac. Right?" Church pointed, "Go on do your Floyd act."

"Few more whiskies for that but too early in the day." He clapped his hands and went to the tap. Nothing. "Uh huh."

"That added to the drama for me. At least blood didn't come out."

"Uh huh," Jimmy flicked a switch above the sink.

"Think that does the hot plate. I..."

Jimmy summoned a hush. "Five, four, three, two." Water spluttered then erupted from the tap.

"Pump," Jimmy grinned. "There is a well but its lower than the tap."

"Ah I see. And I turned it off. I was going to phone the water board. Do you have phones up here?"

Jimmy laughed. "Water board? We do things ourselves. And yes, there could be phones but we choose not to."

"What about emergencies?"

"Sarah says I'm a walking emergency."

"Dunno about that."

"Just be grateful there isn't a generator."

"Meaning?"

"Everyone had one until a new scheme was laid up the glen."

"At least there are tractors."

"Grass sickness put an end to horses."

Church banged his head on the table, "Time machine."

"Right." Jimmy clapped his hands. "Grounding lesson. The pump takes water from the well and feeds a tank in the byre's loft which feeds the house and the water butts in the park. Which is something else I have to ask, I..."

"Park?"

"Fields. It also feeds the outside toilet but that's always air locking and that's another job."

"It's ok. I worked that one out; the bucket beneath the tap."

"Good man. I'll just go out and check the tank. It shuts off with a float switch."

"Can I see?"

"It's dark in the byre. Get your head in the right place first." Jimmy scuttled to the door.

Church began boiling the kettle, seeing then the full

extent of the mess he had created, "A couple of light years away."

His head began to throb, glasses rattled, the floor carried vibrations up to his skull.

Church was ready to scream, to yell at the world.

A blue tractor rolled to the gate. The engine died; vibrations stopped.

He sagged and slid to the door.

"Good afternoon," Church offered a handshake then saw the gigantic hands.

"Well, well, fit like?" A ruddy face glowered.

"Pardon?"

"Aye it's a gay dreich yin."

"Er."

"Did Jimmy spear wi you aboot me putting beasts in the park?"

"Er, I?"

"You'll nae be needing muckle."

"Eh?"

"Aye aye Willy," Jimmy's shout came around the corner.

"Aye aye, my loon," the figure swaggered the length of the building to meet Jimmy.

Church watched them talking, shaking their heads and sucking through teeth; both rocking back on their heels. He could guess what was said when the farmer twirled his finger by his temple with Jimmy nodding.

"Ah well," the farmer regarded Church as he swaggered back to his tractor.

Jimmy waited till it started and rolled away before approaching Church.

"What the hell was that?" Church shivered.

"Willy."

"But what language was...?"

Jimmy stopped him, "It's taken me ten years to work out what everyone is saying. Don't worry about it."

"But you've only been here a year."

"Exactly."

"But what was he saying?"

"A bit more down to earth stuff for you."

"Grounding," Church nodded to the garden.

"Yep. Poppy had fifty acres to manage."

"Fifty?"

"Yep, not much in farming terms but too much for her. She rented it to Willy for his beasts."

"Beasts?"

"Stirks."

"Stirks?"

"Cattle. I didn't think you'd be farming. If it's not worked, the parks would just turn to ruin. So, I sent Willy round to have a blether with you."

"Blether?"

"News, er talk."

"Ok got it. You sent Willy around to chat about renting the fields."

"Hope you don't mind. I know I get annoyed if people try to interfere with my stuff."

"No that's perfect. Appreciate it. Except…."

"Except?"

"The place isn't mine but I'm sure Jasmin appreciates it. And see?"

"See what?"

"I said 'Jasmin' without cracking up. But one more thing."

"Yep?"

"Willy? What would I have done if you didn't happen to be here?"

"Tell him you're English."

"Ok," said Church rubbing his arms. "Look…turning even colder. Coming back in?"

"I need to go," Jimmy gestured with a smile. "But listen," Church felt his hand on his shoulder, "There are plenty of folk here that do like you. We are here."

"Thanks, I'll work away at grounding myself."

"What about more food?"

"Head into town tomorrow; explore and supplies."

"Sounds good.   And if you need a hand with that garden. And anything else."

"Thanks, but I'll give it a go. Something to focus on."

"Ok.   But one more thing.   It took me a wee while to adjust after life in cities.   The local town don't think twice of folk wandering around in work gear. But…"

"But?"

"But before you go anywhere take a look in the mirror."

C hapter 33

Church dropped the box of rattling cans on the stack in the front room. Faces of confused shop assistants drawing a smile, especially the waitress. He sat on the window's ledge, the remains of the candle beside him.

The front door was not properly shut and creaked with a breath of wind.

Church turned to regard the dark flagstones of the lobby and could sense the house breathing. He tried to imagine the old lady found there and what Sarah must have gone through.

He shifted from his perch.

Accepting that the mirror gave sepia toned aging, he checked again that the cuts were not visible after his savage morning shave with a razor Richard had left. He wished he had not looked into the mirror; lingering memories were locked behind the crazed glass. He closed his eyes.

***

"All this darkness; I don't know what to think, Frank." Church sat and wrung his hands.

Frank lent forward in his chair. "You're confused by all of it and feel so weary," his voice conveyed those exact emotions.

Church wanted to cry and had to stop before continuing.

"A fox, a white one, I see that. And a lady with flaming red hair, like it's on fire."

"You see that in your dreams."

"That's the point Frank, that's the whole point, don't know if it's real, if anything is real. Or is this all a dream?"

***

With closed eyes at the mirror, Church saw a woman with hair of fire, a shawl around her shoulders; soaked, she stood beside trees in slanting rain within a circle of light. She had a baby in her arms and placed it in a box beside a white fox on the marble steps of an arched vestibule. She walked away over cobblestones then stopped, turning to face him, a smile of sorrow, her pleading eyes offering a gift of hope. She turned a corner and was gone, as was the fox.

Church opened his eyes to the mirror once more. It held no threat but he struggled to accept it, immediately denied it; her reflection was retained. Behind him, still in her shawl, the woman with red hair was smiling and waving.

"Hi," she spoke.

Church lurched.

"Like, it's only me," Rosemary timidly ducked. "Sarah thought you might need some company."

"Woah...er, that's nice."

"Are you ok?"

"Yeh, er sorry if I gave you a fright."

"I think I gave you one. Didn't mean to freak you out."

"Just not used to this place."

"Different energies," with freckles she was a little girl.

"I guess it's that," Church forced his hands in his pockets. "Lucky, I didn't throw boiling porridge at you."

"Like, I'm not sure what that means."

"Thought gossip would have spread."

"Gossip is a bad scene for me."

"A breath of fresh air."

"That's why I'm here. It's a beautiful afternoon," she offered her hand. "Will we share a walk?"

C hapter 34

Six candles on the floor, their light struggled to raise the heavy shadows to the high ceiling. Standing at hexagonal points around the carving on the floorboards, all six looked down at the naked corpse.

"Untie and dress her," Yefimovich ordered. "Take off the blindfold."

"Is she dead?"

"Definitely, Major; not a breath left in her." The bald giant slipped on his robe and considered the Major. "Your displeasure is a thin disguise."

"A fitting departure," one of the others said.

The Major was being deeply scrutinised.

"A pact, Major. Loyalty to the army or loyalty to us. You have betrayed us, our circle."

"You have to see it through or face consequences."

"But you know, you know the beginning," insisted the Major, "we all thought we would be allies with the Germans. Even the king."

"And now it looks like war."

"And you switched loyalty. Betrayed us. Face the consequences. Consider the choice. Your wife has," he pointed to the corpse.

"Choice? You gave her no choice; it was murder and now you give me no choice."

"You both had the same choice; you or your children."

"We will take our flags with us." The giant Yefimovich furled the flags with the swastika emblem then walked across the room not seeing the watching ghost and picked up a single barrelled shotgun.

C hapter 35

From its long yellow beak, a brush stroke flowed past the bird's eye, extending along its head into a fine plume. The grey feathers down its long neck and its hunched back gave it an ethereal quality. On extended legs it stood; a statue in the shallow pond.

Rosemary took Church's hand to hold him back and whispered, "Do you see it," she was pointing through the thicket of reeds.

Church saw it and the bird sensed him, regarded him for a brief, yet everlasting second, then giving its plaintive cry, it took off to rise into the grey sky; a spectre.

"What was it?" Church did not suggest their hands should part.

"A heron."

"Thought they were fish. Look at the size of its wings, doesn't seem any smaller even though it's in the distance."

"Not so cool though, it's after the frog spawn," she pointed to the lumps of clear jelly amongst the algae.

From the corner of his eye Church watched her, he pulled back just slightly, still holding her hand, so that he could see a little more of her in her shawl. Then he moved closer, her warmth radiating. "Thank you for this."

She turned and smiled.

Flowers in her hair would have completed what he saw.

They walked up the lane, sunken through years of use to be below the ploughed fields, sectioned by rusting and tangled wire, each fence post following them then stopping to be replaced by the next, the banks carpeted with green bushes.

"If you hang around 'till Summer," she said, "we can share wild blaeberries."

"Is that what they are?" Church did not allow thoughts to reach Summer.

"And those are Junipers," she pointed to the smoky green shrubs growing in groups along the line of the lane.

"I've noticed," he said, "we have been going slightly uphill for a long time, yet at every rise there is another incline."

"Soon we will be on top of the world," Rosemary laughed and spun in front of him then waited for his hand.

Church was not inclined to enquire.

"Just enjoy the moment," she smiled.

The lane was approaching a forestry plantation. Even before the canopy of brown and green, the air became dense. Clouds of flying insects crowded him, annoying, their bites not hurting but creating an itchy blemish. He backed up, frustrated, overheating from the effort of swiping the clouds; a mission to destroy each vibrating dot.

"Here," she was offering a small bottle. "It will save you killing them."

He removed the cork and smelt the liquid. It smelt of flowers, divine. It smelt of Rosemary.

"Do I drink it all?"

She put her hand to her mouth and giggled. "Rub it on your skin."

Church did notice that the insects where not troubling her but not needing that proof, he complied.

"Hey it works. But why am I not surprised."

"I remember you and Jimmy arguing that night you burst in. He was talking about these midges and you thought he was talking about midgets. I was thinking of you the other day."

"Oh yeh. I remember. Sarah said the same." He denied any sense of belonging yet Rosemary was thinking of him.

She took his hand once more and led him into the forest track. Deep in the woods and being alongside her came a concept almost alien; shadows held no threat.   They walked the scraped highway of yellow clay, full of tracks and animal scents which led off into private caves of tangled branches; kingdoms in the undergrowth.

"We're here," she announced

They had stepped out into a vast clearing.   The air lifted, escaping to the freedom of a blue sky.

"Wow," he heard his voice.   "We really are at the top of the world."

He took in their surroundings; a plateau of coarse grass with cotton buds, faced by a dark wall at the far end; any bare ground a sullen black.

"This is where they cut the peats."

"Really?"

"At the far bank," he heard her voice; it sounded far off, somehow, "they cut it with special spades.   They say it used to be so busy here."

Church could feel so many tired backs.

"It's really cool; Jimmy and Sarah do it every year.   They cut out bricks and barrow them and lay them to dry and come back in the evenings to turn them.   Willy lends a tractor and cart to take them home.   Beautiful smelly and dusty fuel for free."

"Hard work though."

"Yeh, like, Jimmy has to lay on the kitchen floor and Sarah and me we walk over his back."

"I can picture that."

"But what's really cool is that I get Zimmy for days.   Are you ok, Church?"

"What?   Oh yeh, sorry.   I guess it's your words, your voice and the history here; created so much imagery."

"Far out," Church could feel her breath, warm on his face, smell her oils, "that's a far-out thing to say.   Not freaky though."   He felt her kiss on his cheek.

She backed off and put her hands to her freckled cheeks, "Now I'm blushing."

"I might be as well," he had to laugh it off.

"Now I have special place for you to see."

"It's all special."

She smiled her gratitude.

Church was led into more trees, soon to be led out the other side.

Both halted and gazed.

"Do you like it?" She asked.

"It's stunning."

From the hilltop, their lane curved and dipped, diminishing, taking the eye down to a tree lined loch; its dark waters mirroring a blue sky, the trees, the mountains.

"So hard to see what is real or reflection."

"All is real," he heard her voice. "But there is something else I want you to see."

He was led backwards, sideways, not taking his eyes off the panorama, attracted to a house; an off-white dot perched on the hillside.

"Church?"

"What? Oh sorry." He turned to face Rosemary, so close, her eyes bright; only then did he realise how small she was.

"Say, you seem spaced out; if this is all too much; a bum trip..."

"No, I'm fine." He placed his hands at her freckled face. "I'm fine."

She tilted her head; Jasmin used to do that. "Church? Like, you seem so far away."

Church dipped. "Some things catch up with me sometimes."

Always smiling; she still gazed up at him, "Maybe you should let it all catch up with you."

"Yeh," he nodded to the ground, "running away."

"This may help; this is what I really wanted to share with you," she gestured for him to turn.

His struggle eased.

Exquisite melancholy; dotted with the yellow of wild primrose, he witnessed an earth-covered slab, a huge area, its edges a low wall clad in green.

"Looks like the remains of some building." He surveyed the area. "That must be the entrance," two low pillars clad in the same green. "And what is that beautiful smell?"

"Wild thyme, its growing on the walls, likes the lime."

"Clever lady."

"My brother told me. He's training in archaeology."

"Fascinating."

"He thinks this could have been a priory, thirteenth century."

"My goodness."

"He has been told not to fantasize."

Distant whispering filled his brain.

"I'm blowing your mind." Her words drifted.

"It's this place."

Rosemary stooped and passed him a flower.

"Looks like a small Pansy."

"Nearly right," she said, "many names, sometimes called Heartsease."

Church held the flower.

"Hey," she came close and hugged him.

He buried himself into her shawl and could not control the torrent of tears.

"Just let it all out," she nuzzled his ear.

Eventually the tears stopped, painful emotions washed, he pulled back, only slightly.

Rosemary put a finger on his lips, "Hey, don't even think about saying sorry."

He shrugged, "Yeh, like I say, it catches up with me sometimes." Church hesitated, "And it's crazy but you look so much like someone I keep seeing or think I keep seeing. Does that make sense?"

"Hey," she soothed, "that's enough to freak anyone out. But hey, listen, maybe if you let things catch up, maybe then it will all makes sense."

He wiped his nose on his sleeve, she laughed, "My sweet mother, she used to tell me off for that."

Church laughed and looked back at the remains.

"Ancient memories," he heard Rosemary say.

"Thirteen hundred?" He snatched himself from tears.

"Lots of things have been going down since then," she nodded to herself.

"And someone cares for this place, those flowers."

"That's me. This is my special place."

"Don't blame you. So peaceful."

"Good energies. But peaceful? Hey, let me show you." She pointed to the two pillars at the entrance. "That could be one for you and one for me."

They sat, facing out.

"Isaac was my guide at the beginning. But let us ask our kindred spirits to guide and speak to us both now. Sit upright, poised. Close your eyes and let out a huge breath, breath everything out. Everything."

Church felt inclined not to speak, only listen to the echo of a sweet voice.

Someone's sweet voice. Someone's.

"Try to relax, be aware of where you are.

Be conscious of the space you occupy, your feet, especially your feet; grounding; your contact with this Earth.

Empty your thoughts, let them flow to the ground.

Allow your breath to flow, like a bubbling brook, sometimes fast sometimes slow.

Become sensitive to your surroundings.

Accept the songs of the birds, the sighing of the wind."

He soared; away and into a timeless existence.

Words pulsated; senses tingled; a backward rushing sensation.

"Did you go somewhere nice?"

Church opened his eyes to try and focus on Rosemary. Someone else was there; superimposed, and someone else was speaking; the sun now low in the sky, she was sitting so close, her beautiful smile. She was offering an enamelled mug.

"Spring water, I leave the mug here, drink. Ground yourself."

"Never experienced that before. How long...?"

"Don't measure it by time. Talk it through, only if you want."

"So noisy," he grasped his thoughts, "thought it was quiet here; but the birds, the wind, trees creaking and my own breath; especially my own breath. And silence."

"Accept the noise, and all that's around you. Don't try to fight with it."

"But my thoughts where everywhere at first."

"Monkey on a tree, jumping from one branch to the next."

"But anything else? I can't remember."

"Your journey."

"My journey?

Yeh, I went somewhere...but...oh I don't know. Yeh it was a journey but I can't remember where. Except for a white light, so bright, surrounding."

"That was me."

"You?"

"I placed a white light around us."

"Placed?"

"I visualised it. The intent makes it work. To Protect us."

"Protect?"

"There are wonderful energies here but so easily they could turn dark if we allow them in."

"Too much."

"We can't make the wind go away but we can welcome it and enjoy it. But if it becomes too strong, damaging, destroying, then all we can do is to protect ourselves and give thanks when it's gone."

"Too much."

Her forehead was touching his. "It was a gift given to you and if you can't remember your journey to receive it, then leave it at that. But accept that it was for you, a gift from your angels; your guardian angels. And when it is right you will know what the gift was."

"Yeh," Church rubbed his face, "I read it once; 'don't need answers to understand'."

"That's so cool." Rosemary was back. "Hey," she sang, "try not to tear it apart."

All caught up and slipped away.

It was just him and her.

"But if you don't mind, we need to walk home. Dark soon."

It seemed strange but comfortable to hear that word; 'home.' Although he still welcomed Rosemary's hand, it now implied so much.

Although it had slipped away, the meditation carried clarity.

"How come you know so much of such things?"

"It's in my dear Mother's blood and I allowed Isaac to show me more, use his words, then I carried it on."

"Know it sounds crazy but again it didn't sound like you talking. It was someone else."

"Cool. Say, maybe it was my mother."

"Is it her I see?"

"That would be far out. But like I asked for at the beginning; we channelled our spirit guides or even more cool, maybe it was your guardian angels."

"Guess I dunno what's going on no more but I do know all has been a wonderful thing I've been shown."

And you can find this refuge anytime even if you're somewhere a million miles away, even in your worst nightmare."

"Wonderful words and I think I know what you mean. But what's that place?" They were overlooking the loch again and Church gestured to the grey building, scarred black, perched on the hillside.

"No, don't go there, that is a bad place." Church felt her pulling him. "Too much negativity for any white light."

"Those two trees at the entrance, so dark.

"Cypress, my brother told me. Pillars of sadness in Mediterranean countries."

"Seems familiar, somehow."

"So high, they can reach the stars; heaven. But so dark at the base, the entrance to Hades."

"Welcome to my world."

***

The city park was filled with laughter and as colourful as the cloud of balloons floating by with the seller.

"Is the beautiful baby your'n?"

With sun's warmth, the red-haired lady smiled at the Gypsy and gently rocked the pram, "She is, thank you, her name is Rosemary."

"Magical is Rosemary; their white flowers forever blessed, turned blue. And is that your son?"

"A small boy was pacing the distance between small trees."

"He is. Always measuring and searching."

"He will discover happiness. Buy some lucky heather please Mam."

"Of course," she reached into her purse and passed over silver coins.

"You are a kind lady," the Gypsy studied her. "What do you do?"

"I sign, I dance, I make people smile. And with these hands and with my words, I do my best and try to heal."

"Then you are a gifted lady."

"It's in my dear Mother's blood. Eternal."

"Bless you," the gypsy handed over a sprig, "and bless Rosemary, may she be a dancing child, as free as you."

***

"Purple haze," Church stood at the caravan's door looking in to a cloud; walls draped in dyed muslin. He watched Rosemary in the part that was her kitchen all painted with pink and orange swirls.

"My dream world," Rosemary stirred the pot and nodded to Church, "Please, take your boots off and come in."

Untying his laces, he turned to take in his surroundings; an encampment amongst trees with poles bearing triangles of coloured cloth flapping in a breeze.

"Prayer flags," she whispered.

"So those tents are tepees?"

"Yurts."

"Yurts?"

"Turkish origin."

"Turkish, Mediterranean, monasteries," Church considered, "we travelled the world."

"Hey," Rosemary skipped with her ladle, the caravan danced with her, "and you went to the stars."

"Yeh," Church quietly nodded, "I think I just might have done with that meditation thingy."

"Far out," Rosemary cheered.

"So how many people live here?"

"They come and go."

"And that drumming," he judged not to say that the repetition was annoying.

"Sacred," Rosemary bounced with the rhythm and the floor shook. "Sacred drumming."

"So that building, I can just see the slate roof. Is that the old school?"

"Floyd lives there, in a caravan in the playground."

"And jimmy? Sorry," Church raised his hands, "just trying to get my head around this."

"That's cool," said Rosemary, "I was the same. Jimmy has its own place just up the road."

"Just by coincidence that he is here?"

"There is not such a thing as a coincidence."

Church turned and gazed up, "Hey, hi Isaac."

"Incidences, if they coincide, then it is a significant sign."

"Sign of what?" Church calmly asked and watched Isaac intense face.

"For you to decide." Isaac did not look away, "It is your knowing, your pathway."

"So," Church pondered and smiled cleverly, "Is it a coincidence that you passed when I was talking about coincidences?"

"Soup is ready, you are welcome to join us, Isaac."

'Say no,' Church squeezed his silent wish.

"I must say no," Isaac looked at Church. "Rosemary, I called by to let you know the moon will be right for the sweat lodge in two days.

Church felt Isaac's hand at the foundation of his spine. "Church, you would be most welcome. You should come."

"Sweat lodge?"

Church finally undid his laces and stepped into Rosemary's dream.

"That soup," he put down the spoon, "never tasted anything like it."

"Was it that bad?" She laughed.

"No, I enjoyed it. It was different, that's all."

"Like me?"

She was as vulnerable as anyone; it was then he noticed the reams of paper, some screwed up and thrown, some crammed in piles on shelves.

"One day I'll write my masterpiece," she answered his unspoken question.

"What's the story?"

"Us."

"You've led me like an innocent and happy child all afternoon and I've loved it, please carry on."

"Like, hey, this is a little more down to earth though," she leaned back. "In a former lifetime I played with anthropology and came here out of curiosity only to realise I had been studying life but not living it."

"Woah. Anthropology?"

"That's blown your mind. Hey," she agreed with herself, "that's what happened to me; I blew my mind, didn't fit in, dropped out and reborn."

"Ageless."

"But that's been part of my journey," she eased, "and now I'm understanding what I really want but hey, let me take you on another journey."

He found himself lying on his front, naked on her soft bed. Even with eyes shut, the gentle colours were there. And the smell of heaven. He could sense Rosemary hovering. If she had not explained he would not be able to decipher the warm sensation of oil drizzling over his back and flowing. Her hands were on him catching the liquid before it escaped.

He drifted with the flow of touch; allowing, welcoming, the sensual exploration and pressure of Rosemary.

She was lying on top of him now.

Church could feel her skin, her weight, she slowly danced over him; her arms and legs her whole body. She was shifting her weight to his side and he felt her pull him, instructing him to lay on his back so that she could lay on top; face to face, breath to breath. He kept his eyes closed, relying on the exquisite sensation of touch and the scent of wild flowers to heighten the pleasure; feeling the warmth as he entered her, the pace slowing, in union, using muscles never found, they gently, climaxed together and dissolved into sleep's cloud as one.

C hapter 36

In morning's light, Church dressed and at the doorway, he put on his boots; his hands, his whole body still coated with a film of oil.   He stood to regard Rosemary.   She was wrapped in a tie-dyed muslin sheet, blinking at the light.   They smiled, held hands and as he moved away, their fingers slid apart; a sensation that lingered while he walked over the grass through the encampment in that special silence before anyone else is awake.

He crept past the school building, the headmaster's glare, acknowledging the sleeping caravan where Floyd snored.   Church heard it.

With a feeling of a new beginning, he walked down the lane, taking in his environment as if it were the first time.   It was, almost.   As back as far as England, this was the first time he was able to absorb where he was, the colours, each shade of green, and the smells.   It was the smoke that told him he was entering the domain of Jimmy.   A cockerel bickered with his brood.   He thought he heard the bubbling joy of children.

"Church.   What you up to; sneaking past here this time of morn?   Cuppa?"

Sitting on a bench, Church sipped his tea and followed the line of the lane across the hillside, picking up from where it dipped and rose again or disappeared and emerged from the trees.   He pointed and looked at Jimmy, "That's where we was."

"Up amongst the moss."

"Is that what they call it?"

"Where the peats are cast."

"Peats.   That's it, yes."

"You saw the view and the old priory."

"Yeh," Church nodded that view. "But I..."

"Here you go," Sarah was there, "one each, so no fighting."

"Thank you." Looking up at Sarah's kind eyes fixed with his, Church accepted the two sandwiches, passing one to Jimmy.

"Hey," Church munched while Sarah walked away, "this is good. What is it?"

"Home cured bacon."

"Wow, never tasted anything like it."

"An old whisky barrel full of brine and saltpetre plus some herbs. Chuck bits of pig or lamb in and let it brew."

"As easy as that?"

Jimmy laughed, "Simple yes, but a lot of work on top of anything else."

"And the lettuce?"

Jimmy nodded to the fenced-off cultivated patch.

"And the pig? Don't tell me."

Jimmy nodded and slid the side of his hand across his throat.

"Woah," Church yielded. "But yeh, I can see now. A lot of work." He discreetly noticed the scattering of machinery and half-started building projects. Then he saw the stack of peat bricks and decided not mention his vision of Rosemary and Sarah walking over Jimmy's aching back.

"And now I've got a part time job on top of this lot."

"Really?" Church felt as if he had been caught looking at the site.

"Yeh, plumbing. At the distillery. Lucky to get in there."

"Hey," Church faced Jimmy, "my jibe the other time about you being on the dole..."

"No," Jimmy stopped him. "Need the money and been looking for a job for a long time. Forget that notion."

"Ok," Church slowly stood, "thank you for your

hospitality but before I go I…"

"More tea?" Sarah now had a teapot in hand.

"Yes please," said Jimmy, "Come on Church, it's Sunday. It's a promise Sarah and I made each other at the beginning; one day off a week."

"If, you're sure."

"Please," Sarah looked at Church then to Jimmy, "if it makes Jimmy really have a day off," she pointed to the bench, "sit."

Jimmy waited until Sarah had left. "Now twice you have been interrupted. You had something to say. I'm guessing it's about Rosie."

"What? Rosemary? Yes, I mean no, nothing personal like that."

"Fire away."

"Up above the loch, I guess it's my fascination with buildings…"

"Manse on the hillside."

"Manse?"

"A vague term. Mansion? Sometimes connected with Churches. Excuse the pun."

"It's just that Rosemary…"

"Then it is about Rosie."

"What? No. We are…."

"Ha," Jimmy sang, "just winding you up. What did you want to know?"

"The manse; Rosemary didn't want to talk about it. What's the story?"

"Well," Jimmy nudged an overturned bucket so he could put his feet on it. "It is quite a story and I don't blame Rosie for not wanting to go there."

Church leaned closer.

"You smell like Rosie."

"The manse?"

"The place is old, really old. Between the two wars it was owned by this weird bugger, into the occult and stuff like that.   Story is that he was Russian and got put in jail out in Istanbul or Persia or somewhere like that.

"Jail? For what?"

"All a bit vague but perverted and corrupt stuff. They pinned him down and mutilated his face, cut off his ears or nose or something. Maybe his balls."

"Woah."

"But he escaped, maybe with the loot or relics and ended up buying the manse."

"Woah, that's some weird journey to end up here. And what went on there?"

"Exactly," said Jimmy. "What went on? No one really saw much of anyone but lots of comings and goings and all sorts of rumours about witchcraft and stuff. You can imagine everyone's exaggerated stories.   Anyway, he must have felt too conspicuous up there, or maybe he was on the run.   He still owns the place, or it's in his name but he moved down to England. Your neck of the woods, I believe."

"Really?" Church shrugged. "Then what?"

"Some army Major or General, he rented it. Just before the war."

"The second?"

"Yep. The thing is not long after he moved in; bang. He blew his brains out."

"No."

"Yep, and before he did that, he set fire to the place."

"I thought it looked that way, half a roof and all black."

"The terrible part is his wife."

"What happened to her?"

"This is the worse bit; she must have become trapped in there, burnt alive."

"No wonder Rosemary didn't want to talk about it."

"No one talks about it. I'm only saying this cos you asked."

"Cheers. The place is empty, who owns it now? You said it was still in his name."

"Or his brother."

"Brother?"

"Well rumour has it that the original owner had a brother plus a family left behind in Russia, all torn apart by the revolution."

"Shades of the mad monk. And what happened to him, that original owner, the one that moved down south? Any word of him?"

"Died down there, that's for sure. But rumour has it that his ashes were taken up and placed somewhere up there."

"Some tale." Church shuddered. "Not nice."

"Sure is. People do come and go from time to time. A business circle from down south. But we all keep out of their way. It's all a bit vague and I can't give clear answers." Jimmy looked at Church and laughed, "Bunch of freaks."

"Unbelievable."

"Sure is, and with such a long time ago the tale has probably grown arms and legs." Jimmy looked at Church, "Yeh it sure aint the sort of thing to talk about on a Sunday morn. Change of subject; what do you think of the commune?"

"The hippies? Er. Well, er. Yeh," he slapped his thighs, "if you'd asked me when we first met, I would have given you a different answer but now...I really think the world needs folk like that. Bright colourful folk, not the dark ones like up at the manse."

Jimmy nodded, "I like that. But what did you think of Rosie?"

Church hesitated, "Well, she is different to anyone I've ever met, I have to admit. She took me to another world, another planet. At least our chat has brought me kind of back down to earth. You've opened my eyes to the rich life you have but she..."

"Cleverer than you might think," Jimmy interrupted. "Went to a University."

"What?"

"Aye," said Jimmy, "a Master of something, studied some

sort of an 'ology'."

"A Master's Degree? She got that far? But," Church scratched his head, "she said she just played at it."

"It was definitely an 'ology', one of the youngest, apparently."

"No wonder she had such a way with words...at times."

"When she's not saying *'Hey man cool far out'* you mean. Yep, she told Sarah more about it, she just dropped out for her own reasons, turned her back on it all."

"Floyd a dentist. Rosemary...whatever? Seems everyone has a past," he saw Jimmy look away.

***

At dusk, Church stood at the bridge leaning on Jimmy's lattice of pipe. It was endless, the water running and boiling below, the roar preventing any speck of thought to enter his mind.

C hapter 37

The garden walls allowed Church to retain gratitude. He acknowledged the stack of pruned and cut branches, ready to burn, the garden tidier now.

His lungs felt clear and expanded after the exertion in the garden, the thought of an afternoon's walk to the commune did not trouble him.

And then he stood, in the old school playground, wondering why journeys can pass quicker each time and with no recollection of its passing.

"Hey Floyd." He was hunched in his caravan's doorway.

"Hi there," he waved a limp arm.

"You ok?" Church advanced.

"Bum trip. Get theta way time to time."

"Not good." Church sat on a log close to Floyd. "Can I help?"

"'Preciate that. But no. And I do thank you kindly."

Floyd did not raise his head.

"I'm off to some sweat lodge thing," Church offered. "You coming?"

"That's good that you going. Send my 'pologies."

"You looking forward to Ibiza?"   Church tried. "Sunshine meant to cheer us up."

"Can't get my shit together these days."

"Oh."

"Tomorrow's people. That's what my daddy always used to say. Farming in a dust bowl, always the promise of rain tomorrow; tomorrow's people."

"That's sounds optimistic."

"You try it."

"Meant no offence."

"None taken. So much acid in my young days, messing up my brain."

"Over did it, huh?"

Floyd raised his head. Church saw his eyes. "You done the things I done," Floyd said, "anyone done what I done would overdo it."

"Done? Done what?"

"Out in Nam."

"Nam?"

"After training as a dentist, that's where I went; Nam. Vietnam. Worse thing is, I can't bring myself to feel guilty about things I done."

Church was lost.

"Folk think I'm a good ol boy. Like some joke of a sidekick in an ol cowboy movie."

"I sure folk don't see you that way."

"Now you just get along."

"Hi Floyd, hi Church," Jimmy was there.

Church stood and turned his back to Floyd, cringing and shaking his head to Jimmy, eyes darting in Floyd's direction.

"You ok, Floyd?" Jimmy hollered.

"Hollering aint gonna work today."

"Same old thing?"

"Same ol thing." Floyd lifted himself and plodded into his caravan.

Church felt Jimmy steer him away and heard him whisper, "Gets this way from time to time. Come tomorrow he be fine."

"Tomorrow's people; that's what he said."

C hapter 38

Church was lost in a crowd.

In the Hawthorne's thorny glade, he was back to early days at the orphanage; not knowing what was going on, copying the chattering crowd, hoping he was doing things correctly, expecting a telling-off and trying not to shed a tear.

He retreated into an open-fronted shed, away from the intense heat of the fire, wondering what the black igloo was.

Rosemary was there, he saw her, dancing and laughing around two lads with dreadlocks.

"We got separated," Jimmy was tapping his shoulder.

"Wah? Er hi Jimmy," Church's gaze toward Rosemary was constant.

"Free spirits," he heard Jimmy, "living by different sets of rules; conforming to non-conformity."

"I guess that's what it is."

"I found Isaac and told him about Floyd."

"Yeh, that's a shame." Church gave Jimmy his attention. "What happens here; the fire, and all these folks? And that bloody drumming." He bobbed his head, searching the thicket to ascertain the source.

"It can get on your nerves. Depending on my mood I either love this place or can't abide it."

"Ok?"

"Best way is to just go along with it." Church saw Jimmy's grin, "It gets interesting."

"I'm going to split you two up," soft eyed Sarah stepped between them, "you're too alike."

"You have to be putting me on," Church gawped. Isaac

appeared, in his kaftan and white sash, his glasses and his staff. He brought about a hush and a semblance of order alongside the fire. He opened a flap of tarpaulin; a door into the domed construction, then he moved to stand between that and the fire.

The group formed a wide circle around Isaac. Church obliged and shuffled into a space in the circumference.

"Welcome brothers and sisters," Isaac was solemn. The dreadlocked duo pushed their wooden barrow close to the fire, "Welcome stone gatherers and keepers of the fire." Using long handled pitchforks, the twins braced and placed football sized stones into the fiery heart. "Welcome noble stones."

Isaac thumped the ground with his staff. The drumming stopped. Silence was swallowing.

Without notice the mass moved toward the open-fronted shed. Church watched them. Sarah going inside the shed to chat to a group of kids while pointing to the baby drew his attention to Jimmy who gestured for him to join them.

Everyone began to undress.

Church maintained communication with Jimmy who was smiling and enthusiastically signing for him to undress.

A breeze made his naked body cold on one side and instantly hot from the fire's heat on the other. Making his comfort a priority enabled him to re-join the circle and quickly select a place not too far from the fire. This was obviously a common and well-tried leveller, bringing about jostling and close body contact with false apologies and smiles.

Sharp pebbles amongst the muddied grass cut into his feet, Church investigated, using it to discreetly look about. Skipping the males, he studied all the naked females, different ages and shapes, drawn to Sarah's pendulous breasts, her mass of pubic hair, then to the rounded form of Rosemary who was finally smiling at him.

Her friends, the dreadlocked duo, were still clothed, standing apart. Church disliked them while his eyes followed the circle, then the smoke rising to the freedom of the open sky and he wondered what on earth he was doing to allow himself to become involved in this existence.

Gawky and white skinned, Isaac was also naked, he plunged a long thin branch into the fire and when alight, used the tip to set fire to a bundle of dried grass. He blew out the flames and fanning the smoke with a cluster of feathers, moved to walk around just outside the circle. Church heard Isaac chanting something that he did not bother to understand. He was only aware of Isaac's presence each time he passed his back and admitted that another presence was following; smaller, deeper, darker, mocking.

The circle of individuals spiralled off, following Isaac into the dome, leaving Church with an easy decision of stepping in line. He was the last to enter, save for the entity which elected not to join him. That dirty life force or whatever it was caused Church to glance back; nothing had changed; as still as a photograph. The light through the door was sufficient for all to find their way and sit in a circle on bare earth, their backs close to the sides, all facing a pit in the centre.

His spine curved by the wall of the dome, Church shuffled to adjust himself; a compromise between comfort and not touching the bare bodies each side.

"Welcome brothers, welcome sisters," Isaac chanted. The circle mimicked. Church mumbled; as did the entity outside.

"Welcome stones," the stone gatherers were using their forks to pass in red hot stones and Church quickly moved his bare feet back when the stones were dropped into the centre pit. He fumed at everyone for not alerting him beforehand. It left him wondering about the minds of each.

The flap was closed, it created a darkness that Church had never known. Not even as his eyes adjusted could he see his hand at his face.

"Today," Isaac's quiet words filled the blackness, "we shall have a silent meditation, sending our healing energies out into the universe."

That something was still outside; that entity, a salivating beast; it circled.

Someone cast water on the stones, they hissed.

The entity hissed.

The heat began to rise, so too did the darkness.

A struggle developed for Church, not immediately.

His anticipation of a rewarding meditation and cleansing slowly slipped away. He sweated, the increasing discomfort caused him to wriggle and brush against his companions who he wanted to shove out of his way, wanting to yell, lean back, tear down the walls and escape. Whatever was outside mocked him each time it passed.

"More stones."

A triangle of light, a triangle of sweet air. Vindictively, on forked tips, someone was passing in more red-hot orbs hauled from the fire's dying embers.

The flap was shut, water was cast and torture resumed.

Flying toward a laughing hell, he felt the wind against his face, a burning rush of air, screaming; only for an instant, only for eternity, it lasted. Church opened his eyes to a heavy glow. He stood in a room of large pieces of antique furniture, walls clad in dark wood panels matching the door with two swastika flags of black and red on poles either side. Six people were in that room, all in black robes, they formed a circle over the naked woman who was blindfolded, bound to the floor, spreadeagled. She was not moving.

A dominating bald giant turned and walked toward him, surprisingly swift for his bulk and Church did not have the time or presence of mind to move aside. Church saw the scars on each nostril as he walked straight through him creating a sensation of a rush of air as when someone passes close.

Church was a silent witness; a ghost.

The only but terrible sensation he felt was of purgatory; an understanding that each of those present represented a towering manifestation, dark and threatening, recognisable as the substance of his worst nightmares, swallowing him alive, haunting day and night without end.

A bleak rescue, the ogre passed through him again carrying a shotgun which he thrust into the arms of one of them.

"You've betrayed us, Major, do the honourable thing."

The Major took the gun, it rattled as he pointed it to himself, struggling to reach down to the trigger while the barrel was in his mouth.

"Hurry up man," one barked.

The Major moved quickly, spinning the gun around with the end of the barrel inches from the scarred nose.

"Yefimovich," spat the Major, "you murdered my wife."

"You allowed it.   And you know you wanted it." Yefimovich sneered.   "You both betrayed us.   Both must die. You or your children.   Our code."

"A code you created for your own gain.   Everything for your own gain."

"Our gain, the gain of the Reich."

"You are not from this country, Yefimovich.   You even ran away from yours, leaving your family behind to face a disgusting revolution.   You can never understand.   I must serve my country."

"You enjoyed serving me, you and your wife enjoyed serving me; both to satisfy your taste for young women."

"Corrupt, that's all this is; that's all you are; an excuse to bully rape and torture."   The major jabbed with the shotgun, "Even black magic would seem white and pure alongside you, if you ever elected to practice it."

"You have no idea of what I stand for," Yefimovich sneered.   "And now thanks to your betrayal, all of this has to end."

"The secret service is closing in on you."

"But only here."   Yefimovich turned to his shadowy comrades, "I have found us a haven on England's shores."

The shotgun clicked and Yefimovich seized the element of surprise to yank it back. "Do you really think I would trust you with a loaded gun," the barrel swung down from the stock. The gun was loaded, one shell in its chamber, Yefimovich clicked the barrel back into the stock and ducked to bring the tip under the Major's chin. A devastating explosion. A red mist filled the room. A ghastly corpse dropped with a sodden smack.

The remainder of the group applauded the executioner.

"Pack up everything my dear brothers, we must leave, I hate the word flee but we must. I have a new contact in England, on its shores"

"Closer to our invading brothers," someone cheered. "Who's this contact?"

"A young man with friends in high places."

"We shall get away with murder."

"He should be useful to us for as long as we need him."

"I'll untie and dress the lady," another said, "one last moment to enjoy, going to miss her."

"Don't often find a woman as like-minded. Added another dimension."

The volatile smell of petrol, a skin blistering heat; it tortured then consumed.

Church struggled, wrestled in claustrophobic blackness, a nightmare dragging him back to the swelter of the lodge with no memory of all he had witnessed, except for the lingering company of entities and the crying of tortured souls; all slipping away.

C hapter 39

The chink of the spoon filled the air, Church sat in the kitchen stirring his tea, tepid in the cracked cup.   He gazed into the murky lobby, the hard flagstone floor.   He heard a thud; the remains of an echo when the old lady cracked her head.   The sound ran throughout the hills.   And he could still hear the ignored calls of Jimmy and Sarah inviting him to their home while he escaped from the sweat lodge; desperate to appear unaffected by an oppressive agony, his foot still tender where he trod on a red-hot stone without declaring it.   Church saw only then the disarray of his clothes after dressing himself with the others; companions to each other, not to him.

And outside that dark entity squatted.

The post van passed by, highlighting the extent of isolation.

Time moved in an instant and he heard it before he saw it; the post van hurtling back, crashing through every pothole, the spray of water from the puddles exploding like shrapnel. Church was not affected by the drama but stirred when the white ambulance passed.   He moved and stood at the open doorway receiving an interrogation, such was the look of the driver of the following police car.

Oblivious of what he did during the time; an hour had gone before the ambulance and police car passed on their way out.

Walking down the lane was a painful hobble but he continued until he came across Jimmy at the bridge.   He was leaning over his metal trellis.   That black entity was already there; rejoicing.

He saw Jimmy's eyes; no sign of hope.

Jimmy croaked, "Shotgun. Postie found him. Floyd did it. He's gone."

"Gone?"

"Dead.

Dead."

The slow clunk of a clock, a dripping tap's thud, '... *Dead...* 'Church could do nothing except to watch Jimmy mouth the same flat word, over and over again.

C hapter 40

Church studied Jasmin on her stool at the breakfast bar.

She carried on sipping at her coffee.

"I said…" he slumped.

"I know what you said."

She did not even turn.

"Well?"

No answer.

Church circled to be face on with her, "After all we shared, after all we planned; how can you suddenly announce that you are walking out on me?"

"Walking out? I'm going away to lead a better life, better than this existence."

"I thought we had a good existence."

"Exactly, *you* thought we had a good existence. It might be good for you but when did you ever consider what I may want? It's always poor Church."

"Yeh, rub it in. How can go you just go off with some beach bum?"

"He's a champion surfer."

"Oh brilliant. Send him over to kick sand in my face. Let him try. No doubt he's a brilliant shag."

"Oh yes, far better than you ever could be. No more bickering," she collected her rucksack, "it's pointless. I'm going. Nothing more to say."

"But you're my wife," Church screamed, picked up his mug and threw it. It missed Jasmin, missed the stairs and smashed against the wall. A brown stain ran like tears down the wall; a taunt lasting forever.

"And you're my husband, but that isn't going to stop you going off and playing the 'poor me' with everyone you meet, and it isn't going to stop you shagging that fat hippy cow."

"No," he held his head, increasing the pressure; a clamp, squeezing out the world. "This cannot be. This cannot be." He struggled to comprehend, struggled to breath.

The timeless intake of air inhaled by the stove's lungs drew him to the peat ash of Poppy's kitchen.

The thump at the red door was a shock and it was a test. If he responded, if he went to the lobby and opened the door, it would be another trick, another game played by the monster skulking outside.

Deny it.

"Can I come in?" A sing-song voice, a gargoyle's head; only that part had entered. The rest of it slowly followed. Church was resolute in not reacting to the thing; about four foot tall, dressed in rags. The stench was unbearable.

"It was me that took you back to visit Sarah. Bit of a game. I'm good at that. Confused? But Jimmy sent me. Said it was urgent so I flew here straight away. Can I come right in? You look scared. Promise I won't bite. My name is Egdim." Egdim was offering his downturned hand, "Sniff it if it helps."

"Are you that blackness, always stalking?"

"No, no; that is something far worse than me. Don't worry it will always be there; biding its time."

"Who are you?"

"You know my name backwards. I'm an elemental, your very own creation, bringing to life all your insecurities. I don't feed on your blood, I feed on your weakness."

"If I deny you?"

"You don't have that strength."

"Who said?"

"You know it. But if you had enough strength then I would not exist. But I won't play with you too much. Keep it on your level."

"What do you want?"

"Something else to show you. Be quick."

Church had to go out, to be in clean air.

He stepped out of the door straight into the clearing in the glade; he was back at the sweat lodge, the remnants of his coherent thoughts still present. They were all naked, the circle of people, so was he. The fire was cold. The flap to the lodge was pulled fully open. Someone took his thumb and he turned to look down at that grotesque face. His companion, too, was naked, which increased the stench and he had an erection; enormous.

All the men had erections, the women ogling them; all touching themselves and each other.

Church recognised none.

Egdim chortled, "This is going to be good. Watch," he pointed and held Church back.

Jasmin was there.

She was nude beneath shimmering lace; divine. She walked into the domed structure.

"You stand there," Egdim pointed to the flap, "you can watch before it's your turn."

He was led to the entrance, "Stand aside to let them in."

Unable to respond, unable to destroy; Church could do nothing but witness.

Jasmin lay on her back in the empty pit. She had cast aside her flimsy garment to expose herself.

"Look at that," Egdim danced, "stirring her pudding."

Jasmin was smiling with swirling eyes, one hand was rhythmically moving between her legs, the other churning both breasts. She arched her back, groaning in pleasure, supporting her whole body on the back of her head and her splayed feet. She let out a coarse gasp which Church recognised and watched her turn to be on all fours, her rear facing the door.

One by one the individuals of the circle entered, male and female in turn.

Church turned his face away and squeezed shut his eyes,

denying it all.

"Look at that, Church. She loves it up the arse; big cocks and tarts little fingers."

Church broke free of Egdim's hold, the group sensed this and turned on him. "It's your turn, Church," Egdim was gripping his arm, "swop places with the whore. Take it up the arse."

Jasmin was outside, free of them, he wanted to save her but she sauntered away, her pale body merging with the evening light. He swore, he kicked, he bit groping hands, smashed his fists into faces and lifted himself off the ground, having the satisfaction of kicking someone's teeth, stamping on a head as he freed himself from groping hands to escape to the sky.

He skimmed over a slate rooftop, the sun was setting, tinting the tips of distant mountains a foggy purple, throwing them forward in dark silhouette. The sky blackened, creating such clarity that he could see every star until in sombre darkness he lay, the two wardrobes stationed over him as standing stones.

He buried himself in the sleeping bag, drifting into slumber, with no will to challenge nor make sense.

The bed dipped.

"My poor sweet man." A soothing cloth was tenderly laid over his eyes, he could smell flowers. "I've missed you." Warm and wet, he felt her lips on his, felt her full weight as she lay on top. He could not move, imprisoned by the sleeping bag. She was in full control, her breath deep.

Her weight became unbearable.

"I can't move."

She became heavier.

"Please, you're suffocating."

She stopped moving.

"Please, take off the blindfold."

He wanted to scream when it was snatched away.

Something was squatting on his chest.

It was Egdim, still naked, still erect. He was picking his nose, inspecting his surroundings.

"Look where you are now."

Egdim slid away.

With the weight gone, Church felt cool air on his face, a sensation of freshness.

Looking up he saw the returned stars behind a zig zag of blackened timbers; a burnt roof; one half still intact, trapping the night air. At eye level the debris on the floor seemed huge, scattered all around him. He was in a wood panelled room that had been exposed to the seasons for too long, washed out and crumbling, years of rain flushing away any memory of glowing embers.

He rose, lifted, guided, permitted to pause to witness the loch below, the moon's reflection as real and as clear as the moon above. He was carried out between the two trees; dark spires of unimaginable height, and laid down within the low walls of the flower dotted priory.

Church drifted away into a world of pure darkness. Serenity was eternal. This may be death. And within his obscurity a white fox sat at his feet.

Flickering lights, flickering fingers beyond his eyelids played with him. He thought the ruin was alight again but he was back in the bedroom. Flickering lights persisted. He went to the window; the bonfire was alight. Down there was the grey ghost, looking up to him, pleading, as she orbited the fire, evading the monstrous black presence, ever pursuing.

Stripped of all will, Church buckled. He slipped back to what may be his bed to swirl on the edge of a screaming and deafening maelstrom, darkness forever dragging him; a stygian journey to hell.

With restraints of any truth gone; chaos is set free; a primordial beast to roam once more, leaving no distinction between what is real or what is not; if such a division ever existed; except in imagination.

C hapter 41

Scorched earth was a mutilation on the once cared for lawn. So recently after the fire, the remains still hot, Church was apprehensive to stand on it.

But it was real.

He raked the ash and embers, forming a pile to ensure all charred twigs would be burnt completely; there was enough heat in the centre and a breath of wind caused the embers to glow then burst into flame. The completeness brought satisfaction to Church. Solitude was perfect so was the silence which predictably ran away from the sound of an engine rolling up the lane.

Church turned to see the Land Rover.

"My dear Church," the kind voice travelled to him.

Church struggled for the event to catch up, he was flung back to a time far removed; a previous life. "Richard?"

"I came as soon as I received your letter."

"Letter?"

"Church, my dear friend, you sent me a five-page letter."

"Do you have it?"

"Church my dear chap I…"

"Wait a minute," Church pulled a well-used diary from his back pocket. "Come in."

"My goodness, Church," ticking filled the kitchen, "so many clocks. Everywhere."

Their hands at ten to two, the multitude formed a mocking smile, "Please sit down. I've found it best to be courteous before I check."

He could sense Richard's apprehension as Church

thumbed through his diary, looking at each clock in turn, pencilling entries on a fresh page.

"Right," Church clutched the diary, "You will not have my letter because there is no record of me writing one. I keep a check on the time," he nodded to each of them, "one clock is not enough to safeguard against tricks. And I keep the diary on me," his eyes darted, "no one can tamper with dates."

"Well perhaps you wrote the letter before you started this system."

"Well perhaps I started this system from the day you left."

"Church, please."

"You're not real."

"Of course, I am. Why I have cheese and wine. That's what I brought last time. See, there is proof."

"What did I say in the letter? Did I mention Floyd."

"Floyd? Has he gone to Ibiza? There see, another connection."

Church pulled out his diary, checked the times and scribbled a line.

"It's agreed then; I am real, in fact we both must be. Can't have one without the other. What is this about Floyd?"

"He's dead."

"What?"

"Do you think I wrote you a letter forgetting to tell you that Floyd was dead?"

"We can make sense of this. I mean you must have started your system just before the fire outside, check your well-used diary for that."

"Go back to wherever you come from and tell everyone I have a system in place that is fool proof."

"I shall go," Richard hissed, "but you have not won. Ask your clocks and diary if this was real, or did you imagine it in your distorted brain."

"Richard would never offer that sort of remark. We love each other, you can't touch that."

"You love Jasmin, that's been touched. Oh yes, well and truly touched."

"We used to love each other. We used to. And no one can touch that."

The door slammed and hammers on anvils, ticking filled the emptiness.

Weighed down, he remained on the chair and folded his arms, his head dropping, clocks pounding.

He escaped into a form of sleep.

With dreams.

In vivid colours he saw on the rise a bird flying through two trees into a distant dawn. He stood on grass at a brick wall, feeling temptation to pass through a gate and into a garden.

"Alluring is it not," a tap on his left shoulder.

The garden had a path.

"It leads to purgatory," mocked the voice on his right.

The path led to his orphanage.

"Childhood innocence."

"A farce."

"Security."

"Familiarity."

"Forever trapped in despair."

The clocks ticking intruded.

"And fear," a slap to his face.

"And fear," it chewed in his stomach.

"And fear," the voice was at both ears.

"And fear," it echoed.

"And fear."

Church woke, snatched, immediately aware of where he was. He was outside, standing in the ashes and stabbing through to the soil with a fork, almost breaking the shaft when he levered up a charred clod. The next jab jarred against a buried stone; Church wriggled the fork to lever it until the stone popped out; an eye from its socket. Creatures had survived the heat of the fire. From beneath the stone, pale, devoid of sunlight, grubs wriggled into an alien environment.

"Church, you have been busy, or has it been such a long time since we last saw each other here?"

"Isaac." Church suppressed every emotion, pulled out his diary and checked his wrist watch, nodding smugly to check a different make of watch on his other wrist. "Nope, Isaac, not a mention in my good old diary of us ever meeting here."

"That proves nothing."

"That comment has alerted me."

Isaac took off his glasses and as he cleaned them, seeing his naked eyes, Church was reminded of the stone he had turned over. And just before Isaac put his cleaned glasses back on, Church was able to check that no light-starved maggots were crawling out.

"Excuse me asking, Church. What are you doing here?"

"What am I doing in Poppy's home or what am I doing in this existence?" Church stabbed the ground.

"The former."

"I'm making a rose garden, a sort of remembrance."

Isaac nodded his approval.

"Isaac, you don't seem bothered by my aggressive manner."

"It would require much more before I am affected, beside it is understandable."

"Understandable?"

"Floyd. Jimmy is the same."

"Too right I am," Jimmy was there. "Stopped by to say we are going. Had enough."

"Enough?" Isaac asked.

"Yes," said Jimmy, "if you hadn't conned everyone into thinking that you are some glorious Shaman, I would have saved Floyd."

"And you," said Isaac, "do you think that I am a Shaman?"

"Yes. No. You are not a Shaman but you," Jimmy

spluttered, "walking around as if you own the place."

"But I do."

"And you allow people to stay so you can show them how wonderful you are."

"That would be their perception."

"But not mine and you don't own me or my place and we are giving it all up. It's just one big joke."

"Sorry to hear that Jimmy," was all Church could offer.

"As for you," Jimmy pointed, "wandering around, little boy lost. Sharing seductive glances with my wife, my wife, remember. You and your fancy green oak stairs."

"Aha," Church pounced. "I've never mentioned green oak stairs. You've blown it. Don't need my diary to check on that one."

"Jasmin mentioned it," Isaac intervened.

"Take your nose out of the air, Isaac. You never met Jasmin."

Church simply turned his back and walked into the house.

Poppy was sitting at the table.

She adjusted her beret before commencing the endless stirring of her tea, its clinking filling the warm kitchen. "It's when the corncockles flower that I remember him most."

"Aunt Poppy, please. Not that again, please, no more."

"Then I can say that it must be time for both of us to move on," she did not alter her seated stance, just stared out through the window. "I'm ready now."

"Yes," Church slumped in his chair, "I have to admit you are right."

"Well done," she said.

"But before we leave each other; help me."

"Help you, dear man? How?"

"Answer a few questions, help me understand."

"Don't need answers to understand."

"Please," Church searched the yellowed ceiling, "no games. Just clear answers. It will ease my turmoil"

"Let us try. Shall we?" She was studying him, "Sandy, isn't it?"

"Haven't heard that one for ages. It just proves you are not real because it's never been said up here."

"Have you checked your diary about that?"

"It's in the stove; burnt. Time to move on, you said." Church nodded to the stopped clocks heaped in the sink, water still dribbling out of them.

"Sandy is short for Alexander."

"Didn't know that one."

"Questions? Answers?"

"I no longer know what is real or what is not but there is one certainty."

"That's one more than some have. But tell me."

"There is something following me, can't see it but it's dark and terrible."

Poppy grimly smiled, "I've led an honest and simple life, not harming a soul. That's the presence I leave."

"And something left that dark and ugly presence? How come not everyone sees it?"

"You don't really see it; it is a knowing." Poppy nodded to herself.

"But," Church tutted, "not everyone sees or knows such things, it doesn't bother them."

"Such 'things' as you call it; such things latch on to people, some are aware some aren't. But the effect may still be there. Yes, the effect may still be there; so many frightened souls." Poppy turned to Church, "Heightened awareness is what you have, cultivated throughout your life."

"Someone told me that heightened awareness is paranoia."

"After the war," she said, "soldiers were put out of the way because they saw angels. What would you rather believe?"

"After the war? That's when you came here."

"It was during the war; the land army and I met the one

I love.

"I thought I met the one I love; thought she loved me."

"Time to move on; we agreed."

"But what about the grey ghost?"

"It came to me for help and has been with me for many years. Now it is trusting in you."

"It is all real then?"

"As real as you want me to be," Poppy knocked on the table. "But be wary of the ruin above the loch. Evil is rooted there and it is real."

"I think I know what you mean. But Aunt Poppy don't go yet."

"Sheeit, he's goddam talkin to hisel."

"Didn't even hear us come in."

"Church," said Isaac, "we did knock. May we come in?"

"Think we already have."

The four sat together and conversation became a tangle of words until Church insisted on a halt.

"If you three have all the clever answers," Church scrutinised the impassive faces, then looked to the sink, empty. "What do you think happened to my clocks, the two watches?" They were all real I tell you. I remember buying them," he cursed, "should have kept the receipts, burnt them. Aha, the diary." He forced aside the trio and opened the cold stove's door. "My diary?"

"A diary is on the table," Isaac quietly nodded.

Church desperately flipped through the pages, all empty except for notes relating to his work. "Shit," he rubbed his head, "glad it's not burnt, meant to phone all of these." He looked around the room, searching for clues.

"Aha," he nodded, "Ok, so how come I can tell you what Aunt Poppy looks like? Never met her when she was alive. You saw me talking to her."

"Shit man," Floyd sang, "you was talking with yourself. And don't keep saying I'm dead. This stuff is just freaking me out. I aint dead, am I Isaac?"

"You saw Poppy's ghost," said Isaac. "Nothing unique with seeing a ghost."

"That's true," nodded Jimmy, "Sarah reckons she sees them all the time at that old ruin just up the lane."

"Yeh," Church remembered, "Jasmin said it was haunted. But what about the fire?" Church nodded to the trio, "Yeh, got you with this one. What about the fire?"

"Brats from the commune," Jimmy jerked toward Isaac. "Saw the flames and came to investigate. Caught them running around the fire then they buggered off. Should be able to spot one of em, he got a stone in the back of his head. It looked safe and you were asleep; thought I might as well just go home and back to bed."

"They did a good job," added Isaac.

"And that was last night?" Church was pleading.

"Yep."

"And the sweat lodge was yesterday?" Church saw their faces, "Look I'm sorry but you've no idea what I've been through. Hey I don't know what I've been through."

"And just what am I going through?" Floyd slumped further.

"Yep," said Jimmy, "like I say; after the sweat you just took off when we all came out. Sarah and me, we did shout after you. Sorry we should have thought it through and followed you. You was in a state. But that's why we called by today."

Church turned to Floyd, "And you're really not dead?"

"Shit man, this is freaking me out. I don't rightly know if I am or not." He turned to Isaac. Everyone turned to Isaac.

"Based on all you said, I suggest you went through a healing crisis. It happens after lodges."

"No shit. Means I aint dead. Maybe just havin' a healing crisis."

"Full of many signs," Isaac continued, "for your pathway."

"Yeh," said Jimmy, "looks like you sure are on a new

road."

"Sheeit.   Must be moonshine time."

C hapter 42

Church took his hip flask from inside his jacket and scanned the steamy café before taking a swig.

"Slippery slope."

"Jake?" He looked unwashed which made Church wonder about himself.

"Keep it hidden."

"Yeh, yeh," Church inflated his cheeks and blew. "I'll keep the flask hidden."

"You know that's not what I meant."

"What then?"

"The thoughts, the voices you hear. Learn to live with it and keep it to yourself. Hide it. Coping strategies."

"How did you know...I mean...?"

"Takes one to know one. It's worse when you hear people laugh. And it's in the way you look around, looking for something that just might be there this time. And here she comes."

The door opened and Wallace marched in; Church saw her direct look.

"You look like shit," she had her coffee and was sitting beside him.

"I think that's what the gentleman over there was telling me. He nodded over to his adopted kindred spirit. "Only more politely."

Wallace looked behind her. "Who are you talking about?"

"He was there," Church was relieved to see the empty cup and the sprung bell still moving.

Wallace was close.   Something about her; he felt butterflies.

"Ok," Wallace stood, "that's my lunch break over."

"A five second lunch break?"

"Busy," she said, "I'm glad we met."   Church saw the clear eyes, "It was by chance, was it not."

"Coincidence."

"No such thing.   But come to my office, tomorrow morning at ten.   Lots to discuss."

Church watched her march out and clung to the sides of his chair, feet firmly on the ground.

"Keeping it together," Jake walked back in.   "My mate was passing, gave him a fag.   Owed him."   Church was being considered, "Got any spare?"

"I gave it up again."

"The meds help.   What you on?"

"None."

"Does my head in when they change em."

Church stood and put his hands in his pockets.   "Here." In passing he handed over the half full cigarette packet and the half empty flask.

"Wow.   Cheers, Sandy," he had been given a million pounds.

"Thanks for your words.   Oh, and that stuff in the flask; deadly.   It brings about a madness.   Moonshine madness."

***

'Learn to live with it, hide it; a coping strategy;' Church clung to it.

He was alright that morning, handled himself well in the café.   Or so he thought.   Then thoughts started picking on him, hacking away, demolishing, with voices of growing familiarity.   She was clean, he was dirty, she had noticed.

Why now is the landlord ignoring him?

Hunched over the bar, Church twitched at any suggestion of laughter from the few strangers in what was once *his* pub.

A good plan; use the mirrors beyond the spirits, check that eyes behind him were not aiming at him. But he was caught looking, creating whispered reflections of glances with knowing nods. If they knew he was scared, then why assault him like this? Bullying him. Vindictive. He checked the clock to confirm that time was conforming.

"Church," he heard his name, it was definite this time and the bellows of laughter became the ultimate straw.

He snarled and turned, ready to resolve things once and for all.

"Church."

He brought Richard's smiling face into focus.

"My dear Church, how good to see you. When did you get back?"

"Richard?"

"Are you ok?"

"What?" Yeh, I'm sorry. Been a long drive."

"But you've arrived."

"Think so. Yeh, sorry. Oh, I've just remembered I wasn't going to keep saying sorry to you."

"Really? Don't remember that."

"Wha? No, that's right, it was with Jimmy. That's a good sign. This must be real."

"I'm confused."

"Richard," Church did not relinquish his stare, "how many times did you visit me in Scotland?"

"How Many? Well, yes; you are quite right; I know it was only once. Can only apologise, just couldn't get away, work and all that. Come on," Church felt himself led. "Sit at the table, I'll get a couple of scotches. Don't think they have moonshine."

Church downed the double in one.

"Steady on."

"It's the moonshine, everything seems watered down."

"I think it is," Richard gestured to the landlord. Then he turned, pausing, "Church, you look terrible."

"Everyone keeps telling me. Is it that obvious?"

"Has it been bad for you?"

"You could say that." Church slumped, "I'm hanging on by my fingernails."

"Makes a terrible screech if you slide down the blackboard."

Church laughed, he found it difficult to stop and it was loud, too loud, heads were turning. He moved closer to Richard, ducked, built a wall, a safe encampment. "Sorry," he mumbled and rubbed his nose.

Richard looked sideways at him. "What's all this 'sorry' for? No need."

"It's good to see you, Richard." Church raised himself; feebly assertive and back in his territory. "Seen anything of Nick and Eddie?"

"Apparently, they are across the channel. Keeping low."

"What is it this time?"

"Photocopying pound notes and distributing them."

"Honest?"

"I don't think it is honest," Richard smiled. "Avantha updates me."

"Avantha? Another age." Images tried to invade; he pushed them away before he was able to see them. "But, sorry, I mean. How is she?"

"Who?"

"Avantha."

"She is fine, I believe." Richard checked his watch. "What's your plans?"

***

The bedroom door was heavy with centuries of paint, the hinges groaned as it was pushed open by the tray. It rattled with a tea pot, a cup with saucer and jug of milk. "Good morning. You don't take sugar; am I correct?"

"Richard," Church fought to sit in the consuming bed, "you just don't know how much I appreciate this."

"That's what friends are for."

"Do you really wear striped pyjamas?"

"Mother insists on it and she may call anytime."

"This is a breath of fresh air."

"Walk before you can run."

"Yeh but run I need to, find some clothes, catch up with things."

"I take it then; you haven't been home?"

"Home?"

C hapter 43

Wallace slid open the door, the air was thick with turpentine from the beeswax polish she had applied to the wooden floor the previous night. Before she entered, she bowed to the Buddha statue, the only item in her room. In a corner, it was colossal. It sat upright, legs crossed and tucked under, hands resting together on its lap, palms up. In her white silk tunic and trousers, she walked in bare feet to the glass panels which formed the wall to outside. She slid one of the panels to let in fresh air from her garden to which she bowed. Eyes closed, she felt the rising sun on her face and embraced the warmth. Her garden had four boulders, buried, only their tips showing, interconnected by gravel raked into grooves of motion, intricate arcs, swirls, and waving lines. In the far corner of the garden sat a similar Buddha statue but with its right hand raised, palm out, its left by its side, palm up. One tree grew; a katsura. All was contained by a high grey fence. She bowed to her garden statue, closed the glass panel and lit an incense stick which she placed in a jar in front of the statue in the room. Backing away from it she went to the centre of the floor, bowed again then began a dance of continuous arcs, swirls, turns and dips, mirroring the lines in the gravel in her garden. She moved with increasing swiftness, a blur, then stopped, hands by her sides. She paused for four slowing breaths then sat facing the glass wall, adopting the same position as the statue in the room. Eyes closed, she persisted, her breath continuing as a representation of her fluid dance.

From close by a lone church bell tolled and Wallace smiled even before she opened her eyes. A white fox sat outside looking in at her.

***

"Home sweet home," he sniggered to no one. Church sat in his Volvo looking at the brick building of high arched windows and heavy front door. He grunted and reached to the passenger's sun visor and slid his hand along. He sniggered again; he held the door key.

Tripping over bricks on the path, he rushed behind the car and vomited.

***

He received a curt nod from Wallace. She was looking up at him from her desk. "Good morning, thank you for coming. Is it ok for me to call you Church? Or would you prefer Mister Ashington?"

"You called me shit yesterday."

"But this is business."

"I still feel like shit."

"But today you are clean. Well?"

"What?"

"Church? Mister Ashington?"

"This has all changed," Church looked around the office, "bright, its cheerful."

"Lots of coats of paint."

"Hey, it's dawned on me; the corridor, a new reception area and that weirdo...I mean you have a new receptionist."

"We are still the best of friends."

"And you have a new desk and chair. They finished the light. But...?"

Wallace was smiling now; that feint smile.

"Why are you in Taversham's office? At his desk; well, it's not his desk and that's not his chair."

"Church," Wallace stood to offer a chair, pulling it alongside hers. "Sit."

They sat.

"Church, we have a lot to talk about."

She was close to him. Butterflies started.

"Taversham is dead. Did you know?"

"Dead?"

"Suicide."

"Suicide?"

"Right where you are sitting."

Church stood, rigid.

"Church, this is going to take ages unless you sit and move on from being a parrot."

"Parrot?"

"Stop and sit," Wallace raised her hand. "Why did you say, 'they have finished the light'?"

"Because when we…"

Wallace opened a drawer, pulled out a glass and a bottle of Brandy, "One legacy from him I wasn't going to reject." She poured a large measure. "Talk."

Church leaned his elbows on the desk and swirled the glass. He took a sip and sprayed it out.

"What's wrong?" She dabbed her suit with a tissue.

"Sorry," he choked, waving a dismissing hand. "Driving. This new breathalyser thing."

"There are such things as buses, taxis and," he felt Wallace dab his thigh with the tissue, "one can always walk. I don't even bother to own a car. Talk."

"How did he do it?"

"No. You talk. I fill in the rest."

Church took a deep breath, downed the brandy and looked at her, "After our wee chat in the café. Hey how long ago was that? No matter. I broke in."

"Why?"

"I thought If I could find evidence that he was cheating then I could expose him. Thought he would be too clever to be found out any other way. Sort of blackmail him, beat him at his own game."

Wallace topped up the glass, "Plant a seed and it will grow."

"Seed?"

Wallace raised her eyebrows and twiddled her thumbs. "You set me up for it."

"A gentle push starts momentum."

"My turn. Why did he kill himself?"

"No one knows. But look," she moved closer, "he was up to no good, lots of inappropriate dealings have been discovered. I'll tell you this because you are going to find out anyway; he asked me to come back at night, trying to hook me into something. I don't even want to think about it. When we came here the place had been burgled. Now you've confirmed it was you." she shrugged. "But he tried to blame me then attacked me."

"He attacked you?"

"That was dealt with and I left him here. Next day we came in and he had killed himself. Tried hanging but it went wrong. Garrotted right at your feet."

Church lifted his feet, "Always hated this office." He pointed directly down. "All sorts of weird markings."

"Indeed, there were. A new floor now. But yes, did a bit of research, occult inscriptions and his correspondences show leanings toward Nazism."

Church looked at her, "It all seems like an embarrassing nightmare now, even more embarrassing that I allowed myself to react to it. You probably don't know what I'm talking about. I've been through hell, with voices, darkness and ghosts," he hesitated, "I think it comes from stuff like this."

"Probable."

"You won't understand but that one word is a relief to hear."

"Perhaps I do understand."

"But...talking of dark energy," he sunk. "Jasmin?"

"Please don't tell me you want a reconciliation."

"I know I'm a mess and miss her. But right now," he hid his face in his hands, "I couldn't handle what that would involve."

"That's good because sentimentality muddles. But I'm

pleased to hear you miss her."

"Pleased?"

"You're more rational than you admit."

"What's happening with her?"

"She's in Goa, "Wallace raised her hand, "and don't start the parrot routine."

"I'll say Goa anyway."

Wallace sifted through papers, "It fits in with the hippy trail to India. A place called, er, Anjuna, helping to set up a market, for hippies to sell stuff."

"Hippies?" Church mumbled, "Thought the trail led to Ibiza. More coincidences."

"No such thing. Anyway," Wallace scrutinised more papers. "She wants to sort out an amicable separation, so you need to communicate. Find yourself a solicitor."

"Can't you...oh yeh unethical."

"Plus, I'm winding down."

"Eh?"

"Handing over to another firm and I'm going to rethink my life."

"Really? Seem to be so many rethinking their lives."

"Thinking of buying this place and convert the building to another use."

"If you need an architect.... oh sheeit."

"What?"

"My clients.... I just disappeared off the face of this earth."

Wallace was on the phone. "Hi Popsy. Look I haven't any other clients and need to be out for the remainder of the day."

"Popsy?" Church whispered to himself, "But it was a bloke at reception."

"Popsy, you've done what? My goodness, I've never met anyone who can organise things the way you do. Yes, so take any messages and close early if you want. We'll take the back door. Wallace paused and laughed, "That'll be right."

"Oh sheeit."

"Yes," Wallace put the phone down, "you've already said that."

"No but…"

"You looked like shit when you came in."

"I don't even remember coming in."

"Exactly."

"Manic."

"You're calming now so we are going out to complete the job."

"I but no but…"

"Come on," she stood.

"Can we go back to my place?"

"You never answered my original question," she waited.

"Church.   But what do I call you?"

"Wallace."

C hapter 44

Church paid the taxi driver. "I came here this morning to find clean clothes but don't remember that." He turned to Wallace, beneath an open sky she seemed demure, "Before we go in, I want to say thanks. You don't have to be doing this and I appreciate it. And you sure have a calming presence about you. Yeh," he nodded, "you're alright."

He saw Wallace's boyish face and her eyes, so intense. "Church, when I first saw you, something told me that you were going to be part of my pathway."

"Can't think why."

"Overcome that way of thinking and you will know why."

"Yeh but I'm not the stuff of heroes."

"I'll wait for you."

"Strange thing to say."

Wallace was looking over the building's exterior, "And this place is typical of your art?"

"Nice you call it art." He took a deep breath and opened the door.

"Nice," Wallace took it all in.

Church did not conceal his surprise, "I'm sure I left it in a mess. Is that new? What made her do that?" He pointed in the direction of the French doors; a work desk fitted out with lamp and drawing board. "And she's been packing. Packing?" He scrutinised the writing on the cardboard boxes. 'Records' Better not be mine, not my Thelonious."

"Love the stairs the high ceiling; why it's like a..."

"Cathedral," Church was engulfed by his tears.

**

Wind dipped from a high sky and cut across the trees, fanning through the peat works.   Isaac turned, "It was good to have your company."

"Stay and help if you want," Jimmy nudged Sarah, "we have to clear the drying area before we start cutting."

"Very kind of you but I want to sit at the old priory for a while. Been thinking of Church."

"Oh yeh," said Jimmy, "hope he's ok."

"Exactly," Isaac nodded, "I have been sending him healing. See you later."

"He didn't get the dig about helping," Sarah whispered.

"Hey," Jimmy wiggled his spade, "a double dig."

Sarah grunted, pulling up dried and dead heather. Jimmy puffed and assisted by chopping at the roots with the spade.

"Mister and Missus Grunt and Puff."   Rosemary sang, soothing Zimmy.

Isaac looked down at the loch and called back, "I do not think you should stay long; a storm is threatening."   Dark clouds rolled across the water's face.

Isaac turned through the trees then out to the flower dotted ruin.

He sat, perched on the same low pillar where Church once sat when with Rosemary.

Isaac closed his eyes, breath a shallow rhythm. Across the waters below, the wind increased its pace and depth, surging up the hillside. A darkness obliterated the sun.

**

"Thanks Wallace," hunched over the breakfast bar he felt her hand stroke his back.

"Drink your water," she quietly spoke and looked at him. "You need to get out of here, too much past."

"Full of nightmares for me. So much darkness."

"Yeh," Wallace sipped her water, "There is dark energy here, that's for sure."

"And you feel it? Slowly I'm beginning to understand what '*it*' is."

"Understanding," said Wallace, "that's my pathway, my direction." She turned and Church saw her mischievous smile, "I do go a little off course from time to time."

"I'm sure I'll find out what that means."

"I'm sure you will. Ok," Wallace slapped her sides and looked about, "so It's great that we are here to see your home. But why are we really here?"

Church shook himself, "With poor me wrapped up in my own self-pity; I forgot the main bit. When we did our breaking and entry..."

"We?"

"You don't want to know." Church hesitated, "I found some things."

"And?"

"I've kept them safe."

"Where?"

"In a red box and under my bed."

"Church."

"It's under my bed."

"Church."

He felt a darkness, it flowed down the stairs.

"Church."

It was behind him.

"Church," Wallace's shout reached him. "I'll help you. We need to get the box, pack a few things...not far to walk... come back to my place. Not good here."

Wallace's voice bounced.

Time swung backwards.

Church was moving in retrospect; remembering his actions, unaware of doing them. He had crawled up the stairs to lay on the bedroom floor to summon courage to reach underneath the bed; a lurking hand was ready to snatch his wrist and pull him into the underworld. He had to wrap his fingers around the evasive box and use both hands to withdraw it to clasp it at his chest. Standing over him, Wallace was slamming doors and pulling out drawers to stuff clothing into a bag.

"We should go," he heard distant words.

Pursued, Church was tumbling down the stairs, she was dragging him out through the door. With the key still in the lock, she turned it and Church felt her lead him away.

"Ok Church," air was cool and clear, "we've left it locked in there."

Despite her words, Church knew he would forever be looking behind.

"Hey," Wallace stopped him at the kerb, "you did ok." He felt her arms around him and realised that she, too, was needing the shelter of reassurance. He matched her brief embrace.

"Here's some clothes," she swung the bag. "Don't be surprised if your wife's knickers are amongst them."

"And this is the box." He clutched it away from his body. "Not just me then; you felt it in there. What do you suppose it is?"

"Later." Wallace guided him through enclosed back streets and alleyways of dustbins. "When I'm out jogging," she said, "it's a good way of finding shortcuts."

"Doesn't it worry you?"

"What do you mean?" She screwed her face at him and stopped.

"Alleyways; a girl on your own. Not scared?"

"People need to be scared of me."

"Where you scared back there?" He searched.

"Yes." She marched off.

"It's real then, all these things, not just in my head?" He rushed to keep up.

"In your head but not just in your head, it's everywhere."

"But what if it is just in my head? Slow down a bit," he was panting, struggling to speak.

"If it were just in your head then I would say you are

bonkers." Hands on hips she was making an issue of waiting.

"But what is it, these things that get me scared?   And you."

"Later, I said."

"Hey I know where we are."

A privet hedge crawled like a caterpillar to a high brick wall, Church peered in the gateway to the private grounds. Resinous sap clung to whispered memories; a cherry tree lined avenue led to the house," One of my clients; John Airedale."

"Looks empty, boarded up," Wallace stepped into the entrance.

Church copied and saw the plywood sheets over the windows.

"Looks like work in progress has come to a halt." Wallace led him away but Church stopped after a few yards.

"Guess I need to get my head around what I'm going to do with my jobs."

"Maybe just write a standard letter to all your clients, stall them and give an option of backing down. Minimise the damage to your reputation while you sort out your life."

"Yeh, sounds reasonable. Thanks matron."

"Matron?"

"Just the way you spoke, reminded me of my childhood."

"Well don't call me that again," she smirked, "unless I insist."

"Don't want to go there; the orphanage, I mean."

"That's right, you were raised in an orphanage."

"You know?"   He searched her face for any clue of an expression, "Does that bother you?"

"Don't be silly. No fostering or adoption?"

"Who would have me? But how did you find out?"

"Some bits in your file. And other bits here and there if you know where to look."

"Snooping?"

"Yep." She marched off and turned, "Are you bothered?"

"Nope. I trust you."

"One count of GBH," she said. "That's nothing. Is that how you got the nose."

"Yeh, yeh. Anything else?"

"A babe found in a box. Beyond that is vague."

"Tell me about it."

"What didn't help was that the constable who found you was caught in a hospital bed with a nurse."

"You cannot be serious."

"Sounded like fun. All the paperwork got lost in confusion. Common though, to give abandoned babies names based on where they were found."

"Church, yeh, but Ashington?"

"That was a long way from the hospital you were taken to. Talking of Churches," they turned a corner and were walking down a cobbled lane, a church on their right with trees on the left, leaves rustled by a distant breeze.

"That's my place," she tapped the high grey wooden fence. "Need to go to the front."

Before entering the narrow siding, Church looked over his shoulder, expecting someone to be standing there, at the church entrance.

"Spooked?" Wallace led the way round to her red front door. "Shoes off please. I shower, then it's your turn."

***

"Thanks for the robe." Water was in droplets down his neck. "Always liked the colour charcoal.

Wow."

She sweetly smiled her reply. In a silk robe of white with orange chrysanthemums, Wallace sat across the room kneeling on a cushion at a low table.

"Saw this in a film once," he knelt opposite, "tea ceremony."

"An honour," Wallace poured the tea, bowed and passed him a cup using both hands.

It was then that he took in his surroundings, "A good

stove, top of the range," a room with minimal furniture decorated in black and red. "The style? Cantonese, Japanese, Chinese?"

"A bit of everything. That's me."

"Feels nice, peaceful."

"We have finished our tea; I would like you to see my special place."

He was led to an adjoining room, she slid the door open, he smelt turpentine. She stepped aside. Church looked in but could not bring himself to enter.

"My sanctuary."

Church took in the sunny room, brilliant light reflected off the floor, the enormous buddha, the glass door and her garden. "I don't want to go in and spoil it. It's so...."

"Protecting, calming and holds no fear," she offered the words. "It's where I practice my tai chi and meditate and other stuff."

"Tai chi; that was in that film too and yeh, someone introduced me to meditation."

"What I am trying to do is let you experience the beautiful energy in there. No darkness."

"How?"

"By what is put in and what is allowed to enter. Wind and water, heavenly time, earthly space; all in harmony, nothing dark dare enter; it attracts only light."

"And how do you make it happen?"

"Rituals and tasks with the appropriate intent. But the practitioner must be at one with their own strength."

"And you've learnt all of this."

"Still learning but not in one true discipline."

"Dedication."

"Competing more like. Having two brothers makes you that way."

"You have brothers. Must be nice. But," he looked around again, "this takes discipline."

"Maybe, but too easily distracted." She sidled to him.

"Could have fooled me.   Hey I'm feeling it again; those butterflies, when you get close."   He offered an embrace.

She retreated.   "Could be my energy, my auric field my Chi."

"Chi?"

"Or it can be called Ki and other names, playing with your chakras."

"Playing with my what?   Not sure what that means, it wasn't in that film."

"Enough.   The box."

She led him back to the tea room, covered the table in a white linen sheet, lit incense in a jar at each end and placed the box in the centre.   Silently instructed by Wallace, they sat as they did for tea.

"Shall I open it?"

No response came, Wallace sat, crossed leg with eyes closed, her palms just as the statue in the garden.   Tranquil protection emanated through her, filling the room and encompassing Church.

***

Isaac stirred, only then was he aware of being wet and cold, rain turning to hail.

"We held off disturbing you," looking down at him, Jimmy was there, water running off his rain-stretched tousles. "But the weather is worsening."

"Thank you.   But I think the sun is returning now," he smiled to the sky.

"Please don't tell me you did that."

"I shall not tell you."

***

"That was interesting," Wallace was smiling at him.

"Sure was," Church stretched.   "It seemed right for me just to sit at peace with you and it took me away to a place in Scotland, a special place where someone equally special taught me to meditate, felt like I was back there, sitting with Isaac."

"Well, we are here now and I think we are in a better

place to open the box."

"Er, I think I need to say something."

Wallace had pressed the catch on the box file and the flap was open.

"Photographs," she said, "lots of them. Huh," she inhaled sharply, put her hand to her mouth and peeked over to Church. "That sick bastard."

"That's why I smashed the mirror, it was two-way, I took all the films and the spools, no one really saw them, I've kept it private for your sake, no one else saw them, well Eddie he…"

Wallace was not listening, looking at each photo in turn, pulling sour faces, turning some upside down, "Oh that's a good one of Janice. Are my tits really that small?"

"They look nice."

She stopped and scrutinised Church with an evil eye.

"I didn't have a proper look; the negatives are there."

Wallace looked back over the photos, laying them out on the table, then sharply looked at Church, tears in the corner of her eyes, "How else can I react? What is the choice?"

"Most of them are blurred, if that helps," Church tried.

"Bugger this I'm having a fag." From the table's drawer, she pulled out a tobacco pouch and papers. Signing an offer to Church.

"No, I'm ok. A drink though."

Church sipped his whisky and wondered how Wallace could gulp hers, swallow and then blow out smoke.

"I have a friend," she said, "a Buddhist monk. His aspiration and all that it implies is to be a mountain, so tall but buried deep, with a clear crystal lake at its base. Right now, I am a mole hill in a muddy puddle."

"I'm so sorry."

"Like I said earlier," she looked at her lap, "I'm not that disciplined and so easily distracted. Sometimes I wonder if it's self-destruction."

"It didn't look like it."

"Thought you said you never looked at them." Now

Wallace was snake eyed.

"Well," Church brushed his legs, "I guess we can put them in your stove and no one need never know."

"Especially Janice. Yeh," she sighed, "that monster had to put it in the gutter. I can see what he was up to, gonna try and blackmail me into doing anything. Urrrr," she shuddered and finished her drink.

"But," Church poured more, "no reason for him to kill himself."

"Oh no," Wallace was looking at another photograph; black and white this time, she pulled out another. "Oh please no." She handed them to Church.

Another ornately inscribed circle; laid upon it was a woman, naked, surrounded by candles and bare feet. Squatting on her chest was a brute.   Even in the photograph her expressionless eyes showed she was dead.   The second was of another female, shackled to a heavy chair, her body mutilated.

Neither spoke for a long time.

"Incubus," Wallace eventually whispered.

"Huh?" Church grunted.

"That monster on her chest; an Incubus."

"One of my nightmares."

"That's when it comes; a demon of the night, preying."

Church inspected the photographs, "That floor, it looks like concrete and those walls are brick. Doesn't look familiar."

"Can't burn them; the police."

"What about yours?"

"Let me think about that one." Wallace was searching through the box.   "Much the same as I found on his desk. World war two Nazi propaganda, codes and stuff.   And this," she was holding a large key.   "Any ideas?"

"No. But I know some people who may have."

"Can we trust them?"

"With my life. Although they just might bugger it up."

"Are they nearby?"

"Don't even know what country they are in."

C hapter 45

The tall mast swung, trailing ropes clanged against it; a metronome's blade sweeping an empty sky, as grey as the sea, their horizon a distant union.   The boat's rhythm with the waves was making him drowsy. Sitting wedged in the wooden aft, Nick held on to the lifeless tiller arm and gave Eddie's rear end a lazy nudge with his boot, "Any luck?"

Eddie wriggled out of the hold and held up an oil-soaked engine part, "Fuel pump."

"Well done mate, yep it is the fuel pump."

"Knackered."

"Again. Never mind, help is on its way."

The boat's black hull exaggerated the whiteness of the bow wave as it cut toward their yacht.

"Hello my friends," in his navy-blue jacket, he adjusted his beret.

The engine ticking, a rope was swung across, then a second. The round plastic fenders squeaked as the two craft where tightly secured, fore and aft.

"Hi Jacque."

"Only eight boxes this time," Jacque easily swung one over to receiving arms. "I was being watched."

"If the gunboats appear," Eddie held up the fuel pump, "this is why you are here."

"But you cannot cross without an engine."

"Nick, get out and push."

"Can I still touch the bottom?"

"Uhuh," Jacque gestured and smirked, "I am a surly French fisherman," he put on a comic accent, "I do not understand your funny English jokes."

"A French fisherman with some British University tie holding up his trousers."

"Meet all sorts out here."

"Hey my friends," Jacque's manner deepened. "I tell you this," he gestured to the boxes, "I have contacts now in South America. We can make a lot of money with them."

"Thanks Jacque," Nick dismissed him. "We will stick with the vino."

"Yeh," Eddie added. "A simple life don't need a lot of money."

"You are lucky not to have a wife and five children, then you need money," Jacque shrugged to the sea. "Just you think about it. But for now; what about your boat?"

"Seriously, no problem, a good Easterly, steady high pressure, good forecast."

"Yep, compass bearing dead South."

"North, my friend," Jacque scolded.

"No, Sussex is on the south coast, innit it Nick."

"But I can tow you back and repair the engine."

"Good old Pipedream," Nick patted its gunwales, "this old girl has been to Dunkirk mate."

"And back."

"Twice."

"Nah," Nick was untying and throwing back the ropes, "people may start snooping," he nodded to the boxes.

"You are sure; good luck then." Jacque's boat gently slipped about, then the engine roared and the vessel curved away. "See you next month," he shouted back, "and think about what I said."

"Tell everyone, why don't you," Nick scanned an empty sea.

Diesel exhaust still in the air, Nick skipped along the teak deck. "Bring in the fenders, I'll sort the jib. Then you take the tiller."

"Aye skipper."

Nick pranced back. "Keep her into the wind." He pulled on a rope, hand over hand and the triangular jib slid up the forestay to the mast top, the red canvas flapping violently. "A good breeze. Hold her there." He secured the rope then pulled another and the mainsail unfolded out of its cradle to glide up the towering mast, he gave an extra pull then secured the rope. Both sails were now giant ochre wings of an alarmed captured bird. "Ok, bring her round," he allowed the rope to slide through his hand as the boom swung out over the port side, then he secured the rope. He pulled on and secured an additional rope to fix the front sail.

Both sails set at similar angles, the red canvas filled, the boat leaned and lifted.

"We're flying. Way to go Pipedream." Nick tidied rope's loose ends, laying them out as coils.

"Grandad is up there, smiling down," Eddie grinned at the sky.

"Good old channel chop," the waves grew taller, spray playfully splashing them; a childhood game. "See the Tankers," he pointed to the horizon and switched lights on.

"Remember what Grandad said; steam has to give way to sail."

"Steam?" Eddie laughed. "But this aint a bad way to earn a living is it, Nick."

"Yeh but be nice to get back home."

"At least we saw our dad's graves."

"Job to find em, so many war graves."

"Yeh, too many."

"Cheer up. Glad I wasn't born in France."

"Why? It's been a nice place to stay and lay low."

"Yes, but I can't speak French."

"Hey," Nick looked to Eddie. "South America, you know what Jacque was talking about don't you. Tempting, good money."

"Bad money and what would Grandad say?"

C hapter 46

Still kneeling at the low table, Church watched Wallace's alabaster legs. Standing at the sink, her silk robe was short, offering a hint of a rounded and bare bottom but she did not seem modest, engrossed in wiping the wok.

"That was delicious, Wallace, thank you."

"You are very welcome. I hope you didn't mind no meat."

"Never noticed. Jasmin always wanted us to go vegetarian." He shrugged and looked to the box now in a corner and wrapped in a white sheet.

"She seemed nice," speaking gently, Wallace was looking directly down at him, "I'm sorry this has happened to you."

"It's funny you know," Church ran his hand over the smooth wood of the table, "you mentioned a reconciliation in your office. It hit home how easily I've moved on."

"How easily you think you've moved on."

"Maybe." Church wanted to finish what he was saying, "It's just all the mess that goes with it. And the other stuff," he gestured to the box.

"As long as you are ok about being here."

"Yeh that's a point, getting late. I think I can remember your short cuts to get home."

"If that is what you want but we took your clothes here. Remember?"

"What? Oh yeh. I forgot that bit."

"You would be welcome," Wallace nodded to the wooden slated bench, "the futon rolls out, its mattress and duvet are in the cupboard."

"I've been enough trouble."

"I like you." Wallace was sitting down again, "When you slow down and be just you, I like you and what you are becoming."

"Becoming?"

"Something I see in you. And I like you being here but the last thing I want is to influence whatever is going on for you with Jasmin."

"Can I stay?"

"Please. One more drink," she was filling the two glasses.

"Seems strange."

"What does?" She was looking into his eyes.

"You smoking and drinking. It doesn't fit with all you've shown me."

"I don't normally, but like I've said I'm easily distracted. And," she laughed, "I didn't elect to live as a nun."

"A nunnery," Church smirked, "always fancied that."

"Me too," she smirked back.

"Can I ask you something?"

"Been waiting for this," Wallace was rolling a cigarette.

"You and Janice?"

"Like I said; we are still good friends. Had to put a stop to it."

"Why?

She fluttered her eyelids, "Her husband asked if he could watch."

"Oh. But are you…?"

"Am I what?"

"It's ok by me. I mean…"

"Oh, it's ok by you is it," she reached over and tapped his cheek.

"Well?"

"You've seen the pictures." She yawned, "I've had boyfriends," she was staring at him, "but I get hurt. Women, they don't seem to do that." She yawned again and stretched. Her tunic gaped. Church knew he was caught looking at the exposed mound of a breast. She did not seem to mind, not bothering to cover herself.

"Was a girl your first love? Tell me to shut up if you want."

"It's ok. The first person I made love to, if you can call it that, was a boy. But a lady, Lee, she was my first love."

"What happened?"

Wallace shrugged, "It was fun, used to paint me."

"Paint you?"

"She is an artist and I was her muse, which in itself can never be a permanent thing." With a playful smile, Wallace finally closed her robe. "But we...well she was older and as I grew up, we just moved on. It was ok. Keep in touch now and then. And what about you?"

"My first love? It was in a train."

"Wow."

"Not really."

"Oh?"

"Wasn't like in the old films. Wasn't even a steam train."

"No tea ceremony you mean? Ok," she stood. "In the morning, don't mind me. Get up when you want and eat and drink what you want."

"Yeh, I'll walk home, try and sort stuff out. Need to pick up the car sometime. It's by your office. I think it is?"

"It is. Tell you what, meet for a coffee at one."

"Another five second lunch break?"

She laughed, "You're worth longer now." She pulled the mattress and duvet out of the cupboard. "You can work out how the futon unfolds. Goodnight," she pecked him on the cheek.

***

In the low bed as his night vision mellowed, the silent room filled with light; a moon's glow spreading over the ceiling. He lay on his back, hands lightly clasped over his chest, making him very aware of his rib cage rising and falling, matching his sleep rhythm; in and out of sleep, in and out of dreams he drifted; rising to look down on himself, floating down to look up at himself.

In and out of sleep, in and out of dreams, he passed the night.

And in that night the glow above slid down the wall, shape-shifting into an orb then into a fox of the moon's shade of white. It sat at his feet.

Church could smell coffee then opened his eyes to focus on Wallace. He sat and took the cup she was offering.

"You're not a dream then." He smiled up at her in her white silk tunic and trousers.

Wallace was busy pouring milk into a cereal bowl, taking a few spoonsful before splatting the bowl down, then she slipped of her clothes to let them fall to the floor.

"Sorry," he heard her shout above the shower's hiss, "force of habit. Did it without thinking."

Church did not reply, desperate to retain the image of the hairless body of a nymph dancing to the door.

Recumbent, with the coffee perched on his lap, he drifted away, sounds delicious in the background.

Did he hear a bell's toll? It was another beautiful thing.

"Sleep on," he heard a whisper, "you are exhausted."

***

Church sat in his café; time suspended.

"Hi." He heard a gentle voice. Wallace was stroking his hand.

Church looked at her and forced back the tears. "Here come the butterflies."

Her face glowed, "Me too."

"Really?"

"I shouldn't have said that." She looked to the floor, "You've enough..."

"I'll get coffees."

When he came back Wallace was toying with something and searching his face.

"That's that key," he nodded at it.

"Took it with me and investigated. No idea where it is for."

"Ok, leave it with me."

"How was your morning?" Wallace asked.

"Yeh, sorted out stuff, took up your idea, put my clients on hold. And yours?"

"Yeh fine. I suppose." Elbow on table, she leaned her face on her hand and looked at him. "Put in an offer to buy the place."

"It's going ahead then, your plans. Moving on."

"Seems that way."

"Er, I'll see what I come up with about the key." He hesitated, "Can I walk over later?"

"Please do."

C hapter 47

In dusk's confusing light, Church turned the corner as the lamps came on along the cobbled lane. The uninvited glare made it harder to see. He stopped before the church vestibule. Something made him stop; perhaps an invitation to stand and listen to the bell's lonely toll. He held back his breath. A white fox emerged from the shadows through what must be a gap in Wallace's fence. He had always imagined the fox to be sly but the noble creature moved with grace to the church's doorway and sat as an invitation for Church.

The uplifted direction of the fox's eyes made Church turn to see who was behind. A lady with flames of red hair and wrapped in a shawl was nodding, encouraging that he walk on, giving permission, urging him to take the corner to Wallace's house.

"Sorry I'm late."

Church looked up to see where the gentle touch came from. "Oh sorry, day dreaming."

"Wonder what the neighbours think; a dirty tramp sleeping on my doorstep."

"My hands are clean. Love the suit, by the way."

Wallace helped him separate his back from the door and stand. "Crikey I'm stiff, don't know how long I've slept there. Been working outside my home. Not used to it."

"Please come in," she smiled. "So nice you are here."

They knelt at the table. Wallace almost ripped off her tie and slowed herself, inhaling deeply.

"I remember that feeling with a tie once."

"Hope you don't mind left overs." She forked the

noodles from the wok onto the plates.

"That's great," he nodded to himself, "I'm starving."

"Did you eat today?" Church saw the look.

"Forgot."

"And, I'll ask again, how was it, your day?"

"Busy, lots done," he said between mouthfuls.

"I asked the same thing at the café and had a similar answer but that's not what I meant."

"What then?"

"The last time we were at your home we..."

"Oh yeh, realise that now," he looked at her. "Nothing there. No nasties."

"We need to talk," she gathered the dishes, "but later."

"Another talk."

"I'm irritating you."

"Just intrigued."

"There is another matter more urgent," she nodded to the box.

"Yeh, I had no luck with the key but I guess we should get the police involved. Are there time limits on murder cases?"

"There are not but I would like to find out a bit more myself, see if there are any connections with the building before I take it on. Curiosity."

"And anything more connected with you."

"I'm innocent."

"I know that but more photographs of you would..."

"I can deal with that," she reflected, "just want to find out for myself what has been happening before the police block the way. Its Friday; the building is empty for the weekend.

"Tomorrow it is then."

"I would appreciate you being with me."

"Hey," he grinned, "Friday."

"You said you had some friends who may be of help."

"And it fits. Friday, I fancy a pint. They will probably be there if they are back."

"A pint?"

"Pub."

Wallace stood with the plates, "Would you mind doing the washing up."

"I was going to offer."

She brushed down her suit, "Be out of these bloody clothes, have a shower." She threw her jacket over Church's head. "You're not getting another performance and you need a shower.... Usual routine; after me."

Church splashed out of the shower and wrapped the towel around his waist. He listened for any clues then took a breath and shouted, "I chucked my clothes in the cupboard with the duvet. If your there I'm coming through. Oh my gosh."

Wallace smiled coyly, she twirled slightly, side to side.

"You're so pretty," he saw her, her brushed cropped hair, her in a delicate smock and jeans, a velvet band around her neck.

"Aren't I normally pretty?"

"Extra pretty then."

"I'll accept that," she had a twinkle in her eye.

"Er, I need to get dressed. Er if you don't mind."

"Why worry about me? Nice muscles," she gestured to make Church realise the towel had slipped away. "Now we are equal terms."

***

"Not been in many pubs, that's to say that I've been in only my kind of pub," she led him into an alley. "Not posh I take it."

"What, because it's my pub? Hang on a minute," he stopped her.

Ahead were three youths, pacing and waiting.

"I think we should go another way," Church took her arm.

"You'll be ok," Wallace marched on, "I'll look after you."

"I'm Bill," he jeered this is Rob and this is Joe. "We're three brothers, right. And This is our manor."

"Just let us pass please, Bill."

"Pretty please," Rob sung.

"Pretty please then," Church said.

"They are pretty aint they," Joe joined in and pulled a knife and twirled it close to Wallace's face.

Church moved to step between them. With her arm, Wallace prevented him, head down she turned side on to Joe.

"Come on lads," Church was quiet, "don't do this. Don't need knives."

"Ear, is that a girl or a boy?"

"Bloody queers aint they. Bum boys."

Rob was taunting, hands on hips, legs apart. Church swung his boot; a violent connection with testicles. He moved to Joe but already Wallace had his knife hand behind his back. Joe twitched and yelped. Church ducked beneath Bill's wide swing and came with an uppercut to the chin, he blocked the next punch and followed on with a fist into Bill's face, slamming him into a fence. Church moved with it and punched Bill again in the face, followed by another. "Church," Wallace had his arm. "Enough."

"She's broke my finger," Joe wined.

"Not broken," Wallace sighed, "come here." She took Joe's wrist. Joe's yelp followed a sickening crunch. "Just dislocated. All done."

"Gonna find out where you live," Bill blubbered.

"No," Church hissed and pinned him back to the fence; face to face. "Gonna find out where you live and finish you. For good."

"Here hang on a minute," Rob hobbled to his feet, "I know you. You're Crazy Sandy, Hey," he looked to his brother's, "he's Eddie's mate."

"Oh yeh." Joe had his hand inside his jacket. "Why didn't you say? We would have left you alone."

"Otherwise," said Church, "just what would you have done? A young girl like that? Is this how it is now? Get out of here."

The three mumbled off.

Wallace threw the knife in a dustbin.

"Wallace? You ok? Hey you did great."

"Yeh." Her head was down.

"You sure? Are you hurt?"

She looked up. "When would you have stopped hitting him?"

He dipped. "I know. Do you want to go home?"

"We planned to go to the pub."

"Are you sure you don't want anything stronger?" Church put down his pint and slid the water over to Wallace. He sat beside her. The pub was empty. Her head was still down.

"Earlier," Church offered, "you said we needed to talk."

"Where to start?" Wallace breathed deeply and raised her head to look at him. "Where to start?"

"Hope those boys didn't upset you with their taunting about being a boy."

"I know myself enough to cope with that."

"You did great back there."

"Let's not keep it to that level although I've rarely seen so much anger."

"In me you mean? Yeh it all came out."

"Crazy Sandy?"

"I have a past."

"Where you scared back there?" She asked.

"Nope. I've got my guard up and I want to fight back."

"That's exactly what I was going to talk about earlier on. You said when you were back at your home…"

"Not my home anymore."

"But when you were back there you said there was no threatening darkness. Why?"

"Because I've got my guard up?"

"Yes. You are becoming aware and becoming at one with your own inner strength. No one, nothing can get in. It just needs permanence."

"But why," he wrung his hands, "why is that darkness following, that thing; how does it scare and torture so?"

"Because it knows every weakness every secret in your heart and in your soul. And how to exploit it."

"Think Egdim said something like that."

"Who?"

"No matter."

"But, Church, there is something else I feel I need to say. I..."

"May I intrude?"

"Wha...?" Church sprung to his feet, "Richard," he hugged him. "Wow so good to see you." He saw that Richard was already ignoring him. "Richard, this is..."

"Hello Wallace," Richard offered his hand, "if I may say; you look charming."

"You know each other?"

"My dear Church, have you not noticed that this young ladies' teeth flash when she smiles. Just like mine."

"Richard is my new dentist," Wallace explained, "life goes on."

"Hey Church," the slap on the back hurt more than usual.

"Hey Church," the second was worse.

"Eddie, Nick," said Richard. "You're back."

"Box of vino beside your back door."

"I shall pay you with the pound notes with which you paid me."

Church watched Richard begin to woo Wallace and was about to intervene.

"Church," Nick whispered in his ear, "nice to see you back, mate. Anything we can do, just say."

"Actually," said Church, "I need to talk with you both."

"I know," Eddie raised both hands, "their mum just phoned me."

"What's it all coming too, guys? It wasn't like that in our day."

"What would Grandad say," said Eddie, "that's just what we told 'em."

"Their old man is in jail though," Nick joined in," but we will take 'em under our wing.   Hey Eddie, we could be their; what was the word?"

"Mentor."

"Yeh things have changed alright," Eddie looked up. "Gonna give up on the channel crossing; be messing with dangerous boys.   Don't want any of that stuff over here."

"We fancy running sailing classes.   Get some nice birds," Nick gestured over to Wallace.   "Who's that then? Richard got another one in tow."

"She is so lovely," added Eddie.

Church felt emotions he had never encountered; fringing on panic and anger.   He pushed his way in.

"Richard, I'll buy you a drink."   He pulled him away allowing Nick and Eddie to swoop on Wallace.

"I am glad you did that," Richard looked serious.

"Why?"   Church held back a jealous anger.

"Because I want to ask how you are?"

"What?   Oh yes, sorry.   Yeh I'm getting along a lot better.   Wallace she...."

"Yes, Wallace, she certainly is...."

Nick and Eddie pounced on Richard, shouting and jostling.

"Nick."   Church flatly commanded, "Give Richard his wallet back."

Church checked over to Wallace.

She smiled and shrugged.

"Hang on," Eddie pointed, "seen her before."

"Yeh," Nick added, "seems familiar."

"Where was it?"   Church was scrutinised.

"Drop it," he snapped.

"Say no more, Boss."

"But we'll go and chat her up."

"Yeh but listen guys don't push the haven't we seen you

before. Ok?"

"No worries there."

Church signed the turning of a key and pointed to the pair who were sitting each side of Wallace. She gave a clear look of disbelief but showed them the key.

"It's German," Church heard the bellow through the crowd.

"I recognise you've been struggling but aside from that, how are things in Scotland?" Richard was shouting the lengthy sentence above the growing din.

"It's a long story."

"I can imagine. Still, plenty of moonshine? And how is dear Floyd?"

"Alive, I think."

"Immortal."

A scream distracted them.

Nick and Eddie both rolled across the floor to end up propped against the juke box, Wallace signing her innocence to Church.

"I think it's time to go. Love you, Richard."

"Love you too."

***

Church lay on the bed, stroking his lips where Wallace had kissed him goodnight. Her whisper still echoing. His hand on his stomach, he allowed the butterflies to flirt.

The church bell tolled just once. Its pulsating ring was never-fading.

The luminous glow began over the ceiling. Forearm over his brow, he drifted into sleep's threshold.

A shape manifested, wakening him. Pale, it held no threat as it slid toward him on all fours.

The slats creaked as it moved in behind him, its body conforming full length to his.

"I've been screwed up and confused," Wallace sighed.

"What's wrong?"

"It's driving me crazy," Wallace whispered, "another

night of you in here and me alone."

"I'm glad you are here," he whispered, still not moving, feeling her warmth along his back, their breath in rhyme.

"Are you sure? I mean you have your marriage to...."

"Without doubt."

"That's good, because there is something, I must tell you."

It caused no alarm.

"I've been holding it back and it so hurt me not being able to tell you. And was wanting to tell you in the pub.

And maybe I do it too easily; far too easily.

But.

Church, I'm developing feelings for you, strong feelings."

C hapter 48

Rosemary rocked in the chair and fondly rubbed her stomach, "The pendulum says it's a boy."

Sarah smiled, "Now you have what you want."

"Are you sure it's his?   Sorry," Jimmy ducked beneath Sarah's glare.

"No hassle," Rosemary beamed. "There has been no one else. I just knew he had to be the one."

"But you seem so friendly with all the boys.   The dreadlock duo...I mean...."

"Jimmy." Sarah pointed to the door.

"It's cool."   Rosemary nodded to herself, "Yeh, I like being friends with everyone. Yeh, but just friends."

"So, it won't be born with dreadlocks then," Jimmy ran.

"I had a feeling there would be a connection between you. But..." Sarah humbly suggested, "You will need to tell him."

C hapter 49

Wallace lay across his Chest, "I've been feeling you breathe," she said. "I can tell you are awake now."

"I love you, too."

"Those are your words" she whispered. "And you don't have to say that," Wallace whispered, "just because I touched on it."

"I do. Finally, I'm able to see it, admit to it. I've…" He was stopped by Wallace tapping his chest."

"Slow down."

"Said I've been manic."

"We are both confused. Simply enjoy and share whatever we have."

She skipped from the bed, naked; Church watched the elusive woodland nymph; enchanting.

"How can anyone not love that?" She did not hear him above the coffee grinder.

C hapter 50

"Boiler suit?"

Jostled by indignant pedestrians on their Saturday shop, all four crammed toward the door.

Wallace shrugged at Church, "Dressing up nights from my days with Lee."

"What's she on about?"

Eddie quizzed Nick and Church quizzed Wallace.

"Is this quiz night?" She asked.

"Don't want to know, well not now anyway. But still 'Taversham'?" Church nodded to the sign etched into the glass.

"On my to do list," she stuck out the tip of her tongue.

"And that's my bag. Are my clothes still in it? Jasmin's knickers?"

"What you two been up to? Nick, what they been up to?"

"In a spare drawer." She opened the bag enough for Church to see the red box.

Nick was bending to investigate the door, "Bloody hell it's a new lock."

"That's a euro cylinder," chirped Eddie, "anti snap, top of the range."

Nick looked up to Wallace, touching his forelock, "Sorry Matron, may have to break the glass."

"Gonna make a hell of a noise," Eddie stepped in, "explode it will."

Wallace folded her arms and shook her head at Church. "Why don't we go around the back?" She gestured to the café,

"We are being watched."

Nick and Eddie waved to the window, "Our mates."

"That makes it alright does it," Wallace raised her eyebrows.

"Didn't know there was a back way in." Whistling a display of innocence, they sauntered, following Church and Wallace along the side passage.

Church was mouthing, "Dressing up nights?"

"Bloody hell," repeated Nick, tapping the back door, "it's a new lock."

"That's a euro cylinder," Eddie added, "anti snap, top of the range."

Nick bent and looked up to Wallace, "Sorry Matron...."

"Stop." She halted everything. "This is a wind up, isn't it, Church."

"He put us up to it."

"You did bring the key?"

Wallace clicked the lock open.

"Crikey," Nick jabbed Eddie, pointing along the corridor, "all different."

"That's because we came in the backdoor this time."

"Yeh but all decorated and cheered up. Carpet and all. Where did he top himself, Sandy?"

"Thought it was going to be creepy but it's nice."

"Woman's touch."

"Right," Nick clapped his hands, "to work." He turned to Wallace, "Got that key, Matron?"

"Nick," Church stopped him. "We've finished the windup, it's Wallace."

"I don't know," Wallace took Church's arm, "I'm beginning to like 'Matron'."

"See," Eddie sang, "we had a good old chat in the pub, didn't we Matron?"

"And Matron sent us flying."

"Didn't hurt. And Matron is going to learn us."

"Will you stop this," Wallace raised her hands and

controlled her smile.

"Yeh, come on guys," Church waded in. "Need to find if the key fits anything in this building."

The pair took off, tapping walls.

He turned to Wallace, "I'm sorry. But honest when you really know these guys, they…"

Wallace stopped him, "I see through them, I realised it in the pub. They cheered up my confused thoughts. Your friends are beautiful and all around them becomes beautiful. And clever. Hey, Nick," she caught his attention and loudly whispered, "that panel your tapping; it's a door."

"Might be a secret one."

"Yeh, were clever; we went to Infant School. Just had a thought though," Eddie produced a magnifying glass and examined the key, "definitely German," he turned to Wallace. "Fancy a boat trip up the Rhine?"

"And I've just had a thought," Church turned to Wallace. "Those photographs," he paused and nodded to her, "those two black and white photographs."

"I know the ones." She held up the bag.

"They showed a concrete floor and a brick wall. If it relates to this key; these floors are all wooden."

"A cellar."

"Let's check that office again," Nick tried the door.

"No need," said Wallace. "A new floor, nothing there."

"What about in here."

"That's my old office. Feel free."

Nick stuck his head in. "Crikey a safe. Missed that one." He walked in and jumped. "Don't sound very hollow."

"What about the reception?" Eddie suggested.

"Concrete," Wallace pondered, "Church, you look troubled."

"You ok boss?"

"He gets that way. He gets these feelings, you see."

"Yeh, remember when we borrowed that car."

"That's right, he had one of his feelings just before he

crashed it."

"Nice motor that was."

"Whenever," Church raised a finger. "Whenever..."

"Yes," Nick rolled his hands and prompted, "whenever...."

"Whenever," Church repeated.

"Whenever," Eddie joined in.

Wallace hid her head.

"Is she crying?

"Right hang on a minute, guys," Church moved along the corridor.

"Church," Wallace insisted, "don't say 'whenever'."

"Whenever," he paced, finger still in the air, nodding with certainty, "whenever I walked this corridor...When it was dark and gloomy...I always used to think I was going to fall down a deep hole."

Nick and Eddie dropped to their knees, tugging at the carpet, "Don't worry, Matron," Eddie pressed together the torn strip as if stopping a bleeding wound and looked along the corridor length, "got a cousin."

"And he's a carpet fitter," Wallace tugged her end.

Hands on hips all four scanned the bare boards.

"Hope there is a cellar," Nick spoke first.

"Yeh," Eddie gestured to the rolled-up mess, "that's where we can hide that."

"This is nice wood," said Wallace, "now there's decent lighting."

"Come up nice," Church agreed, "sanding and polishing."

"That's my story then," hands on hips, Wallace agreed with herself.

"Found it," Nick pointed.

"Saw it first."

"Oh yes," Wallace moved closer.

"That's good old fashion putty."

Blending in and flush with the discoloured floorboards,

was the shape of a filled in key hole.

Nick pulled a gimlet and began picking, Eddie was down with him, blowing away the debris. They toiled; picking, a pause, a blow, picking a pause…; a coordinated team.

Church felt Wallace's hand in his. "Hi" she whispered. "We've not had a minute."

"Here come the butterflies. You ok," he asked.

"I am. You?"

"Think so. Wondering what we will find?"

"And I've just remembered," Wallace ducked.

"What's that?"

"Taversham confronted me here, he did mention there being a cellar." She looked to Church, "But you knew it was there."

"So maybe I'm not going mad."

"We know that," she touched his arm.

"Thanks for that. But," he raised his voice, "listen guys," Church stopped them. "We don't know what we're going to find…"

"Trust us, Sandy," Nick stopped him, "You know us and we know you," he turned to Wallace, "and your family from now on. So, whatever happens is between us."

"Yeh," Eddie finished off, "we go back a lifetime. The old way."

Nick looked to Eddie, "We sound like Grandad."

"Family," Church felt Wallace's head gently on his shoulder. "And I can begin to understand your torture."

"Eh?"

"I forgot Taversham told me but you knew there was a cellar there."

"Just knew."

"And you live with that 'knowing'?"

C hapter 51

"I can't lay that trip on him," Rosemary rocked, secretly smiled, and placed both hands on her stomach, "so much hassle."

"I know it's what you've wanted for a long time," Sarah gently spoke. "And you would be a wonderful mother on your own. But he has a right to know. A son without a father; is that fair on anyone?"

"If he does not know," Jimmy suggested, "it won't bother him"

"But he will know," Isaac was there, "Church will know."

"Yeh that's cool," Rosemary nodded, "Church has that gift. But if that gift tells him that he has a son who has the love he never had, then he will be happy. Won't he?"

C hapter 52

"Right Nick," on his knees, Eddie grunted. "Gotta turn the key gently, seized lock..."

"...Snapped key shank."

"Bloody hell," Eddie rolled, almost somersaulting.

"German workmanship, that is," Nick turned his head to Church. "It's open." With the heel of his hand, he nudged the gimlet into a gap and gently applied pressure. "Must be German hinges." The heavy flap started to lift and Church grabbed a hold. In one curved motion the cellar door banged against the wall revealing a square black hole.

"Aint going in there," Eddie cringed.

"He means it," Nick seemed sure that Wallace would understand. "His Mum used to lock him in the cupboard under the stairs."

"Did anyone bring a torch?"

"Always wondered what this was for," Wallace flicked a wall switch above the opening.

"German bulb and all."

Church stared down at the wooden flight of stairs, a yellow glow coming up from the abyss.

All four looked at each other. "Typical bunch of men." Wallace moved.

"Ladies first," Nick tried.

"Oh no," Church heard Wallace's cry coming up from below and sped to follow.

In musty space they both stood facing the spot lit chair, still with leather straps for wrists and ankles.

"That was in the photograph, and the brick wall. We've

found it."

"Poor soul," Wallace was talking to the empty chair.

Church took her shoulders, "Wait upstairs. Please."

"It's ok," she patted his hand. "Thanks."

"Strange smell down here, familiar."

"Don't smell it."

"Linseed oil, I think."

Church dipped under the corridor's floor joists, dust leaking through the gaps in the floorboards that formed the low ceiling. He inspected the damp corners of the cellar, avoiding the washed-out painted circle at his feet.

"You alright down there?"

"Yeh guys," Church quietly spoke.

"Shall we put the kettle on?"

"In my old office."

"Are there any biscuits?"

Against the leeched brick wall, a sideboard had been arranged as an altar with cloth and candlesticks. And a wooden box, which Church opened.

"Newspaper cuttings," he said, "missing girls, unexplained deaths.   And," he held them up, "more photographs." Chin on his shoulder, Wallace looked over.

"I know that girl," he whispered at the innocent face, her grey eyes, her hair in ringlets. "I know her, from somewhere."

"And this?" Wallace reached in and held up another photograph.

"Can't be."

"What?"

Church took and held up the picture of a white house perched on a steep hillside, two dark trees at the entrance. Wallace took it from him. "You know this place?"

Church remained motionless.

"Beneath the two trees is where my ashes will forever be," she read the words inscribed in black ink on the back. "This is old. It has a name; 'Yevimo..Yefimovich'?"

"That's the same name on one of these cuttings of deaths," Church found it to confirm the names.

"What about this one then?" Wallace showed him another photograph, a group of five in black robes. An ugly scrawl, there were names under each.

"Taversham," Church nodded. "Recognised him anyway and there's Yefimovich, his face is a bit blurred but he's the stuff of my worst nightmare."

"Police can work on that one." Wallace rubbed her arms and looked about, "Sealed up for a long time."

"Maybe this explains Taversham's suicide. So many terrors locked away."

Wallace reached down and opened the doors to the alter. "Empty."

"Doesn't seem to be anything else," Church scanned the cellar.

"How are you doing?"

"I know what you mean but surprisingly I'm ok." Church looked at her. "Lot to get my head round though; those two photographs. Coincidences, yet again. And another thing."

"What?"

"Who took the photo of the group of five?"

"Right, I know what to do." She pulled the red box from the bag and carefully placed the contents in the cupboard beneath the alter top, putting the red box back in its bag. "Memorise that girl's face if you need to but they need to go back in their box."

"Tea break," the shout ran down the steps.

***

"Do we have our story straight," Wallace checked their faces.

"We came here," munched Eddie, "to lend a hand lifting the rug because you realized after the carpet was laid you wanted bare boards."

"In retrospect," Nick added.

"That's a good word, Nick. Remember that one."

"Found trapdoor," said Nick.

"You always wondered where that key in your drawer fitted."

"We sorted the lock for you."

"You found photographs and other stuff."

"We haven't seen em."

"Thought you best call police."

"And we know nothing about the original break in."

"Our fingerprints are not a problem because we admit to being here today."

"Sorted."

"Only one problem," Wallace looked at the pair.

"Wassat?"

"You've eaten all the biscuits and your feet are on my desk."

***

In a subdued light, lying beside him on his makeshift bed, Wallace stroked his face and whispered, "You rushed down that cellar to protect me."

"Seemed only right."

"Not used to that."

"Perhaps you should get used to it."

"But when we came out of the cellar it was as if you weren't there."

"Yeh," Church slid across to be closer to her. "Those two photographs."

"And you think that it is the house you saw up in Scotland?" She stroked his chest.

"Positive," Church searched Wallace's eyes. "Nothing surprises me anymore."

"And the other?"

"Seen it before."

"It?" Wallace paused, "The girl you mean?"

"No, the photograph," he frowned.

"You need to relax Church, close your eyes."

Wallace pulled the cover away to expose his bare torso.

"Wow that's amazing."

"No peeking."

"How many hands do you have?"

Church opened his eyes and looked at her serene face with that glint of mischief. Her hand was hovering and sweeping over his body in smooth motion; inches from his skin.

"Never felt nothing like that before."

"You try." She shifted her position so that both their bodies could be explored in the same way. It was a struggle for him not to touch her but without such contact, not a word spoken, with half-closed eyes, they drifted.

"I'm sorry," eventually Church spoke, "that was something I've never experienced before. But what is that scratching?" He searched the room then her.

A scent of musk filled the air.

"It's coming from my garden," she said. "It's Shady."

"Shady?"

"A white fox visits, becoming tamer, whished it would come in."

"This is bizarre but maybe one problem solved."

"Meaning?"

"I sometimes see a white fox, never sure if I'm awake or dreaming."

"One in the real world and one in your dreams? Why am I not surprised? They make good spirit guides."

"Spirit guides? Heard that one before."

"With us from the day of our birth and before. A fox chose to be your spirit guide."

"Like a guardian Angel?"

"Yeh, why not. But you seem so calm about it."

"You mean I'm not freaking out? Don't know what it would take to freak me out now. But you called him Shady; what's the story?"

"Neighbours say there's always been foxes here. And from time to time a white pup is born. This one allows me to live in his realm. I do feed it, that may have a lot to do with it. And I hope it puts him off killing anything."

"What do you feed it?"

He felt Wallace's breath as she murmured, "Cat food but don't tell him."

Her breath lingered at his ear.

They passed the night, sleeping intermittently, sharing a closeness. And perhaps in a dream, the fox lay at their feet.

Chapter 53

At Wallace's doorstep, Church held onto her before finally speaking, "Not giving you my full attention this morn."

"Both in different places with all this going on.   Just glad to have you around."

"Hope so."

"But," she pulled away, "I need to go, open up and check with the police."

"What happened to Sunday?"

"Time seems twisted.   What's your plans, Church?"

Outstretched arms, he felt her tiny hands in his and saw her smile.   "See if I can get my head around that girl's photo."

"Let me know If you discover anything, we can pass it on.   Hey, the guys do know the police may call?"

"They will run rings around them."

"I'll call in and see them, just in case."

"Why?   Don't worry."

"I'm not," Wallace kissed his cheek and turned.

He stopped her, "One more thing."

"Uh huh?"

"What happened with Taversham's body?"

"I didn't want to even think about it.   But his cronies, his circle or whatever it was; they took over."

C hapter 54

The sticky tape rasped as Church pulled it from the cardboard. In red felt tip she had written it; the word on the box lid; *'Photographs.'* Touching Jasmin's hand-written word hurt. Seeing pictures of shared memories was worse; far worse; that smile, those eyes.

'Exquisite memories,' he remembered her sadly saying that once.

He twisted it into a chore. And it did not matter if the corners became turned, only allowing himself to touch the image of something he could cope with. He was rummaging deeper until it became easier to tip the box upside down. Like playing cards, the remnants of the pack slid out, each slice going back further until it made sense. It was easy to pick out the image of Mimosa. It was her.

Shut away memories; one by one he placed each photograph in the box.

***

Church rolled a cigarette and chucked the tobacco tin across the café, "Thank you, Jake," he shouted then whispered to himself, "think he lives here."

"Not easy to give it up, is it Sandy. See the police have been across at that solicitor this morning."

"Oh well."

"Nice looking girl that. Different but very nice."

Church stubbed out his cigarette. For the third time he checked that the photograph of Mimosa was in the envelope, pushed the chair back and stood.

He sat down again.

Looking across the road, despite the steamy window, it was easy to pick out the figure of Wallace, he had to peer harder to confirm that it was Richard she was hugging.

"Did she hug me this morning?"

Richard was pointing and waving an envelope to two suit clad young men, identical, efficiently walking toward the office door to shake hands with Richard who passed over the envelope, leaving Wallace to warmly embrace and kiss the two men.   Church closed his eyes then opened them in time to catch Wallace going in with the two through the office front door. She was checking that no one had seen them before she turned the sign to say; '*closed.*'

And why did she have to see Nick and Eddie?   *His* friends.

Church retrieved, straightened, then relit his cigarette butt from the ashtray, he had to borrow a pen from the unsmiling waitress to scrawl across the envelope containing the photograph of Mimosa.

C hapter 55

"Aunt Poppy, I thought you were moving on."

"Back again we are."

"The grey ghost; I know who she is."

"Ah so the ghost is a 'she' but you already knew that if you learnt to trust in yourself."

"But I know who she is. Knew it a long time ago."

"We knew you would remember seeing her before."

"Who knew?"

"Mimosa and I."

"Aunt Poppy," Church fought back an urge to thump the table, "I am so angry right now. In no mood for games. If you knew who she was why did you not tell me? I have had enough."

Poppy darkened. "No one has helped Mimosa find peace, that's what she craves. We knew it would be you but you had to find your strength first. And you had to find it your own way, no other way."

"But how do I help her find peace?"

"You know."

"I don't know anything anymore."

"So many have tried to help and support you, only to be met by your indifference."

A wave of light passed through the kitchen.

Church saw Poppy looking at him, "Your mother loved you, yet you go through life feeling worthless, that's not why she had to depart."

"Then why did she?"

"She surrendered her love for you in the hope you would

be cared for. She knew she could not do that; such a tortured person, such a tortured soul."

"Why didn't she find a way of telling me that?"

"She has, oh she has. And it's taken you long, too long, for you to finally see."

"She has?"

"By the church where she left you, you saw her with the fox, urging you to go on."

"That church, by Wallace? Is that where she abandoned me?"

"Abandoned; a nice word for you. Takes away your responsibility."

"I really did see her? That was my mother?"

"Her soul. She wanted you to see where you must be."

"With Wallace? Someone else who has betrayed me."

"Abandoned, betrayed, a nice collection of words for you."

Church slowed his world. He closed his eyes.

"I am tired now," he heard Poppy, "I have to go but you will see me again when the time is right."

"Thank you," Church whispered.

"No need to thank me." She paused, "Listen to me and understand this; all the words you heard were from you, not me."

Church opened his eyes wondering if she were ever there.

C hapter 56

"Sarah," Jimmy was breathless, stumbling into the kitchen, "Look busy, he's coming what do we...?"

"Church," Sarah sang over Jimmy's words, "what a pleasant surprise."

"Hi," Jimmy bobbed. "Come in. How you doing?"

Church crashed down into a chair and punched his thighs. "Angry and pissed off. Just had to come up here."

"Can we help," Sarah dried her hands, "cup of tea?"

"Tea would be great, thanks." He considered the pair, "Some entrance, eh?"

"Just be yourself, but don't wake the baby. I mean... don't mention the baby..." Jimmy stole Sarah's towel and wiped the bath.

"It's still there then." He saw Jimmy's desperation. "Ok, ok, I'm calming down."

"A long drive," Sarah passed the cup.

"I apologise," said Church, "shouldn't come into your home like this."

"It's ok," said Jimmy, "why you is fambily now."

"Yeh," Church blew into his cup. "Must be nice to have a family."

"One day," Sarah glanced to Jimmy. Church noticed.

"Jimmy," Church asked, "can I talk with you?"

"Do you want me to leave?" Sarah stood.

"No, please. It's a bit grim but not private, unless I want to keep my insanity private."

"Nah," Jimmy waved, "we're all mad. Fire away."

"I know we've talked about it before but I just need to get

it clear. The mansion on the hill."

"Yep. See fire away. Must have known."

"Jimmy," Sarah scolded.

"The Russian bloke that owned it."

"The one I told you about, with the cut off balls?"

"Oh Jimmy," Sarah sighed and looked up.

"He died down in England. The thing is, were his ashes taken back up here?"

"I know I said they were but not really sure."

"Are other people's ashes taken there, not local people obviously but those connected with the ruin?"

Jimmy untangled his tousled hair and looked to Sarah. "I really don't know but it certainly fits with rumours, and like I said to you when we spoke of the place, people have been seen coming and going from time to time."

"Can we ask why?" Sarah tried.

"You wouldn't believe me."

"Isaac might."

"Good idea. How is he? Floyd and...," Church did not have to sense anything; it was obvious, "...how is Rosemary?"

"Rosemary has gone off to Ibiza," Sarah looked to Jimmy, "the two lads are with her, seeing over her. She was going to hitchhike but Floyd lent them the money. They flew last week."

"Wow, Floyd not with them?"

"He said he is one of tomorrow's people."

"Yeh," Church stared to the floor, "she's gone, and with those two lads; adds to it all."

C hapter 57

Walking over the grass through the commune, Church was reminded of a principal he had learnt at college; before deciding where to lay paths, see by tracks where people have walked most.

He saw the well-trodden path to Rosemary's caravan then walked to the campervan.

"Isaac," he rapped on the metal door.

"A coincidence is here, hello Church."

"Hello Isaac," Church accepted the long hug.

"Please come in and thank you for taking your boots off."

"Been trained." Church walked into a fog of garlic.

"I am going to eat; would you like some brown rice."

"If that is ok."

"Of course. How have you been? I have been very conscious of you recently. And now you are on a mission."

"What makes you say that?"

"You are on fire; your energy is charged."

"You can feel that?"

"And see it."

"I had a friend who could pass her hand over me and it was electric. Is that the same?"

"Especially if you have an attraction. Is that why you are on fire?"

"I am angry and seeking answers."

"A crisis. Please sit," Isaac beckoned. "To continue; we all have an energy field around us."

"She mentioned chakras."

"Specific centres in and around our bodies. If we are flat everything is flat and out of balance."

"And I am electric?"

"And out of balance."

"This energy field, how far does it extend."

"An enlightened question; no boundaries, everlasting, infinite, timeless.

"And when we die?"

"The energy is still there, unrestrained, unleashed."

"Are there good energies and bad energies?"

"Are there saints and sinners?"

"Can places have its own energy?"

"Everything has its own energy; earth, stones, crystals and specific lines and points on this planet; extending throughout the universe."

"How do we drive bad energies away from places and when someone bad dies how can we do away with their bad energies? Exorcism?"

"My friend, you are troubled because you are gifted; aware of so much but have no understanding."

"That's why I'm angry," Church ground his teeth. "Had enough bullshit. Seeking answers."

"Eat in silence now. Then come and see me in the morning."

C hapter 58

The fire crisped overhanging Hawthorn leaves. Church backed away. "Doesn't seem right, Isaac; no one else here and we've lit their fire."

"We can rectify that another day," Isaac was considering Church. "Now you have to select stones."

"Select?"

"Take the wheelbarrow, go amongst the trees and pause. The stones will call to you, it is them you must select. Do it with intent."

"A month ago, I would have taken the piss, gone into the trees and called as if I was enticing back a lost animal."

"That would not be far removed.

Now you must speak no more.

Leave your mind empty and open."

That the barrow tyre was deflated could have made it a labour but Church was resolute. He picked up stones, guided by a reclaimed instinct, feeling the glorious past of each, finding it impossible to discard any but in the end returned with stones that he felt had chosen him.

"You placed your trust in your intuition," Isaac was passing him a pitchfork. "Please be careful and place them into the heart of your fire."

Church quickly learnt to go low but the heat was searing, brightness blinding.

"Now, please undress and stand before me."

Naked, arms out from his side he watched and remembered Isaac lighting the grass.

"Sage grass is purifying."

Church closed his eyes listening to the humming chant, knowing, reassured, that Isaac was fanning the smoke around him, a shadow before his closed eyes each time he passed in front. Many times, that shadow passed.

"Do not be afraid," Isaac read his thoughts. "You are protected. Now, please go into the lodge, choose where you sit and I will pass in four stones; earth, air, fire and water. And in your darkness ask your spirit guide to appear and lead. I will be outside, but you will not need me."

It was easy for Church to dismiss any creeping apprehension, dismiss any apparition conjured from his previous experience in the lodge. He sat crossed legged opposite the rectangle of light that created a shaft of luminescence to the pit in the centre. The stones were red hot, Isaac forked them in one at a time and Church welcomed them, closing his eyes, hearing the hiss of steam as water was dribbled. He welcomed the depth of darkness as the flap was closed, the heat embracing his body.

He sat in limbo, a sphere of light around him.

The light intensified, magnificent, spiralling in to become an orb at his feet, shape-shifting to become a white animal; a fox. The way ahead was a tunnel of darkness, the fox entered and waited, looking behind until Church began to follow. He floated through blackness, the fox his only reference until, in a fog beginning to clear, Church stood at still water's edge. The fox had gone. Floating toward him came a small boat propelled by a sack-clothed boatman poling the water's depth until the craft reached him, gliding into the shingled bank. Church saw a silver coin glimmering in the shallows and ignored it. Water lapping beneath the boat was the only voice while they crossed until the boat touched the shingled bank on the other side. The water offered no sensation at his ankles. The ferryman did not turn but pointed with outstretched finger. Church was commanded to walk up the hillside. Despite going up, the sensation was that of going deeper and deeper into blackness, denying female wraiths who silently enticed him to deviate by performing every act of his most secret fantasies, shocked by three figures hanging by their necks in alcoves of blackness.

Church moved on, wrapped in darkness.

He stood between two trees of unimaginable height at their tips and unspeakable blackness at their bases. 'Ifeg,' he heard the hint of a whisper; it emanated from the ivy suffocating the trees, tendrils reaching ever higher. A contemptuous laugh played a persistent tune. Cross legged between the monoliths he sat, unmovable, defiant of whatever dared emerge from the blood-black roots. Undertones of a murmur came from deep down. Church challenged it, challenged the grip tightening on his ankles and around his throat.

Like smoke, blood-black shadows endeavoured to rise, moaning, fading, admitting to the finality of a death.

Soundless now, the shadows retreated to beneath the trees from where no light came and no light dare enter.

The fox returned and sat until Church wanted to move, they walked away together. Church turned to see himself still sitting there; a part of him, a permanent sentinel.

He was led into a mist, falling drizzle forming an incandescent glow around the street lamp. The fox sat at an entrance to a stone-built antechamber with a box beside it. Church lifted the baby, seeing his eyes shimmering. He felt the baby snuggle into his warmth. Behind closed eyes Church saw a lady in a shawl, hair of flames. With pleading arms, pleading eyes, she approached to become part of a shared embrace; an embrace that was infinite.

Unashamed of his nakedness, he embraced Isaac, the embers of the fire rising to a starlit sky.

C hapter 59

The spade slid into soil cast crimson by the colours and sounds of the setting sun, Church turned over the last divot to complete the circular garden bed. His collarless shirt, found in one of the wardrobes, clung with perspiration to his body. The ache in his muscles was redemption.

He gathered his coat from beneath the beech tree and over his shoulder he carried the spade, leaving it at the red door with his boots. He entered the flag stoned lobby, his socked feet leaving footprints of dampness into the kitchen.

Inevitably something scratched at the door, he turned and opened it.

"I didn't want you or anyone to come running after me, Richard."

"And I don't want to be a walk-on cliché, Church. I was just passing through and got caught in the rain."

"Beyond here lies nothing. And it's not raining."

"It may."

"Please come in, you are welcome."

"I know."

It was unique, that feeling of not wanting to gulp down the offered share of wine but Church eventually conceded that he was hungry, although he took a long time to display it before gnawing on his half of the French loaf.

"I think they remembered me, the other time I bought their bread, cheese and wine."

"I know you are studying me, Richard."

"I read the note."

"The note?"

"The one you scrawled on the envelope with a photograph inside."

"And you read it."

"They were her brothers," Richard insisted, "long lost twins, a reconciliation, coming to share in the finances of her plans for the building."

"And you where there."

"It's what they do.   They helped me plan my new business. I'd arranged to meet and pass on accounts to them."

"In an office doorway."

"Such is their approach."

"And in that doorway, you and her shared a loving embrace."

"And she embraced her brothers.   Besides, I was concerned, the police had been earlier."

"Did she say anything about that?"

"Only that something ghastly had happened some time ago. She said it was in the hands of detectives and would pass the photograph on with your explanation of who it was."

"But it was a loving embrace you shared, Richard."

"You and I, we love each other, that does not mean that we are going to fall into bed together."

Church sensed tension in Richard's pause.

"Church, I've done a lot of bad things, even once tried suicide, but I would never betray you. And I've never known anyone to be in love with someone as she is with you. She knew she should have held back; too much too soon for you. She understands. And we understand your frailty, you've been betrayed before and don't trust it won't happen again."

"Sounds like you've had a cosy chat. You had a cosy chat with Jasmin."

"Nick and Eddie wanted to come and beat sense into you. I'm beginning to see their point."

"She had to go and see them."

"Dammit Church," spittle flew.   Richard thumped the table, "Stop this. She is not a possession. Such a vibrant soul, that gift should never be destroyed."

"I've often wondered if I could have made a living with my fists. My guard is up but I don't want to hurt anyone."

"You've gone the distance, Church. And it certainly is not the case of the ref raising someone's hand to say they have won. Or is it?"

"Putting it that way makes me see that this is not meant to be a fight."

"There is no defeat but such a loss."

Church turned to Richard, "What now?"

"Church, I'm so very tired."

"Where did you sleep when last you were here?"

"Under Jimmy's table mostly."

"That's good because I'd hate it if something happened between us and I had no memory of it."

"Church? Do we have you back?"

C hapter 60

"May I come in, Sarah?" Church saw apprehension, "I'm in a better mood."

"Please do," she dried her hands and swept clothes from a chair. "I'll make some space on the table, there's tea on the go," she darted around the kitchen, "somewhere."

Zimmy began to cry from his pram and Sarah's whole being said it; '*last straw.*' "Shall I take him?" Without a reply, Church was there, carefully scooping him up and bringing him to his chest.

"You have the knack."

"Don't know how," Church sat and enjoyed the contact with the passive baby, knowing that Sarah was considering what to say as she smiled at him.

"He's more than precious. Zimmy is our third."

"Really?" So quickly Church felt foolish and stopped himself searching for the others.

"We were grateful, the last boy lived for a week, the first well…"

"I'm so sorry. I always felt there was a sadness about you." He recalled once hearing a distant joy of children.

"That's why we came up here."

"A new start."

"Please don't say at least we've got Zimmy."

"It doesn't work like that; I know that much and I'm so sorry. And here's me been dumping all my stuff on you. I'm so sorry."

"Jimmy's not here," Sarah breathed it all away.

"I know I met him; he sent me on up to you."

"Oh really."

"Which reminds me," he balanced and pulled out a package with its stamp attached.

"Aha, postie said you had a parcel."

"Did he now?"

"He also said he saw that posh Englishman with you. Richard?"

"Oh me. He was just passing through, going to see if there is life beyond here."

"I can hear him saying that."

"Anyway," Church held up the package, "a sort of thank you, an apology and a favour."

"Can't think what."

"Seeds, got them from Exchange and Mart, corncockles."

"Corncockles," Sarah put her hand to her chest, "why that's so kind, but they were Gran's special flower."

"I know," he closed his eyes for a second, "but please don't ask how. The thing is I wouldn't know where to start and Jimmy said you would know."

"Did he," Sarah sung.

"I guess that's why he sent me to you."

Sarah did not respond.

"I also chatted with him about a rose garden in Poppy's front lawn."

"And?"

"Well, we agreed that it would be too much to ask someone, anyone, to look after it when I'm gone. So, we will put in on hold till things are more settled. Poppy knows; the thought is there."

"I really appreciate the corncockles."

"I guess you can scatter them anywhere, you know best." He smiled at her, "I know you were close to Aunt Poppy; it's for you both. For everyone."

"Thanks; so kind."

They both closed their eyes and without physical

contact, they held each other in an endless silence.

"Aunt Poppy?" Sarah was bright.

"Your Gran. But Aunt Poppy, that's what I like to call her when she visits."

Sarah softly moved in to stroke Zimmy's head. Church could feel the touch flowing onto the back of his hand and feel the warmth of her caring face, so close to his.

"Church, I think I'm beginning to see the world you live in; it must be beautiful but so hard coping."

"Someone else recently said much the same." He paused. "She's pregnant, isn't she? Rosemary."

"Yes," Sarah nodded with eyes closed. "That's why Jimmy sent you here, so I could tell you."

"And I know what you are going to tell me."

"She could never fully explain why but she was so desperate to have her own child. After she quit her studies, she felt free but aimless; until now. But please don't think you were used. She doesn't want anyone else in her life, no father by her side; just her and her boy."

"Thought it will be a boy."

"She knew you were the one who had to be the father; I think she saw your gifts and knew the baby would be as beautiful as you. You were an orphan and she saw it as a chance to give your son the love of a mother; something that you never had."

"But I know now that my mother did love me."

Both allowed tears to roll.

He soothed the wakening Zimmy, "Will they stay in Ibiza?"

"No plans, but Rosemary wants you to know where they are always and doesn't want to block you. Her son needs a father."

"But not a permanent one," Church quietly smiled. "I'm not bitter and I understand, but can't put it into words."

"I think we all understand, somehow. But only because we know each other."

"I would like to send them money."

"Money and seeing the boy is all up to you and Rosemary. And you know I don't have to say this, Church, but…"

"I'm the father, there is no one else." Church nodded, "I know. Those guys with dreadlocks they…"

"Just friends looking over her." Sarah exhaled loudly, "Phew."

In passing Zimmy over, Church cupped both her hands, "I love you."

"I know," Sarah laughed timidly. "I think we shared that in our eyes a few times."

"I love all of you."

"And Jimmy thinks the world of you but…"

"He can't handle this sort of thing."

"He did struggle to comprehend."

"I can hear his words."

Sarah laughed, "He thinks you should have free access to the boy and…"

"And to Rosemary's tits," Church said it for her.

"I said you two were alike. But I'm so relieved that you took it as I prayed you would."

"A couple of days ago I would have lost it."

"You do seem different, easier to see the real you."

"At last."

"But," Sarah hesitated, "you mentioned going?"

"Soon."

C hapter 61

Church looked down the valley; the loch was crystal. He saw the police cars at the old ruin and had seen enough. He turned to the site of the priory and pulled out the last of the weeds growing amongst the yellow primrose. As had been explained, he pinched off as many dead heads of flowers as he dared. *'Tough old buggers, like you and my man,'* he heard Sarah's words, *'let them go to seed every seven years; the flowers I mean.'*

A warm wind rustled last winter's dead leaves, tugging them from their resting places amongst the divots. With the breeze came a scent, a familiar scent, that of an animal. He stood, stretched his back and looked back along the path he had taken.

A white fox sprung and bound toward him, shimmering then rising, becoming a figure in white, floating, dressed in a long cheesecloth dress. With her smile, she came.

Chapter 62

"Sheeit Jimmy and sheeit dear lady, they was ghosts I tell you. And Isaac never said a word, he just pointed up the track."

"A man of few words," Jimmy spoke knowingly.

"A lady in white, man she was beautiful and there was two men although I might have been seeing double, so it could have been one men."

"Where?" Jimmy asked.

"Up the track, I tell yer. Isaac pointed them up the track. They ignored me, kept backing away."

"I wonder why," Sarah mumbled.

"Did they speak to Isaac?" Jimmy was now shouting to Floyd.

"Never heard nothing," now Floyd was shouting, "on account of I wiz trying to find the jar I dropped and they got too far away to listen."

"Was your jar empty?" Jimmy nodded to Sarah.

"Maybe."

C hapter 63

The sun's warmth penetrated the bark of the pines, the gum softened and its scented oils evaporated, mixing into the air around them, neither letting go of the other.   Church could feel that same warmth down his back and every part of her clinging to him, her breath as rich as red wine, just as intoxicating.

"Shady told me it was time to come."

"And he was right, Wallace, he was right."

"I always imagined Scotland to be cold," Wallace breathed down his neck.

"It forever has been," he kissed her thin lips, "I have begun to like it here," Church looked at Wallace, "but to be true we two do not belong here."

"Only if you are sure, Church."

"I'm sure."

"You seem different, feel different," she smiled at him.

"I vanquished my demons."

"I'm pleased, as long as I wasn't on the list."

"No, and I'm sorry," he bowed then raised his head, "that was my insecurities. But not now. And it's time for me to say my goodbyes. But if you want you can say hello and meet my companions before we move on."

"I would love to share that."

"The police were there earlier," he nodded across the clear air to the valley side as they walked on.

"Of course, I can see it now. But my goodness this is a beautiful place." She looked behind.

"Possibly that is the ruins of a priory, except it is not a

ruin. It's alive still."

"And those flowers?"   Church could see that Wallace was more than just mildly curious.

"I have so much to tell you."

"And I have so much to say."

"No secrets, but so much time to do it."

"That just swept me away to an infinite horizon."

"Can I come too?"

"Hold my hand all the way.   But where are we going?" Wallace clung to him and looked up, "Not that I care."

"We can go down to Aunt Poppy's for food, "then we can meet up with folk."

"Aunt Poppy? Will she be there, will she mind me being with you?"

"Oh yes, she will be there and no, she won't mind. This should get the better of her.

Hey, Wallace, just thought it through. How did you get here?"

"My brothers, they took me up."

"Kind, be nice to meet them."

"They have travelled on, meeting up with Richard to explore."

"Ahah," Church swung his head up and down. "Richard did a reconnaissance."

"Sort of but I would have come to you no matter what anyone tried to say."

"Spare me what Richard said about me."

"Ok."

"But what did he say?"

"Well, he was wrong. You're not Mister Grumpy."

"I was. But the three of them are setting off up North?"

"Lock up the women."

"They are like Richard then?"

"Triplets."

"Just curious, but Richard did he…?"

"Try it on with me?   He was about to but as soon as I

C.P. HILTON

told him you and I were an item, he backed straight off."

"Love that man.   Hey, but how did you find me way up here in the wilds?"

"Two of em.   They tumbled out of the bushes."

"One tall one, one crazy one?"

"Couldn't put it any better.   Now the tall was a mute.   He didn't speak only sign."

"That's Isaac.   He can talk but his last words to me was that he is taking a vow of silence for a week.   Bugger, I'm supposed to inform folk.   Do it later."

"A vow of silence, that is so cool.   But the other one...."

C hapter 64

Wallace was deeply scrutinised. With no threat in the room, Church was drifting in and out of sweet slumber; listening.

"All dressed in white like thet. Sheeit. I thought you was one of 'em ghosts. Never seen one afore, ghosts that is. All these fellers have."

"Are you a Hollywood actor?" Wallace shouted. "Have you been in any John Wayne films?"

"Jimmy? What she says?"

Jimmy acted dumb.

"And where is the other one that slick fellar that was with you?"

"He's my brother and there are two; twins."

"See," he turned to Jimmy again, "I teld yer I wasn't seeing double. And what happened to Ricardo? Is he under the table agin?"

"They have all gone off exploring," Sarah joined in with shouting, "up North."

"Trailblazing? Wish they'd said, could have lent them a borrow of my gun."

"Next time," shouted Jimmy, "you go with them."

Sarah turned to Jimmy and mouthed, "Think Floyd is getting worse."

"I aint," Floyd coyly smiled.

"He is putting you on," Isaac spontaneously spoke, "all of you. If only you knew of the secluded conversations we have had."

"Isaac, shush," Jimmy squeaked and flapped his hands, "your vow of silence."

"I have made an exception, but I will not tell anyone. Wallace, it is such a pleasure to meet you; so beautiful."

"You really are," Sarah smiled to Church.

"Now," said Isaac, "I am going back to my silence."

"Wallace?" Floyd asked, "Is that yer name?"

"Yes."

"First or last?" Sarah smiled at her.

"Both."

"What?" Church woke.

"My name is Wallace Wallace."

"Eh?"

"My family name is Wallace; my mother and father had already had a set of twins. I was only one so they gave me twin names as compensation. Nice of them."

"Never thought to ask that one. Like it." Church settled back. "What are your brother's names."

"Brian."

"Both of them?"

"Of course."

"Yes," Church yawned, "no threat in this room." He drifted into a simple domain.

C hapter 65

The besom's bristles stirred the dust, drifting through each room and up the stairs. Church swept the small pile into the dustpan and sprinkled it out through the open door, it blew back in. He gathered the food and put it in a box alongside a note on the kitchen table and placed the plastic bag with his clothes another inch nearer to the lobby.

"It's time."

He turned; she was waiting for him to say it first.

"Goodbye, Aunt Poppy."

"Just for now."

"How do I hug a ghost?"

Poppy placed her hand over her heart.

"When again you meet with Jasmin, tell her she searched with the wrong person and in the wrong place to belong. Tell her to take her sari back to Ceylon."

"Sari? She got married in one."

"I know."

"A shame you could not manage, I would have met you then."

"I can see it now."

"The sari? I don't know what you mean."

"Her mother does and you will know what words to use at the time."

"Her mother?"

"Tell her to listen at her grave."

"I'm sorry I never visited your grave."

"I'm here."

"And I'm sorry I never met your husband."

"He's here." She faded.

Church locked the door and placed the key under the pot of freshly growing lavender.

"Thanks Wallace, for waiting."

She smiled her reply, forever in sunshine by the gate.

***

A grey figure watched Church place a sprig of lavender by Mimosa's headstone, he bowed to the other two stones, hesitating at Willow's, then he cast a second sprig into the wind drifting over grassy mounds.

"I listened; we now know what happened," he whispered to the fading ghost. Distant, it now held a baby in her arms; content. "I hope that is enough."

He turned to Wallace. In dappled light, head to one side she was watching, smiling, sitting on the bench, yellow daffodils behind her. Church sat next to her. She moved to be close, he felt her tremble.

She had her eyes closed now, "So good to be with you."

He put his arm around her and breathed into her ear, "Got them butterflies."

"Me too. Who was the second sprig for?"

"My mum."

"Shame you don't know where she is."

"Always with me, but maybe one day."

He saw Wallace tenderly touch the bench, "I remember," she laughed quietly, "I remember I met my first true love on a bench like this."

"Lee, you spoke of her. Was she nice?"

"Oh yes. And now I have another love; truer." He felt her stroking his face, felt her breath.

"What about your family?"

"What made you ask that?" Wallace turned and they both watched an elderly couple shuffling on sticks toward them. So slow; It would take a lifetime for them to reach the bench.

"I take it you had family problems having girlfriends."

"My brothers took it worse but we are ok now."

"Wallace," he paused, "talking of families, there is something you need to know."

"I think we should give them our seat," Wallace stood and gestured to the old couple.

"Allow me to help, if I may," Church stood and supported the frail arm of the lady as she sat.

With long fingers; she patted his hand. A penetrating stare from the depths of age-old eyes, Church dissolved under the scrutiny of a face somehow so familiar. The gentleman was also looking at him through his glasses perched on a wrinkled and large nose, a benevolent smile.

"Thank you, young man," she spoke with a joyful laugh.

"You young folk make a lovely couple," he croaked waving his hands as if conducting an orchestra.

"Now," the old lady insisted, "don't let us keep you."

"Just you be on your way. May God bless and keep you always," he smiled at Church.

"That was nice," Wallace nestled into Church as they walked away. "You were going to tell me something about families."

Church looked back at the couple, "I will tell you later, I need to. But I was also going to talk about one day meeting your parents."

"You just did."

***

The smell of turpentine was an associated memory. Kneeling before the Buddha he watched her. She, too, was naked; an elf floating across the room to place a candle beside them. Its glow matched the twilight beyond the glass. Layers of beeswax softened the hardwood floor as he lowered her light body. He knelt over her, laying her on her back. She gently complied as he hovered his fingertips inches over her body, sometimes allowing a fleeting brush of contact, causing her skin, her lips, her delicate nose, her nipples to quiver, matched by her breath. Delicately, he passed his hand between her legs, she moaned quietly, their gaze entwined, a complete uniting, he lay on top of her, aware of how delicate she was. She raised her legs about him, her arms too, gently drawing him down.

C hapter 66

"This is something else," Church put his arm around Wallace.

She rested her head on his shoulder, "A beginning."

"Just obliterating the word Taversham off the window is enough. But plain glass?"

"Smokey. Nothing to hide."

"Yep, see your point."

"But I would like you to help me design the inside. Rustic. Fresh energy, especially the cellar."

"Sage grass."

"Coffee?"

The café across the road was empty as usual, apart from; "Hi Jake," Church chucked him a pack of tobacco.

"Cheers Church."

"How you doing, Jake? Plenty to moan about?" He shouted then whispered to Wallace, "Still working out who he is."

"Who is he then? Been puzzled, too."

"Dunno."

"Yes, thank you," Jake replied. He looked to Wallace, "Strange seeing you without a suit on, used to look cool. Nice you still wearing the hat though. A fedora, is it not."

"I did pack one suit in my suitcase."

"Going away? Thought you would be. What's it going to become?" He gestured out through the window.

"New age stuff," Wallace nodded.

"Buddhas and crystals and stuff like that?"

"Nice one," said Wallace, "you got it in one."

"Be nice to smell incense down the streets," said Jake.

"Good energies. Got some friends in Scotland into that sort of thing. Living in a commune."

Church shrunk, "Please don't let this be happening."

"Don't bang your head like that," with one hand Wallace stopped him with the other she rolled a cigarette. "Damage the table. Fancy something stronger?"

"Pub."

Two raised glasses clinked, "To us," they said in harmony.

Wallace slid a bunch of keys over the table. "Ok Nick, ok Eddie; keep an eye on the old office and my place. And feed the fox."

"Yes Matron," Eddie touched his forelock.

"Old bill came round again."

"What you done now?" Church raised his eyebrows.

"No nuffink like that.   Its coz we cooperated so well assisting them in their enquiries...."

"They gonna turn a blind eye to what we been up to. But I told em we aint been up to nufink."

Church turned to Wallace, "What do you suppose will happen?"

"Well," Wallace sat back with hands behind her hat, "all goes back years, but they will work at digging into it and see what happens."

"As long as they don't dig up our garden but least, we are in the clear," Eddie piped in.

"Of course," Wallace looked at Church, "we are innocent."

"Time to go?" Church offered to stand.

"One more drink," Wallace adjusted her fedora.

"You two really going to Timbuctoo?"

"Nepal," said Church.   "Overland on an express from Marrakech to Casablanca," he looked down, muttering to himself, "I think that's the way? Or is it the other way? Soon find out.   But we're gonna track down supplies of Buddha statues and stuff like that. We'll be back before you know it."

"But on our journey," said Wallace, "a slight diversion."

***

With the yachts sway, Nick nudged Church, "She's got that boiler suit on again. But what's Eddie saying?"

"Gulls miss," Eddie swiped one away when it threatened to swoop across the blue sky toward his melting ice cream cone. "Not seagulls just gulls." He leaned closer and whispered in a low rumble, "And if you really want to impress; see these ropes; on yachts they're called sheets."

The boat rocked when Nick and Eddie disembarked, leaping onto the pontoon. Church started the engine, it roared then subsided to a gentle chug with diesel exhaust filling the air.

"Going a treat," Nick shouted above the noise, "new fuel pump," He came eye to eye with Church. "Mate, take care around Biscay."

"Cast off," Church finally said it.

Eddie stuck a finger in his mouth then raised it to the sky, "North is that way," he laughed and pointed out to sea.

"Ibiza here we come," Wallace gripped the tiller, "you need to tell me what to do, remember."

Church looked up, "No wind so we'll keep her on the engine until we're out, it will become choppy, hope you don't become sea sick if you do it will pass, promise." He searched her face, "Scared?"

"Not with you by me."

"Always. Hey been meaning to ask you this." Church tidied ropes.

"Yeh tidy them sheets Church."

"What? No listen; those photographs, the ones of you and Janice, what happened to them?"

"They were all blurred so I sold them to Nick and Eddie."
"Sold?"

"Nice little earner, they said. I did keep the nice one of Janice though. I did it that night I threw the pair across the pub. Remember?"

"Yet another lifetime."   He laughed to himself, "Another confession."

"How many more? Go on."

"That same night; I kept the nice one of you." He smiled at the boiler suit, "And talking of confessions; dressing up nights?"

"Got to keep some things a mystery." Swaying with the boat, Wallace smiled and looked behind at the blue air, the matching sea, the receding coastline, then looked to the horizon ahead. "Hope Rosemary will like me."

"She will. And thanks once again."

"She sounds lovely. May even become interesting."

C hapter 67

Beneath a thin canopy of clouds, the air was hot, increasingly hot each day and humid.

Jasmin rubbed sun cream over her deeply tanned face and arms. "It doesn't seem that long ago when you would have rubbed this all over me and ripped this off me," she adjusted her long sapphire silk strip and tucked it in at her cleavage. She squinted against the glare reflected off the low rolling surf in the background and looked straight into Justin's coppery face, his green eyes. "I want to walk the clifftops to Baga. Please come, it's what we share. Then we can walk the long beach at Candolim."

Justin scuffed the sand with his bare feet and searched over her shoulder to the beach hut.

"She's still in there, Justin. Are you coming?"

A habit now, he used his fingers to comb his long hair over the receding forehead line. "It's Wednesday tomorrow lots to sort out."

"The market takes care of itself. We are outsiders from day one. Remember?"

"That's how you feel, not me. Take care when you walk, stay away from the edge, those stones are like ball bearings."

"How convenient that would be."

Sneering did not suit her.

"And cross the river by the bridge, Jasmin, don't wade on your own."

"I didn't know you cared. Anymore."

"And leave me some money."

Red kites circled, carried on thermals reflected off the

soft red cliff face at the back of the beach. Jasmin did skate on the rounded yellow stones but she knew that would happen. She gave up trying to catch up with the small group of laughing friends and turned to look back on Anjuna's small bay; the sand scarred by outcrops of straight edge rocks. Justin was down there, skipping and spinning with the blond girl.

"Do I deserve this?"

Chapter 68

Across the green mountain, carrying the perfume of wild herbs, a stream flowed down to the sea. Beneath an azure sky, Church slumbered at its estuary. He stirred from a monstrous dream. He awoke to force it away, an ebbing sensation of something dark coming out of the sea, sweeping over the land.

He sat in silver sand. "We've got to go," he shouted through the air, cloth tents distorted into shimmering mirages by the blazing heat.

"What?" Sun golden naked, Rosemary and Wallace stopped building their sandcastle, looked at each other then turned to him.

"Believe me, something terrible is going to happen and we have to go back to England."

They collected their sarongs wrapping them around their waists and walked the small beach to Church.

A baby began to wail and gently, Church gathered him from his muslin shade.

"What's wrong?" Wallace's worried voice was genuine. Caused by laughing in bright sun, the delicate lines around her blue eyes were paler than the rest of her salt-baked, skin.

"I mean like, yeh, this is beginning to freak me out," abundantly freckled, Rosemary took the giggling baby from Church.

Standing now, he put his hands in the pockets of his cut-off jeans and shrugged, "I know and I'm sorry," he scratched his bleached hair and looked inland to the green hill, "something bad is coming. We cannot stay. We need to put our stuff in the dingy and row it out to the boat." Restless, Pipedream was tethered to an anchor one hundred yards out in the crystal waters of the bay.

"You cannot stay?" All turned to the sing song voice. "You leaving?" The green shirted dumpy man was fingering his black moustache and questioning the three faces.

"Carlos," Wallace sighed, "Church wants us to go."

"Why?" Carlos raised both hands to the air. "You happy here."

"I'm sorry, I know what I'm asking but..."

The demeanour of Carlos changed, he beckoned Church aside and murmured, his breath strong with yesterday's onion's. "Be very careful Mister Church, I don't know how you know but yes, I come quick to tell you, someone very bad is coming." He tilted his head to the hills.

Dervishes; dust rose and spun along the track; dust devils following the pale jeep.

It came to a halt at the stream's edge.

"Hello my friends," the weasel threw away his cigar and in his military boots, splashed across the water offering a hand. "Hello Mister Church, I am Pablo."

Pablo was forced to stand mid-stream.

Church had moved to stand between him, the girls, and his baby. "You know my name."

Pablo waved his arms, dismissively, "Everyone know everyone."

"I don't know you."

"That is why I am here, to introduce myself." He looked beyond Church, "Ah but I don't know the beautiful ladies, ah and you have a baby. So delicate."

Without turning Church knew Rosemary would be covering herself, clutching baby Van and backing away. And Wallace would be prepared, standing side on, arms by her side and head slightly down. He stood square on.

"Pablo," Carlos stepped in. "These are good people."

Pablo grunted Carlos aside.

Church saw through a false smile, "My friend," Pablo

gestured with both hands, "I think we are, how you say? Starting on the wrong feet and my boot is leaking. Can I cross?"

The devil must be invited. Church did not budge, becoming aware of the heavy shape in the back of the jeep.

A warm breeze rippled the sea and flowed up the stream, blowing sand off the beach. "No time," said Church, "we need to go now, this wind could increase."

"Ah but that is what I wanted to talk about. Your boat, she is a fine one."

"Not for sale."

"No no, please, you misunderstand. You are from England. Yes?"

Church did not respond; he could deal with the weasel but was waiting to see if whoever was in the jeep was coming out.

"If you decide you sail back to England you could come and see me first. Some packages to take. A good price would be waiting when you hand it over to my associates."

"Packages?"

"Exported goods."

"What if I keep them and set up my own import-export?"

"That would not be wise."

"I tell you what," Church coldly suggested, "perhaps it would be wise for you to see the size of the boat's hold."

"Ah now you are interested."

"Perhaps we should row out together."

"That is sounding promising"

"What I can promise you is that only one of us will be rowing back."

Church stepped into the stream; weasel stepped back.

"What disgust me most," Church mocked, "is that you don't give a shit if your packages end up inside rich or poor, adults or kids."

"You have just made a very big mistake for yourselves,"

in a tantrum, the weasel stomped back to his jeep.

Church waited while the jeep started, struggled to turn with grating gears, then sped away, dust following.

"Wow," Wallace stepped in front of Church. "Next time wear a poncho, hat and spurs. And a cigar to chomp on."

Church spat from the side of his mouth, "Is that how you do it?"

"That was far out," Rosemary bounced baby Van.

"You no scared?" Carlos looked it.

"I was scared alright," Church sagged, "Angels must have sent that wind. But I was more scared of what was in the jeep."

"Not sure what that was," Wallace turned to where the jeep had faded into the distance.

"Mister Church," Carlos nodded, "they are bad people. We are just lucky he came alone."

"Alone? But no matter, we will go. But Carlos; you will be ok?"

"I am from a very big family; they already know not to bother us."

"You want us to take our tents down?"

"No, just leave it," Carlos laughed and raised his hands, jubilant. "More will come. What you call them; Gringos? I can rent them."

"Ok, if you are sure. We will leave everything here for you to pick and choose."

Carlos hugged them one at a time, leaving Church till last, "You look after them."

"I will," he kissed Carlos on both cheeks. "Please say adios to Margaretta. I am sorry we have to leave this way."

"She will understand. But yes, now you must go."

"Pronto."

Church rowed the dingy, seeing the two girls turned heads, all leaving Carlos, fading into the distance.

"Sad," said Wallace.

"Our Shangri-La," Rosemary hugged her.

Church tied the dingy to a dangling rope on the yacht's side and shinned up to roll out a ladder, reach down for Van and watch the two board in well-practised style.

"We will go back to Ibiza to take on water," he said.

"Church," Wallace commanded, "raise anchor. Rosemary make Van safe; we can't risk another drop on his head. Then maybe you should take some rest. I'm gonna use the engine, make a quick getaway, just in case. I'll bring her out into open water, so no one can sneak up."

"Aye aye, Matron," Church saluted as Wallace fired her into life.

***

The setting sun rolled out a red path up the jetty. Masts in the harbour seemed as three hundred lances in the forlorn sky of a fading day; an army encampment ready for battle at dawn. Wallace turned off the tap and pulled the hose from the boats fresh water inlet. The air was not chilly, but after their short voyage and used to the heat, all three started to shiver. They stepped down into the cabin and huddled under a blanket.

"Nice way to keep warm," Church sadly smiled.

"Saves dressing," Wallace winked.

"Think he needs changing," Rosemary cuddled in with Van.

Reaching from under the blanket to the table, Church filled three enamelled mugs with whisky.

"Cheers." They clunked mugs.

The sound left.

No one wanted to speak, hiding in their mugs, Van asleep.

"Guess this is crunch time," Church said it to himself.

"Too beautiful to spoil," Wallace stared through the walls of the cabin while Rosemary lay her head on her shoulder.

Church stretched over to Rosemary for Van and lent back to rest the baby on his chest.

"You two have created a gifted child," Wallace smiled.

"I knew we would," Rosemary sighed, "meant to be."

"Rosemary," said Church, "this has all been so good. But I said it before, I respect your wish of not wanting the tie of mother, father, and son. You just wanted the freedom of you and Van. Now is the time to go back to the commune here in Ibiza. If that is what you want?"

"Is it what you both want?" Wallace intervened.

"I know what I want," Church replied, "but have no right to...."

"But I've so fallen in love with both of you," said Rosemary.

"Me too," added Wallace.

"And I reckon I feel that more than anyone. But reality could hit in anytime," Church challenged.

"But this is real."

Wallace stood, the blanket slipped away and she took Rosemary's hand. "Let's make this easy, get it over with."

Rosemary took Van and she was led by Wallace out on deck. Church felt the boat rock as they stepped off. Head down, he listened to the low murmur of water beneath the boat. The harbour was deep, deep and welcoming, an endless murmur without consequence. He drifted down, swallowed; time without end.

The boat rocked again.

With the baby the two slid under the blanket, one each side of Church.

"Sorted," Wallace said. He felt her arm draw him close, felt her warmth.

"Inevitable," Rosemary added. He felt her too. And the baby was returned to his chest. "We four are one."

"I am so grateful we are staying together," said Church. "As long as we are all sure."

"I know we need to get back anyway, long overdue to sort out everything we left," said Wallace. "And we want to follow you. But were following you blindly."

"Yeh," Rosemary added, "I mean you were right, we had

to leave behind our Shangri-La."

"But it's the rest," Wallace continued.

"I know," Church whispered. "Back at our beach, I dreamed of something terrible approaching, not just that slime of a weasel, something beyond that; something is happening back home. I remember Grandad telling tales of monsters coming out from the sea. Well, that's the only way I can describe it; coming to our shores back home."

"That's good enough for me," Wallace squeezed his hand beneath the blanket.

"Far out."

C hapter 69

Rosemary slumbered, head to her chest, yet her arms showed no sign of allowing her baby to slip.

Wallace sipped her whisky and looked around the timber-beamed pub then considered Church.

"It's strange for me being back here. What must it be like for you?"

"A light year journey," he smiled into the distance.

"Perhaps I've said it before," she said, "but you are so different from the frightened invisible boy I first met. Saw it in you then; the real you. Said I would wait."

"I remember those words," Church nodded to himself. "Thanks for having faith in me then. And now. But what of you?" He looked at Wallace, "Where are you now?"

"With you."

"Robinson Crusoe, I presume. Although you look more like Tarzan."

"Richard, my love." Church stood, all three stood and hugged him.

"I remember you," Rosemary smiled. "Moonshine madness."

"Ah yes," said Richard, "that night we stumbled into Jimmy's." Richard held his head.

"Hello lovely man."

"Wallace," Richard stood back to behold, "an angel."

"She is, they both are," said Church, "and so is he." He gathered his son. "This is Van."

"Short for Caravan," Rosemary nodded in a most serious manner.

Richard took Van and cooing, snuggled him into his shoulder.

"That I never would have believed," Wallace smiled.

"Beautiful just," Church also smiled.

"Your tans are magnificent," said Richard.

"All over," Wallace nodded.

"Inevitable."

"Painful at first."

"Rosemary's oils helped."

"In many ways."

"Please," Richard left them to their trialogue, "let me order drinks," he offered Van back, "lots of drinks.   Have you eaten because they serve food now, in a basket?"

"Food in a basket?"

"I'll have soup."

"Where are the two?"   Church asked Richard.

"We need to talk."

***

"We encountered the same thing," said Church, "had to leave in a hurry. And I know Nick and Eddie talked about some French guy hassling them. Or trying to."

"Jacque is his name."

Church nodded to himself, "I remember now."

"Now they are at the cusp of accepting a deal."   Richard lent forward, elbows on knees, "It's like a black and heavy mood has taken them."

"Couldn't have said it better myself."

"Here they come now."

***

The car park was freezing, Church knew it was partly due to being no longer in the Med. And it was dark, very dark. He knew where the switch was for outside lights.

"What's wrong with you?" Eddie whined.

"Some welcome," Nick joined in.

Church grabbed them both by the neck, "What do you two think you are playing at?"

They both squeezed his wrists, easily releasing the hold.

"Told you, didn't I Eddie. Who grassed then? That bleeding Dick, I bet."

"Easy money. What's wrong in that?"

"What's wrong in that? Drug peddling? Listen to yourselves."

"Yeh it's alright for you, shagging two whores at once, a bastard in tow."

"And loads of money. No worries about paying for anything."

Through night's darkness, Church's fist was led in a straight line to the sound of Nick's voice and he felt a well-remembered connection with teeth and lips. He followed with a swing which thumped into Eddie's ear. He took one step back and heard a swish of wild swings with blind curses.

"Stop." It was Wallace.

The car park lights came on.

Eddie lurched toward Church who head butted him, finishing with a knee in his chest. Nick hesitated at the sight of a barricade of fists, a fixed stare, eye to eye.

"Is that it?" Wallace asked. "All done, are we?"

"I aint," Nick spat blood.

"Would you like me to finish it then?" Wallace stood before him, fists at her waist, voice potent, "This goes beyond just a playground fight. What on earth do you think you two are playing at? Don't think I'm going to lead Church off by his ear. This is serious stuff boys, no more games."

"And this is not a stalemate," Richard stepped in. "It can only end one way. I shall notify the police."

"Bluffing. That Dick's bluffing."

"He's not," Church said. "You've blown our old way right out of the window. I'll be the one to call the police."

"And its Richard, if you don't mind."

"And Rosemary and I are not whores," Wallace said it and Church felt the discreet tug of her hand.

"Yeh, I know," Nick grunted.

"And your boy is not a bastard." Eddie joined in. "But you are for smacking me one."

"A question," Richard asked, "I'm cold. Can anyone see the harm of going over to my place? To talk?"

"No," Church called a halt. "We're tired, especially Rosemary and Van."

"Tell you what," Wallace suggested. "What about my old office, tomorrow at two?"

"We'll get Rosemary and Van," Church said. "You two treat Richard with respect."

"Or else." Wallace hissed like a cat then whispered in Church's ear as they walked the car park, "Can I be your whore?"

"Thought I was your bitch."

C hapter 70

"You were right, Church," letters were swept aside as her front door was opened, "our return is long overdue."

"Oh wow," Rosemary peered in, "cool energy. This is too much."

"Come in, please. All of you." Wallace peered in, "Place feels so small now."

"I'll make some tea," Church piled up the envelopes, "Do you mind If I sort through these?"

"Go ahead, this is your forwarding address." Wallace was steering Rosemary, "I'll show you round."

"Need to sort Van though."

***

Church yawned and stretched; his legs locked in a kneel at the low table. The hysterics from the two girls in the shower, then the giggles and low rhythmic murmur from the bedroom had all stopped. Blinking, he looked toward the bedroom door and tidied the array of papers, their opened envelopes. A separate stack for Wallace. In numb silence he crept toward the door and peered into dancing candlelight. Van was asleep in a cardboard box. Then he witnessed the closeness shown by the embrace of Wallace and Rosemary sleeping under the duvet in the bed.

He crept back to the cupboard to pull out the mattress.

***

In a morning's peculiar light, paper rustled beside him on the pillow, squinting to focus, he read the scribble.

'See you at one W x
Back soon R x'

He dozed into the morning, clutching the scrap of paper which kept slipping from his grasp.

"Hi," Rosemary beamed in her denim dress, her hair heavy and wet.   She balanced two cups, shuffling in bare feet toward him.   The smell of coffee intermingled with the gentleness of flowers preceded her.

"Bliss," he sat up and kissed Rosemary full on the lips as she slid into the bed, still balancing the cups.

He stroked her hand and took time to consider her, sitting beside him.

"Don't take me wrong," he said.

"Never."

"But I feel like I don't really know you," he tried. "Suddenly a stranger.   Feels like we have all become strangers, even I to myself."

"I and I."

"Or maybe we always were strangers but never noticed until we finally stopped."

"We are close though," her voice had a dreamlike quality, "all of us."

"That is undeniable. But…"

"Yeh there is something," she said.

"Just say it, no worry."

"I'm tired," she sagged with obvious relief.   "Ibiza was too much."

"A far cry from the simple life up in the glens?"

"Right on.   And when Van was born," she was smiling at him, "it was beautiful but I didn't know what a busy scene it would be."

"Maybe I should have been there, from day one"

"Hey, I'm not laying that on you," she put her coffee down and rested her head on his shoulder.

"And then we came along," he whispered, "and whisked you away island hopping."

"And that was so cool," she sounded far away.

"I know." He reflected quietly, "Your face, it was like the sun when you opened your caravan door."

"And with Wallace too. Wow she is just far out. She was born to be by your side."

"You were close last night."

"We missed you; you should have joined us."

"Too close to intrude."

"She missed you most."

"That kind of puts you on the outside," he tried to see her face.

"Kind of." She lifted her head, he saw her eyes, radiant. "Wallace and me, when we made sandcastles, we spoke a lot."

"I noticed, always glancing over to me."

"Hey we both love you."

"But." He conceded.

"Hey, it's not like that but I know you prefer stuff laid out."

"Lay it out then."

"I couldn't return and stay in Ibiza anymore and we both wanted us to share a little more time. We didn't have to ask to know that's what you wanted."

"That's true," he said. "But this is leading up to something."

"Before Van was born, I've said that I..."

"Yeh, I know you wanted a life; just you with Van."

"With no heavy ties," she sounded wistful.

"And this is getting heavy?"

"No. But I think deep in my heart, one day I will feel that way; a bad scene."

"You make it so easy for me to admit it; yeh it could become heavy between us."

"And it would be a shame to end up that way. So..."

"So?" Church held his breath.

"Wallace has agreed that I live here for the moment. Van and me, we need to be grounded. And I need a rest, get myself together."

"A good truth."

"It's cool you said that.   She said I could help run her new age shop, kind of part time.   Yay," she waved her hands, "I know I have a baby brain, but she said her twins would look over me.   And you never know," she quietly laughed, "I may even finish writing my masterpiece."

"Masterpiece? Oh yes, back in your caravan, all those papers...anthropology."

"Way, way back is now coming forward.   I'm going to send word to Sarah, asking her to send up all my notes."

"'*Par avion*'."

"Of course."

"But that's you and it sounds like Wallace is ready to move on. I wonder where that leaves me?"

"That's up to you and Wallace to decide, isn't it?   But, hey, I mean I don't want you to go."

"Not right now," he said.

"No, not right now."

"I'm ok," he rose from the bed and saw her worried face looking up at him, "honest it will all be fine.   Think I'll go out and go for a walk, sea air."

C hapter 71

Church remembered as a boy being confused as to whether the railings on the beach road were green or blue; such was his life's complications. But he still remembered in his gut that fear, vanquished today, yet permanently with him in those days. The road was still as busy, maybe even more so; wide and bright with people, the sky reflecting a vivid sea. He leaned over to look down to the pathway outside the numerous arches below, hearing the waves rolling onto the shore. He had always wanted to count them, every wave, by picking up a stone from the beach for each one, to see how high a pile he could create. He was tempted to go down there. He never really wanted to.

He walked on.

Pulled from childhood fantasies he knew where he stood and looked through the sweeping traffic over the broad road to the black railings, the seven steps leading to the black door which was ajar. A grey ghost flitted by the upstairs bay window and within seconds she was stepping out through the front door in a flowing grey dress. He tried to duck, dissolve into the clusters of passers-by but boldly weaving through the cars, she was coming straight for him.

"Hello, Church." Jasmin was up close and different. She was taller, her skin dark; adding to that overseas mystery and enhancing iridescent eyes. "My goodness," she touched his arm, "you look great, grown your hair and that tan really suits you."

"Thank you," Church touched the back of her hand still on his arm. "And you, you look so different. Great though."

"Yeh," she loudly exhaled, "guess we are both different." Jasmin gestured to a bench being vacated, "Do you have time? Or desire?"

"I sorted through your letters from your solicitor," he sat at his end of the bench.

"What do you think?"

"Sounds good. Too easy."

"Better than the alternative," she tilted her head.

He knew that pose.

"How's things for you?" He beat her to it.

"I'm okay now," she nodded to herself, "I'm ok."

"Problems?"

"He turned out to be a bastard. After my money."

"Oh. I am sorry to hear that," Church felt a rising discomfort, almost guilt about his life, now so good.

"I've guessed you've moved on," she offered. "You look like you have."

"Come through it."

"What he did to me made me realise what I did to you," she looked down to her sandals.

He copied and saw brown skin, painted toe nails, gold ankle chain; it spoke of the long journey she must have walked. Then he realised she was searching his face.

"You didn't deserve it," she said, "you were no bastard. I am glad we met; I want to apologise."

"No need. Looking back, it was the right thing. We met when we were almost young and grew up growing apart."

"Nice way of seeing it."

"And now?" He asked, "How are you now?"

"But how are you first?"

"Yeh I am ok, Jasmin, honest. And to be even more honest, it would help if I knew you were ok."

Her shoulders sagged, "Guess it's a learned behaviour from my Mum; these days I seem to be always wishing." She turned and he did not flinch. "No right to place burdens on you."

"Try."

"It seems like I'm chasing shadows?"

"I used to have shadows chasing me. But try this; turn it into chasing butterflies and when you catch one be very careful, they are so fragile and precious. Then let it go and you go with it."

"Wow," she scuffed her sandals on the pavement, "you really have changed."

"And there is something else, it's all to do with being on your pathway and if you are constantly wading upstream and things go wrong, change direction."

"How do you know this stuff?"

"A long pathway." This time he did flinch under her puzzled scrutiny and blurted, "It's not by coincidence we met. I've a message, you must search in Ceylon. Take the sari."

"Message? Ceylon? Sri Lanka?" She looked bemused, "Are you sure you're well?"

"I know, I know," he held up his hands, "wait and see until it makes sense. Try a visit to your Mum's grave."

She nodded and sort of smiled to herself in acceptance, considering her own private thoughts. "Yeh," she softened, "that does kind of fit. A lot went on for me at mum's grave." She turned to him, "Did you know that?"

Church gave a shrug.

"I remember now; the sari is wrapped in tissues with dried flowers and Mum's letters. Photos too. Maybe I should read mum's letters from Ceylon."

"I think you should, I'm sure she won't mind." He looked at her, "Maybe she wants you to."

"Maybe that's why she kept them." She quietly laughed to herself, "Alice suspected a romance." Her mood changed, "Never did send any photos to Alice and she's not getting them now. Bad blood; Dad always reckoned. But yeh, the sari, yeh," she was nodding enthusiastically, "yeh, it's all in a box."

"I noticed you packed. Lots of stuff in boxes."

"Yeh seems ages when I packed, still there though.

Waiting. What about your stuff?"

"Forget it, nothing I need. Not even my records. Oh," he said, "thanks for replacing the desk I smashed."

"Least I could do. Didn't blame you; think I got off lightly." She turned and raised a smile, "Thank you, Church. The sari, the letters, given me a plan, a purpose. Feels right, somehow. Yeh. Ceylon. Investments out there to be checked out and...Thank you."

"We've granted each other permission to move on then?" Church searched for her response.

"Sounds about right," she put on sunglasses, stood and offered an outstretched hand.

Church cupped her hand in both of his and held her that way for a moment; a moment of sadness. Their hands slid apart; she left and took the sadness. He watched her walk away. Perhaps she knew how not to prolong their parting, she went down the steps to be out of sight, to the arches below.

C hapter 72

In that boiler suit, too large, cute but pensive, Wallace was pacing, chewing on a pencil; he saw her through the glass door. She jumped with excitement, letting him in to throw her arms around him.

"Oh, I've missed you."

"No doubt there," he looked around what was the reception; papers and boxes strewn. "This is too much for my brain. Where did we leave the boat?"

"Take a look in the office. No don't," she tugged at his arm.

"Shipment from Nepal?" He won the tug of war by pushing to throw her off balance.

"I feel so bad." Wallace subdued face called a halt.

"All broken?"

"No. Nick and Eddie; all opened, packaging list all ticked, invoices all arranged in organised system."

"Oh shit." Suddenly his knuckle hurt.

"We've got an hour."

"I can handle them. We can sort it."

"So," she brightened. "How was your morning?"

"Fine," he swept his boot over the dusty floor. "Went to my old place."

"No ghosts?"

"Nope, all gone. Sealed up in boxes."

"Boxes still there, then. Anything else?"

"Yeh sorted out stuff, papers from the ex."

"Hope that's ok."

"Yeh," he looked to the ceiling then straight at Wallace.

"We gonna agree that she will dig into her investments and give me the value of the house we built. Cash. That's all."

"That's all?"

"That came out wrong. I'm happy with that; more than happy. I don't want to slice too much into her family inheritance; gonna sign it all off my hands."

"You could acquire a bigger share but guess it's a man thing."

"She wants to hang on to all other properties," he said. "See where she wants to go."

"As long as you are happy with that."

"Yeh makes it easy to move on."

"Church," she took his hand, "what about emotionally."

"She's my ex," his hand slipped.

"Ok," she was lingering with him in that space.

He looked at her, "Yeh, there is something else."

"Tell me."

"Went for a walk, bumped into her. Was meant to be."

"Her?

"Jasmin."

"Really? Is she back?"

"On her own."

"Oh dear," as she said that he saw that Wallace did not take her eyes off his face.

"They split up."

"How do you feel about that?"

"I'll be ok."

"Is she ok?"

"Confused is the word," he considered it. "But yeh, she will be ok...in the end."

"I think I know what you mean," she gave a nod. "How was the rest of your morning?"

"Rest of the morning?" He sniffed, "Is that not enough?"

"You're right. Sorry."

"I'm fine," he grabbed her hand back. "No worries. Did

287

the washing up."

"And?"

"Left em to dry."

"And that's it?"   Hands were on hips; she shook her head.

"There is something," he hesitated.

"Yes?"

"We need to agree on what to do with the nappies. But what about you and this place? Any plans?"

"Well," she sounded reluctant, "if you're still willing, we need to begin by designing a layout."

"Will the Brians want to be involved?"

"Be more interested in a business plan, going to help with finances of setting it up. I can deal with that."

"Sounds good. A bit of an onslaught though."

"True, but once we start and be done then we can see what's next."

Silence crept.

"Best involve Rosemary?" Wallace offered.

"Oh?" He shrugged. "Ok?"

"She didn't talk with you?"

"We spoke."

"And was she okay? Are you Ok?"

"Funny is it not, she out of all of us have direction."

"And are you ok with what she said?"

"Yeh, she needs to be grounded and take a rest; for Van's sake, too."

"As long as you don't think she and I conspired."

"Not conspired; you just got things moving. And I can see what you've done, broken it down into easy stages; that 'man thing', again."

"And you're ok with that approach?"

"Yeh."

"You're more than a man;" she was looking up at his face, "a dream man. But where does that leave us?"

"Ok if you want me to lay it on the line," he sauntered

toward the window, "Jasmin is around but she doesn't come into the equation. Rosemary's been straight with me from day one and no hassle there. Because," he spontaneously held Wallace, "I just want to be with you. Just you and I."

"Oh Church," she buried her head in his chest, soon becoming damp with tears. "That's all I wanted to hear."

"What's going on?" He gently held her, hearing her muffled words, still clinging.

"So many changes; coming back home, transitions, your marriage, Jasmin, Rosemary and Van, all coming into your life and going; didn't know what you would end up like at the other end."

"While you patiently wait?" He stroked her hair.

"I want to."

"I simply want to be with you."

"I just get scared."

"Thought you would know me by now," he said.

"Still get scared."

"Maybe you're not as self-assured as folk see you." He closed his eyes.

"And I thought you would know me by now."

"Could be that there's gonna be lots more crunch times to come; with one certainty."

"Which is?"

"You and I as one."

"I and I."

"That's what Rosemary said."

"So, we're agreed."

He squeezed into her, looked over at the room and sighed. "But not so sure about being bogged down with all of this."

"Me too," she still clung, "let's get this place sorted. Try and keep it fun."

"Need more adventures."

"Gonna get one." Wallace let go and pointed to across the road. "Here they come."

"Let me do the talking," Church stepped forward.

***

"When I first met you two," Wallace lectured, "I thought you gave so much beauty in your very own weird way. That's why we intervened."

"By beating us up," Eddie retaliated.

"Yeh," said Nick, "when Church went off the rails, we never beat him up."

"But we was always there for him," added Eddie.

"Yeh and we fed Shady."

"And we looked after your places."

"Yeh," Nick mocked, "loads of places."

"Even had to sort someone out who was casing the shop."

"He wasn't one of our lot."

"And," Wallace joined in, "you sorted the shipment from Nepal, for which I thank you. "

"Yes yes," Church held up his hands. "We know all of this and we are here for you. But what's going on? Hey? What happened to your plans with teaching sailing?"

"You took the boat."

"Remember?"

"What about those three brothers?" Asked Church. "You were gonna be their mentors."

"They moved on."

"I moved on," Church said.

"You left us behind."

"Reality kicked in."

"Drugs?" Church mocked, "Some reality."

"What about that moonshine stuff then?"

"Just as bad."

"That's not sold to kids or anyone for that matter. But listen." Church herded the two in, "We can't let this happen, not on our territory."

"It's happening everywhere."

"Can't stop the tide."

"Canute tried it."

"Around here."

"No one knows exactly where it was though," Wallace intervened. "He only did it to demonstrate he could not do it. It was to show that even being a king has limitations."

"Really? I never saw it that way," said Nick.

"Nor me," Eddie showed respect for Wallace.

"Should make it into a film," Wallace nodded knowingly.

"Saturday morning pictures."

"What are you three on about?" Church searched Wallace's face and she stuck out the tip of her tongue. "What do we do with Jacque?"

"Hawkhurst Wreckers are we."

"Need to teach him a lesson. Blow up his boat."

"He got wife and kids."

"Stop him."

"Trap him."

"Sirens," said Wallace.

"Sirens?"

"Mermaids, enticing sailors on to rocks," Wallace stared at Church.

"Think I get it."

"S'pose you caught us in time, Church. We never did anything bad."

"Well not really bad."

"We got it wrong didn't we, Matron. Please don't lock me in the cupboard under the stairs."

"Church, mate, are we forgiven?"

"Perhaps I'm the one to be asking that. But you two need to die. But before you do, set up a meeting with Jacque. Has to be at night. Let's say in five days. In the Wreckers Bar. Then you die."

"But before that," said Wallace, "you and I, Church; there is somewhere else we need to go."

C hapter 73

Straight black hair, dark glasses, PVC chequered minidress in long boots; Church ogled her pointed tits from the bar. She sat alone at a table with a glass of red wine. She looked French; she gave him that impression and she looked like she was waiting for someone.

"What?" Church screwed his face. Drink in hand, a drunken man was advancing on his French girl, starting to chat her up. "Is this for real?" He jumped from the stool.

"Frank?" He dragged him away. "Is it really you? It's Church, Church Ashington. You were my shrink."

Frank tried to shake free from the grip on his arm. "What do you think you are doing?" He was being forced to the bar under a whining protest. "You're hurting me."

"Gonna buy you a drink," Church looked back at the girl, still there, unperturbed, alone again.

"Listen," Frank griped, also looking back at the girl, "I do not acknowledge my clients outside of work."

"Just an unacknowledged pint."

A man came in; navy-blue jacket and beret with a manner unmistakably connected to boats. He smiled at the bird and nearly tripped walking to the bar. The bird looked the other way, hard to get; as French girls are.

Church heard him order a lager; he had a posh French accent.

"Listen," Frank persisted.

"Are you married, Frank?"

"I am but I don't see what business that is of yours."

"I suggest you stop eying up that innocent young girl

and piss off home then."

Frank backed down, sneering and swaggering to the door.

"And thank you for your help, Frank," Church shouted, "I'm cured."

Jacque, it had to be Jacque, he was about to make his play with the bird. Boldly, Jaque sat at her table. More drinks came. Every time someone came into the pub, Jacque turned, continuously looking at the clock behind the bar, progressively giving more attention to the girl who was clearly becoming tipsy. Church was caught looking at her; she made eye contact through dark glasses as she bent to squeeze Jacque's leg and whisper something in his ear.

They were leaving.

Church slowly counted five then followed them out to the street. A fog had crept in from the sea, muffling sound and creating three dimensional shadows. The two ahead now had murky doubles, larger and ominous. A familiar spectre followed him. Other shadows emerged of no origin, dwelling in the streets to throttle victims in a Victorian smog.

***

Church was aware of Wallace's scrutiny, even though she was behind him. Or was it someone, or something else?

"How do you feel, Church?"

"Not as bad as I felt at the top of the steps." He looked around the cellar in its ancient light.

Chalk marks and methodical tabs by forensic remained. And distant sounds clung; of tortured souls and mocking laughter.

"I can still hear it," he said.

"I feel it too."

"But it doesn't scare me, doesn't haunt me like it did before."

"Just sealing it up aint gonna work."

Church held Wallace and felt her welcome, "We just have to turn it into a better place and hope." He gazed at her,

"And I think now would be a good time for me to tell you that without any doubt, I love you dearly."

"Thank you for saying that. And I love you."

They continued their unity in silence.

Wallace put the flowers in a vase Church now held. He placed it on the sideboard that was the alter. Using a cigarette lighter, he heated a charcoal disc, not minding burnt fingertips until the charcoal glowed, deep red. He dropped it into a saucer by the flowers and Wallace sprinkled granules of Frankincense resin over the glow.

The scent of heaven; smoke filled the cellar.

Church and Wallace held each other before leaving the depths of the cellar; their embrace ever-present.

***

From the fog a hand grasped his shoulder, Church spun with a raised fist.

"I need to talk with you," Frank slurred. "How did you become cured?"

"Make an appointment." Church steered him away and caught a glimpse of the couple turning a corner. Running, he caught up then slowed his pace, recovering to follow them into darker back roads and then an alley. It looked familiar; Church remembered it from a walk with Wallace. He put on balaclava and gloves.

The couple stopped. She made it happen and she was allowing Jacque to press her against the fence.

The fog had dissipated but a sense of menace encroached, suffocating; Church felt for the safety of the girl. Ahead of them a dustbin lid clattered, then a second, then a third. Two more behind. Church moved fast to shove Jacque from the girl. It became evident that the French man was not used to violence; he cried a peculiar wail when Church hit him on the nose. Church did not follow with more but put his arm around his neck, drawing him close to breath into his face.

"Listen to me, Frenchie," Church hissed.

Jacque twitched. Three figures ahead, two from behind;

they were coming. All silent, all with balaclavas. And there was something else; that persisting presence.

"You do not belong here. Take yourself and your business away from our manor. Do you understand me?"

"I do not know what you are talking about."

"We do the business around here. We don't need you."

"I do not know what you are saying."

"Your name is Jacque, is it not."

"Who told you?"

"Nick and Eddie."

"Ah so you know my friends," Jacques eyes were desperate, "we can chat and we can come to an arrangement. That is why I am here, to talk with them."

"Can't be done."

"But surely."

"They have been made to disappear. Be careful when you are trawling, you may find them."

"You have killed such lovely boys?"

"Would you like to join them?"

"But I have a wife and children."

"Then honour that and stop your games."

"It is not games. You do not understand, these people once they have a hold. They won't let me go."

"Not if you don't have a boat."

"You have damaged my boat? My livelihood?"

"I give you a chance. Sell your boat, take up a new profession. Or if you like we can sink it, with you on it."

"That is impossible."

"You have no choice. We have already given the coastguard your boat's name and details of your smuggling. They are waiting for you when next you take to the sea. Your vessel needs to be clean of everything; really clean of everything. So now you had better run or very soon you won't be able to walk."

He fled without any consideration for the girl who advanced on him. They became entangled until he threw her back to the fence then vanish.

"Wow boss," Nick took off his balaclava.

"That was some acting," Eddie did the same.

"Who was acting?" Even though his head was coated in sweat, Church left his balaclava on and called to the remaining, "You three boys head off now and don't get any ideas. There some cash in your letterbox, it's for your Mum, remember."

"When do we die?"

"Will it hurt?"

Church laughed, "You're reprieved. But remember the deal? Tell it to me so I know you've got it sussed."

"Catch the morning train to London then Aberdeen."

"A bloke called Jimmy will meet us."

"If he got my letter in time," Church added.

"Why didn't you phone him?"

"No phone's up there."

"Bloody hell."

"What sort of place are you sending us too?"

"Is it really fancy dress?"

"It would help you fit in."

"We always tell our mums its fancy dress if we're all going to a do."

"Stick to telling me the plan."

"We lay low at Aunt Pippi's place for at least six months."

"Write a thank you note to Jasmin."

"'*Par avion*'."

"Poppy, not Pippi."

"How come you got an aunt?"

"Yes," insisted Church, "and you do some work there, sort the place the way Grandad showed you how to do things. Maybe even plant a rose garden. I owe it to her. And you owe it to yourselves and Grandad."

"Hate gardening."

"What about the bird?" Eddie's whisper was coarse. She still hid in shadows.

"Tasty."

"She can come with us."

"Alright darling?"   The pair gave a thumbs up.

"I'll see to her."

"How many women you need?"

"Bye," Church shooed them away.   "Stay out of trouble and give my love to everyone up there.   And if you come back early;" Church retained them with his words, "I *will* kill you."

Hands on hips, the French girl pranced and threw her head back, speaking with a phoney accent.   "Do you think it will work?"

"*Work?*" He mimicked her strange pronunciation.

"What?"

"You said '*work.*'

"Yes, I know I did."

"Well, I doubt if it will *work* for long.   But at least it gives some breathing space and keeps those two out of trouble."

"Out of trouble?   Up there with that lot?"

"Heaven help all of them."   He put his arm around her and kissed her violently ramming his tongue deep in her mouth.   She matched him until he pulled away and saw her look up at him, pleading for air.   "You did great, Wallace."

"Church," she said, "I must admit, I was scared.   That fog, those shadows.   Glad you were there."

"Jacque was scared."   Church searched, "There was something else around him; that menace still to come.   What was it though?"

"Maybe it depends on what your demons are."

"I vanquished mine once."

She slurped, Church nudged her; she was laughing, tormenting.

"Don't you like my tongue in your ear, Mister."

"I love it; but how am I supposed to hear what you are saying?"

He felt her hand between his legs, "Is that better, Mister? Can you hear me know?"

"Much better," he held her wrist to slow her down, "but I still don't know what you said."

"I said; at least I can show my face around this place without being spotted as one of a gang."

"You need to change first," he groped her false breasts, "harlot."

"This wig itches like hell," she tugged at it. "But not straight away." She rubbed her groin against his. "Keep the balaclava on. I wondered why your ears were furry."

"Rosemary will freak out."

"We could go back to the shop."

"What's wrong with here?" Church dipped to run his hand up her skirt. "No panties? A bit risky with a bloke like that."

"Took em off at the fence, folded them tightly and put 'em in Jacque's inside jacket pocket as he ran past me. A technique Nick and Eddie taught me way back when we first met."

"Really? A souvenir for Jacque?"

"Planting evidence. Just a little something for his wife to find."

C hapter 74

"Tell me again," Church wiped the paintbrush over her boiler suit. Purple emulsion splattered the café's chair. The waitress frowned.

"Lee needs a place," Wallace took over, "to sell her paintings."

***

"Do you think we should cut down on our alcohol intake?"

"Not tonight," Wallace downed her double and stood with both empty glasses, "same again."

"Was that a rhetorical question?" Church laughed, "I asked a copper that once."

"And?"

"Wallace," he reached up to her, "relax."

"Lee said that to me once, it was the first time we met. In her studio."

"I remember it, oh so well."

Church smelt Patchouli and turned to the husky voice.

"Lee," Wallace flung her arms around her making it difficult for Church to have a proper look at the ex-lover.

'Funny,' Church thought, 'If Lee was a bloke, I'd have decked him by now.' He feigned clearing his throat.

"Oh sorry," Wallace still had an arm around her, "Church, this is Lee."

Church stood and offered his hand to the mature lady, shocked, no confused, by the way it was accepted; soft and delicately brushing, palm to palm. A gorgeous smile and hair as short and silver as Wallace's.

"Well, well, wow," came the same husky voice. "Nice.

Nice to meet you, Church."

"I'll get some drinks," he said, "give you a chance to catch up."

"Thank you," Lee smiled, "whisky would be nice."

Church caught Wallace's wink, "Lee has it neat, that's how I got a taste for it."

"Taste for what though?" Wishing he had kept his gob shut but pleased that no other quips were offered, Church stood at the bar watching the two in close conversation with Wallace laughing and brushing her hand over Lee's hair.

"It's wonderful," he distributed the drinks, "the closeness you two still have. If Jasmin was to walk in, I can't imagine it being like this."

For an undenied instant he wished Jasmin was there.

"We sorted ourselves," said Lee, "we both knew it was time to move on."

"Still friends," Wallace held Lee's hand on the table. "And," she looked at Lee, "Church and I have another friend and we all agreed it's time to move on."

"Rosemary," Church began to rock to and fro.

"It's a long story," said Wallace.

"A very long story."

"My mum said I shouldn't tell stories."

All heads turned.

"Richard."

He had a tray full of drinks, "I assessed your glasses and assumed. Good evening," he offered his hand to Lee. "Richard."

"Lee."

"Nice handshake, Lee. And like the hair."

"Something I've promised myself."

"And you went and did it," Wallace flapped her hands with excitement.

"Scintillating," Richard smiled.

"Never had the chance to really catch up, Richard," Church nudged him as he sat, "You were heading North with the Brians. Rape and pillage?"

"Don't want to talk about it but I thank you for bringing it up now, my dear Church."

"Is it true you are all banned from Scotland?"

"Richard," Wallace intervened, "Lee is an artist and we are arranging for her to rent part of the premises."

"Ah," Richard offered to stand, "then I am intruding."

"No, you're ok." Church looked at the other two, "Unless you want privacy."

"In a pub?" Lee offered, "Richard, stay. Please."

"Actually, Lee," said Wallace, "I think I'm right in saying you want to give it a try."

"Sure."

"Well," Wallace continued, "our time is limited and anyway it would be my brothers who would be the best to negotiate a deal."

"Aha," Church woke, "Richard knows the Brians."

"A go between," suggested Lee.

"I say," in prayer, Richard drummed his fingers together, "a go between; an Edwardian melodrama is evolving."

"Knew you'd like that."

"Lee, you're an artist?" Richard flirted.

"I paint; photorealism."

"Ah," Richard nodded, "hyperrealism. I'm rather taken by Feuerman, of course."

"Of course," Lee approved.

"But I rather fancy some of Mclean's work."

Wallace shook her head and raised her eyes to the ceiling while Church sidled to whisper, "I've worked it out."

"Worked what out?"

"Richard; he doesn't just appear here, in this pub, by the dreaded coincidence."

"What then?"

"Obvious. He lives opposite and must sit and gawp through the lace curtains of his wee lead-paned window to see who comes and goes."

"Would you all like to come back to my studio," Lee was asking everyone, "to see my work?"

"I'm ordering a taxi," Richard was walking to the bar.

***

"I'll get more coffees," Church gestured to the waitress. "Do you think Lee and Richard had a good night after we left? I'm wondering what would have happened if Richard had not appeared."

"Church." Wallace wagged a finger, "How many complications do you want in one lifetime? He's wasting his time anyway, if that's what he wants."

"Why?"

"Lee is attracted to women and women only."

"Cool. That was a nice nude of you by the way. Like a photograph. Thought there would be more like that."

The waitress thumped the coffees down and shoving a cloth under Church's nose, pointed to the splattered paint from Wallace's boiler suit.

"Never got round to it," Wallace continued from Church's comment, "easily distracted."

"You never did elaborate on dressing up nights with that boiler suit of yours."

"Like explaining the illusion of Shady and seeing a ghost who looks like Rosemary; some things are best left to the imagination. But," she hesitated, "maybe I'm becoming old-fashioned but I'm not so sure if I want a nude of me on display."

"No problem, been bought."

"Private collector?" She quizzed him.

"Maybe. Still have a photo of you. "But at least that's Lee sorted."

"Rosemary will do her best with new age stuff," Church sat back.

"Popsy will organise."

"Is Popsy a bloke?"

"A brilliant organiser."

"The two Brians will be sleeping partners."

"Sleeping with Richard?"

"A perfect environment for Van's upbringing."

"Aint gonna make us rich."

"Who cares?"

"When's the next tide?"

"High tide is at two twenty-eight, a strong ebb," someone behind them spoke from the back of his throat.

"Oh, hi there Jake."

"Been lots going on," Jake nodded, "but your back."

"Just for a while," said Church.

"See you got a new coat, Church."

"Yeh," it was over the back of his chair.

"Donkey jacket," said Wallace, "for sea voyages."

"If I go overboard in it," Church hinted, "I'll go straight to the bottom."

"Nice. Did sort of keep an eye on the place, then two lads started to have a go at me. Accused me of casing the joint."

"Wonder what that was all about?" Wallace shrank.

"Won't happen again," said Church. "But tell me, Jake, you are a knowledgeable man; if the sun sets in the West, is there a place beyond the horizon where it is rising in the West?"

"Go past the shops, downhill all the way to water, it nearly always is, head West, reach the horizon, then ask again."

Church wondered; was Jake smiling?

"That's exactly what we will do," said Wallace.

C hapter 75

Church watched Rosemary.

Drawing her shawl around her, she smiled down at the marble steps then moved back to take in the vestibule.

"Like, this is where I've been coming," she was dreamy, "every morning since we arrived."

"Even in the pouring rain," he said, "remember your hair being wet."

It was dry now, she pulled it away from her face and he saw her smiling at him.

"Your hair is like fire and from time to time I have a vision of my mother standing here; so much like you."

"That is so far out," she said. "I saw her as well, and all of this. It was when I gave birth. I knew what I was seeing. The white fox as well."

"I don't really understand what it means, you looking so like my mother and the fox in my dreams and for real."

"Yeh," Rosemary was gazing into nowhere, "like twins from a higher level."

"Maybe even your mother comes into it; that time I meditated up at the peats. Believable and beautiful."

"Guess we don't need answers to understand but hey, I can give our son the love you never had."

"I'll always believe now that my mother loved me. Just wasn't there."

"That's so cool. But she was with you, in your heart. But think on this," he felt Rosemary's hand at his chest, "we will always be here for you; at this spot. And meditating with Van in Wallace's sanctuary we will be sending our love."

Church gently laughed, "Van should be able to handle anything, growing up with that around him."

"Gifted, that's for sure," she nodded.

"He already is." Church gave his son one last kiss on his forehead, cherished his sleeping face and gave him back to Rosemary.

"Good bye, my dear lady."

"Only for now," she said, "your son has a father, I will never deny you that."

"There is so much more I want to say."

"It is those words not said that linger longest in the heart."

"What about this one," he said, "whenever I smell wild flowers you will be there."

"That's cool," she said, "and it runs in Van's veins."

They embraced and she watched him walk over the cobblestones. Wallace was waiting for him, Shady slipping away.

Church and Wallace held hands, turned the corner and were gone.

**

"Wait for me," he heard the whisper.

It became cooler.

Church pulled up the collar of his donkey jacket and turned around; Wallace was no longer there, slipped from his hand and he was lost.

The lane was lined by a hedge; a mix of small trees and bushes. Approaching, shimmering as a mirage, was a figure in an army greatcoat, a duffle bag slung over his shoulder. Wordlessly they passed, heads turning, constantly looking at each other. A tough guy, Church felt that he knew him, so familiar, like himself but older, greying hair. He steadied himself and leaned on something; it was a wooden fence rail, sectioning off a ruin of bricks with embedded charred timbers.

Church closed his eyes then he opened them to the sound of gulls screeching above; the sky and sea a wide expanse.

"Wallace, you disappeared," Church stood poised, ready to board the yacht and stared at her. "You put your suit back on."

"One last time," smiled Wallace, blue eyes shimmering beneath her fedora, "something told me, I had to go back. One last time. Saw Jake, gave him tobacco and then...Guess what?"

"Will I scream now?"

"Saw someone in the café...looked so much like you only older. And a stunning lady with dreadlocks."

"Think I had a vision of the same guy. Will we head back?"

"Left Rosemary to sort it."

"Am I dreaming this?"

"Could be."

"Maybe we should head back."

"Let's finish this dream first."

EPILOGUE

Daffodils in bloom behind him, the ginger-headed young man sat at the bench before the three headstones looking at the small marble plaque added on beside them. The perfume of white flowers in a vase rolled across the path.

"Jasmine," he inhaled it. "I think she likes the flowers. She did find happiness didn't she, Mum? Dad always said that."

She smiled to herself, "Don't think they ever really stopped loving each other."

He reached to adjust her shawl, checking once more that the brake was on the wheelchair.

"Van, don't fuss," bones creaked as she readjusted his worrying and looked at him through ancient eyes. "But Jasmin lived a peaceful and happy life in Ceylon."

"Sri Lanka, Mum." He closed his eyes and saw the pyre, the numerous mourners. "Dad became more and more sure that Jasmin's mother had a lover in Sri Lanka and that lover was Jasmin's father. That's her connection with the place; deep in her soul.

"You look tired," she was still looking at him from the depths of her eyes.

"It's the injection, Mum, same effect again."

"Sit back down. Close your eyes, we have time. Always have time."

He closed his eyes and sadness engulfed; a lament in deep dusk; a path meandering through a garden dotted with white flowers leading to the veranda of a bungalow, someone was forever waiting; a ghost in a white sari. He saw it and felt the heat in the air laden with exotic perfume.

He opened his eyes.

"You slept."

"Yeh, I did Mum. And I dreamed." He rubbed his nose, "Dad's gift, or a curse."

"A beautiful gift. But we should go. I must finish writing my masterpiece."

"Heard that before." Pushing the wheelchair, he looked back. "And she never had family?"

"No and I think what she left your father was a gift of gratitude for her granted freedom, touched with a plea for forgiveness."

"Guilt," he sighed, "a curse."

"Oh now," she drawled, "don't you start laying any heavy trips on yourself. Life's not short enough for that; that's what Floyd used to say. Be cool." She waved her stick, "So many gifts. Just like your father."

"Some gift though. Tell me the way back; you know the shortcuts."

"Had a good guide."

He pushed the chair through side roads down alleyways of dustbins until they came to the church doorway.

Grey hair tumbling, she cast aside her shawl, gathered her stick and shuffled to stoop at the marble steps of the vestibule, trees rustling in a distant wind behind her.

"Never been inside have we, Mum."

"This is our place," leaning on her stick she lowered her head and sighed. He touched her hand and felt her warmth, the smell of wildflowers around her.

"Sorry we are late," the shout reached them before they saw the spirited aged lady in a suit come round the corner. "His fault." Not as agile, a wayward gentleman struggled to keep up, hobbling over the cobbles.

"Hi Dad, hi Wallace. How did it go?"

"No problems, Van," her blue eyes winking at him, Wallace gently spoke through thin wrinkled lips. "Hello my sweet Rosemary," she adjusted her shawl.

Rosemary tutted, "Don't fuss, I've said.   I am not a cripple."

"Raspberry ripple, Eddie used to call you," Wallace kissed and embraced her.

"Hello, Van," Church warmly hugged him.

"So," Van puffed his cheeks, "that's us all had our three

jabs. Should be safe now."

"How was it at the cemetery?" Church quietly asked.

"I put the flowers there, Dad. It felt right."

"He saw things," Rosemary added.

"Good things, I hope."

"Yes Dad," Van nodded, "good things. But are you sure about this?"

"You know I am. You worry too much, Van."

"I still say it's because we dropped you on your head when you were a baby in the yacht."

"But Dad, only when you go away do I worry. In case you never come back."

"Well," Church said, "One day I won't and it's getting nearer. But for now; be grateful."

"Dad, you know I am."

"Grateful to be alive," Wallace said it.

"Sorry many friends now gone."

"Terrible times."

"Never saw that coming, did you Church."

"Well," Church gently swayed. "Remember that time I dragged us away from our Shangri-La?"

"Our paradise in the sun, you mean. Way back when."

"I often wondered what I really saw coming."

"But that's what you say whenever there's been a disaster."

The mood sunk.

"Hey," Church clapped his hands, "Is this what our friends would have wanted? Let the four of us shuffle off to the pub."

"Can't"

"What? Oh sheeit; bloody lockdown."

"Got a full bottle of whisky hidden at home."

"Half full. Found it last night."

"There's always the moonshine."

Church took Van aside and hugged him again. "It's not been easy but still they are good times."

"More to come, Dad.   And you really are ok for me to sell?"

"We've been over it too many times. Haven't we."

"That's a rhetorical question, Church," Wallace butted in.

"Come on guys, let's get home and plan our next adventure."

"Well, this time," Van exhaled, "tell me before you set off anywhere."

"Van the man, stop worrying."

"Dad," Van buckled, "don't call me Van the man."

"Yeh, seeya later, Van the man."

"Later the better."

"Love you, too."

"Far out."

***

Timeless; the air whistled through her white bedroom it caused Mimosa's floral dress to billow like a cloud. A darkness descended.

She turned, "Alice."

"That's right Mimosa, well done." Mimosa was looking at Alice's companion, "And this is Ali."

"Alice and Ali," Mimosa found that amusing.

Ali was silent.

"Shall we play some more games on the bed and Ali can join in." She was squeezing her hand with each word, tugging her. "And then a surprise, Ali will take you to meet Taversham."

"Taversham," Mimosa frowned.

"That's right and you can play with a group of his friends."

"What fun we shall have." Ali finally spoke; in a voice too loud. "You are so young, Mimosa. Love the ringlets in your hair. Like mine," he pointed to his curly blond crop. "Smile."

The flash alarmed Mimosa but she smiled.

"Ali is a photographer; he can take lots of pictures of us playing."

The cold air finally died.

***

Van dipped his head, walked out of the haunted bedroom, closing the door. He locked it.

At the front door he locked that, too, rattling the door handle, checking it twice; it was the clunk of a clock without any source in the empty hall that nurtured his uncertainty. He walked down seven steps, the black railings were badly corroded, crumbling. He did not touch them but adjusted the 'For Sale' sign.

Van crossed the quiet wide road and walked down to the arches below. Deserted; not there now but a memory promising to return; a carnival atmosphere buzzed, pushing the sea into the background. He stepped onto the beach to regard the locked-up arches, hearing the waves behind him rolling onto the beach.

He began picking up stones and stacking them for each wave he counted.

END

For Wallace.

Printed in Great Britain
by Amazon

28242884R00175